POISON IS A

WOMAN'S WEAPON

LILY GREEN Mysteries

BOOK TWO

PRUDENCE AMBERGAST

For Wilbur

Reminiscence & Anticipation

Lily Green swept a lock of curly red hair out of her eyes as she leaned forward to read the advertisement in the *Milford Advertiser*. Her hair promptly fell back into place, but Lily ignored it in order to give full attention to the bold square of print in front of her. The advertisement said it all: it trumpeted the wonderful Milford village fayre, to be held that coming Saturday, where Lily was to be in charge of the book stall.

This, she considered, was a very important job. But the final sentence in the bold little square was the most important of all; it summed up all that had happened and all that was yet to unfold. Lily read for a second time with pride swelling in her heart: '*The Milford Village Fayre is to be held in the grounds of Fig Tree Hall, thanks to the generosity of the new owner'*.

Glancing over to where the elderly Head Librarian, Mr Lucas, sat diligently absorbed in the card index box, Lily let her mind wander back to how it had all happened, only eight months before. On an equally quiet Wednesday afternoon, a similar advertisement appeared in the *Milford Advertiser* for a murder mystery weekend at the mysterious Fig Tree Hall, hosted by the previous owners, Major Reginald and Lady Felicity Manners-Gore . . .

A foul-smelling old man approached the desk, breaking into Lily's happy reminiscence. His gnarled fingers handed over a crumpled library card and a hardback book with a tatty olive-green dust jacket. Lily duly stamped the book, handing both back without comment. She was not in the mood to prolong the encounter, striking up a conversation with Bert Buttermere about his chosen volume on ballroom dancing.

Lily felt instantly sorry for any potential partner Bert, a perpetual bachelor, may choose – unless she suffered from anosmia or he had a damn good wash before donning his dancing shoes. Bert shoved the book into his string shopping bag, ambling away with all the grace and coordination of a rusty one-wheeled bicycle.

Settling back into a comfortable position – leaning on the desk, elbows bent with her head resting on her hands – Lily tried to recapture her daydream, although Ida Pritchard was now prowling the romance section. Without warning, the older woman approached.

"Anything new in?"

Lily shook her head, knowing how Ida loved a good romance novel.

"Shame," Ida muttered, shoulders drooping in her elderly winter coat. "Didn't you and Peter meet in a rather romantic way?" she asked with interest, knowing full well that they met the previous year at the Fig Tree Hall murder mystery weekend.

Lily nodded. She had attended the event with great hopes of coming out of her shell and perhaps meeting someone who loved reading detective novels as much as she did. Her mother intermittently reminded that, at the ripe old age of twenty-two, Lily was in danger of being *left on the shelf.* Consequently, Lily increasingly dreamed of meeting someone just right *one day*, like the heroines in her favourite Miss Pringle mystery novels always seemed to do without even trying.

"Go on, what exactly happened?" Ida encouraged.

"Well, it came as a complete surprise to meet Constable Beresford there. He has such kind blue eyes that crinkle at the edges when he smiles, so I could tell he was nice. I soon discovered that he's also generous and rather funny."

Ida gave a wistful look. "Kind, funny and rich! So how did he discover Fig Tree Hall was his?"

Lily drew in a long breath to recount the tale. "It was all very unexpected, as these things usually are. The original owner of the

Hall was the famous inventor and scientist, Professor Thaddeus Ambrose. His son, Nathaniel, died of scarlet fever, aged six, while his daughter, Dorcas, was packed off to boarding school in America by her unscrupulous uncle, Ezra."

"I remember Evelyn Ambrose dying some years back. Such as shame when the boy passed too. Why wasn't the Hall just sold when Ambrose disappeared?" Ida asked bluntly.

"It was . . . Professor Ambrose's solicitor tracked down a distant relative. Major Manners-Gore was offered the Hall as, for some unfathomable reason, there didn't seem to be a will lodged with the solicitor, so Ambrose died intestate."

"It's a bad business," Ida muttered, shaking her head. And where does Peter come into it all?"

"Peter's mother, Nella, has worked as Cook up at the Hall for over thirty years. Ignoring her indiscretion, Peter's emerged as the true heir to Fig Tree Hall twenty-five years later."

"Ahhh!" Ida exclaimed knowingly. "And the fraud in the local papers?"

"The murder mystery clues uncovered that the Major and his manipulative friend, Dr Bailey, had actually been living off the Professor's income from his inventions for a quarter of a century. As you know, the fraudsters were unceremoniously removed from the Hall and, after a fair trial, sent to prison. Peter was stunned to find he's the new owner."

"Well, good for him! And here you are, eight months later and engaged . . ."

"We are indeed," Lily confirmed, knowing Ida wanted details of when she should buy a fancy big hat for the wedding.

"Couldn't make it up, could you? Inheriting a gothic mansion set in several acres with its own chapel in the grounds . . . Do you spend much time there?"

Lily visited the Hall most evenings to re-catalogue the vast library, a task she absolutely loved. She was currently working on the flora and fauna section, incorporating numerous very ancient and out of print leather-bound works. And it was at this stage in her happy recollections that Lily smiled, peering at the old Victorian clock that ticked away on the library wall.

"Oh, I try to get over there when I can, Mrs Pritchard."

Only an hour to go and Lily could catch the number 34 bus, spending another happy evening with the two things she loved most in the world – Peter Beresford and his wonderful private library.

♥

Constable Peter Beresford glanced at his watch after daydreaming of promotion again. He felt he certainly deserved it on account of him solving the mystery of the missing Professor Ambrose at Fig Tree Hall, mummified after many years in a secret room behind the library.

He had once longed for some excitement in his career – a bank robbery or a smuggling operation in Milford. This wish had come true with some very unexpected consequences after his discovery: Major Reginald Manners-Gore and old ally, Dr Simeon Bailey, had actually been defrauding him, Peter, out of his inheritance. The telephone rang shrilly and Peter automatically answered the call before his brain had engaged fully. "Fig Tree Hall," he announced, realising he was still at work.

A muted giggle was instantly recognisable as belonging to Lily. "Can't speak for long," she whispered, "just to say I'll be over after work."

Peter cradled the receiver in his hand, peering over one shoulder. Detective Constable Brian Cribbens and Sergeant Tom Whittaker were immersed in some paperwork, so he judged it safe to reply softly, "Great, I'll see you later." Brevity seemed necessary since their engagement as his workmates had taken to teasing him: *You'll soon be gaining a wife, landing yourself in all sorts of difficulties you could have avoided if you hadn't proposed in the first place. . .* They had also begun calling him 'The Lord of the Manor' whenever possible, something Peter took in good part but wondered if they would ever tire of.

Nella Barnes, staying on as Cook when Peter took possession of his inheritance, was thrilled at the engagement, never missing an opportunity to suggest she begin making the wedding cake. Peter and Lily frequently explained they were in no rush to set a date for their marriage, happy to have a reasonably long engagement, purely contented to be betrothed to one another to the exclusion of all others.

With his thoughts now travelling back to the murder mystery weekend, Peter was still amazed by how it had all come about: his mother's relationship with Thaddeus Ambrose, the father he had never known; taking possession of the Hall after the Major's long-term fraud and embezzlement activity; the unexpected steady income from his father's inventions and, of course, meeting Lily Green. When he put it all in a nutshell like that it was mind-blowing. And it had certainly knocked the desire for a bit of excitement through his police work into a cocked hat.

♥

The forthcoming Milford village fayre was a source of excitement for most of the residents as the grounds of Fig Tree Hall had been out of bounds before now. The Major and his wife, Lady Felicity, had always kept themselves at arm's length from the real world.

Discussing the previous owners one evening, Lily told Peter what she'd heard from a library patron. "Being former successful thespians, they continued to live some sort of strange fantasy existence after leaving the theatre, dreamily still treading the boards at Drury Lane. As a consequence, Major Reginald and Lady Felicity gained this reputation for being reclusive as well as unfriendly. According to the gossip-mongers, all kinds of dubious goings-on occurred here at the Hall."

Peter nodded. "The news that the Major had spent Ambrose's money very freely didn't come as a complete surprise to the locals."

"And how they treated Nella . . ."

Constable Beresford had been a familiar figure in the village, man and boy. Gossip long-fuelled the belief that Peter was the clever professor's son, born out of wedlock to Nella Barnes. For many months around the birth, a village girl helped out at the Hall, freely speaking the truth to anyone who would listen. Nella strongly enforced the idea that Peter's father had died during the war, that the villagers' muckraking was vicious and insulting. Eventually, she stopped trying to make people believe something they simply were not prepared to accept.

Since moving into the Hall, Peter (having thusly proved the villagers' suspicions correct) encouraged that bygones be bygones. His offer to open up the grounds of Fig Tree Hall for the village fayre was, he hoped, part of this process.

Diane Pargitter, larger than life and overly accustomed to treading on other peoples' corns, suddenly found herself widowed and penniless. She could not bring herself to accept that Frank (due to a cruel twist of fate) was no longer available to consult over life's big decisions. Indeed, had it not been for her hectoring enthusiasm to attend the Fig Tree Hall murder mystery weekend the previous autumn, there was a very great possibility he would still been alive today.

Word in the village of Milford put it about that Frank Pargitter had not actually been that good with money, failing to squirrel anything aside for a rainy day or his wife's future, should anything untoward occur. And as a life insurance salesman, this had proved to be a fatal flaw. Diane often spent her evenings wondering how it had all come to this: pacing the living room angrily, usually ranting to the empty room about the unfairness of it all and how (she would bet), no one else had ever been plunged into this highly unacceptable position.

The house, bought with an inheritance Diane received from her father, had been their home for almost twenty-five years. There were no words to describe the despair of having to let it go; the injustice that Frank had been so careless in dying like that without a fully paid-up insurance policy. There was sadness too, but not for the loss of Frank particularly. Diane decided the entire world was against her. And the loss of the home she thought was protected seemed the biggest blow of them all.

Waking that morning with steely determination not to plunge into wishy-washy wallowing, Diane accepted that a new path in life had to be forged. She kept herself busy, packing up everything she wanted to keep, donating much to the Oxfam shop in Milford High Street. The possessions she chose to retain held memories going back to her childhood as (Diane hated to admit), there was very little from her marriage that she wished to keep.

The pottery anniversary owl with bejewelled eyes and a quirky tilt of the head was the exception. The very last thing to be boxed up, he now sat alone on the bare mantle shelf, reminding Diane of better times. Now there was a buyer for the house, urging her out so that they (a young family with two lively children) could get in, Diane felt a cool detachment from her former home. The house sale was a business transaction, and she was graciously allowed to stay on until she and the owl had somewhere else to go.

A further bone of irritating contention concerned a recent summons to attend Fig Tree Hall from the unexpected new owner. Diane perceived this as undoubtedly another snub after the gothic pile had pulled the rug from under her. But curiosity over what might be revealed pricked her enough to attend, just to discover why she was, no doubt, the subject of yet another unpleasant outcome.

The kitchen at Fig Tree Hall was full of nervous energy, although this was due totally to the excitable young maid, Kitty Walker. "I know we're doing the refreshment tent," she enthused to Nella, sliding her petite frame past the much larger woman to stand, animated as a jumping bean by the oak kitchen dresser, "but I just don't think I can wait until Saturday! There's going to be a fortune teller and donkey rides, stalls, a coconut-shy and everything!" she blurted, her hazel eyes glowing like amber coals.

"Well, you're just going to have to," Nella pointed out crossly as she placed the pastry lid on a huge chicken pie, judging that she seemed to be the only one interested in getting the evening meal ready on time. She swiped a hand over her forehead to remove a wisp of silvery grey hair, almost knocking off her round, owlish spectacles. With feet throbbing a persistent tattoo after standing for most of the afternoon, Nella longed to deposit her sturdy frame into one of the comfortable kitchen chairs.

Now that her son owned Fig Tree Hall, a few things had changed, one being that Nella cooked the same meals for everyone, although Peter had taken to eating his in the formal dining room with Lily, if she was joining them.

"I hope the fayre's not going to get too out of hand – people trying to get inside the Hall to look around, that sort of thing," Sebastian Treadmill, forty-something thin and rangy butler-cum-valet remarked acidly.

"Yes, because then you might have to shift yourself and actually do some work for a change," Nella retorted. "Now that would be a novelty!"

Seb gave her a hurt look, but soon got over the insult, busying himself pouring a cup of tea from a giant brown teapot in the centre of the kitchen table. He neglected to enquire whether Nella or Kitty wanted to join him.

"I'm just saying – security could be an issue if I'm busy organising the parking and someone strays too far into the grounds. You never know what people might do, given the chance to–"

"If it's anyone, it'll be a nosey villager with a fondant fancy in their hand, curious to get a closer look, not a gang of robbers with crowbars you'll have to tackle single-handed," Nella scoffed.

"Let's hope you're right," Seb muttered darkly.

In the luxurious foyer of The Crown Hotel, a slender blonde dressed in a smart tweed two-piece, a rose-pink blouse and black high heeled boots approached the reception area. Pausing, she removed her tortoiseshell sunglasses to reveal a pair of dazzling green eyes. She announced in a confident American drawl, "I'd like a double room for the week."

The young receptionist beheld the vision of loveliness before him, musing that they definitely didn't get many of her sort in Milford.

"Certainly. May I take your name, please?" He gripped a pen tightly in his right hand, breathing in a waft of musky perfume as he prepared to write her details in the register.

"It's Barbara Andrews, Mrs Barbara Andrews," the extremely attractive woman provided seductively from between frosted coffee-coloured lips.

"Room number 24 is available," the receptionist said without missing a beat or breaking eye contact, handing her a key attached to a Crown Hotel key fob. "Could you sign here, please? Your room is on the second floor and there's a lift just over there. I can have your luggage sent up." He indicated the far corner of the foyer housing a very large potted palm, almost obscuring the area he wanted her to see.

The woman smiled broadly, wanting to say, "You mean the *elevator*?" but stopping herself. She took up the pen in her left hand, hesitating for a moment before signing her name.

"On holiday in Milford, are you?" the receptionist enquired, assessing that the woman – somewhere in her mid-thirties – was rather wealthy, judging by her jewellery. He saw it as his duty to be interested in the guests' comings and goings.

The attractive Mrs Andrews smiled again, lifting her tapestry travel bag. "Something like that," she replied before disappearing in

the direction of the potted palm and the lift
beyond it.

Coffee Cake & Lacking Leaflets

Friday 19th May, 1958

Felicity Manners-Gore, formerly the self-titled *Lady* Felicity and resident of Fig Tree Hall, sighed as she appraised her new business partner – the robust, vicious-tongued and devoutly cake-loving Diane Pargitter. The unlikely pair met as a result of a murder mystery weekend, where Diane's unfortunate husband departed this life after drinking fig wood tea: a tonic for the healthy but to be avoided in the case of a dicky ticker. Poor Frank suffered a heart attack and died in front of the library fireplace, casting a dampener on the murder mystery activities.

In a hugely generous gesture, Peter, as the new owner of the Hall, had bought Felicity and Diane the leasehold on a small tea shop in Wenham – the next village over from Milford on the map – as both women were homeless and had unfortunately lost their husbands.

Nella Barnes agreed (after some persuasion, given that Felicity's husband had denied Peter his rightful inheritance for so many years), to share her recipes with the two women. Neither was well acquainted with the smooth, efficient running of a kitchen nor, it had to be said, running a business.

Felicity Manners-Gore had rarely set foot in the kitchen at Fig Tree Hall, becoming very used to being waited upon hand and foot by the three resident staff members, never questioning how the Major could have afforded them. Now, with her husband imprisoned for five years for fraud, she had to make the best of a bad situation, recognising that Peter had, in fact, been extremely kind.

Diane Pargitter, already of the opinion that the world owed her a living, was equally stunned when Peter invited her with Felicity to the Hall to discuss a business proposition. They learned that the Wenham tea shop lease had already been purchased. With no insurance pay-out for Frank's demise, Diane had little choice other than to accept the generous offer, despite a growing dread that her inexpertise in the kitchen was about to become public knowledge.

Many delaying tactics stalled the opening of the new tea shop, including several months spent by Diane and Felicity with Nella

Barnes, trying to master the art of cake and pastry making. In Peter's opinion, the two women seemed in no particular hurry to get the premises habitable (each having a bedroom over the shop), or to gain enough confidence and practice to actually run the shop as a business.

The most pressing problem for Diane – aside from the fact she had absolutely no talent for producing pastries and cakes – was that the new venture needed a name.

Felicity experienced a flicker of doubt that she was personally up to running a business and especially, to running one with a selfish woman who seemed to upset other people as a hobby. Diane Pargitter – it had to be said, did not take prisoners, calling a spade a spade.

Both women stood in the empty little shop, taking in the newly-painted stark white walls, bare shelves, un-stocked counter, and several little wooden tables stacked with chairs.

Diane placed her hands emphatically on rounded hips and summed it all up with one question: "Is this it then?"

"It would seem so, yes." Felicity responded with irritation.

"So, we've got to set this place up as a tea shop and do what Nella showed us, offering   refreshments   to   visiting customers?" Diane's dark piggy eyes narrowed.

"Again, yes."

Diane pulled down one of the stacked chairs, sinking heavily into it as the news seemed to hit her for the first time. "But, I didn't think it would all be so *empty*. I suppose I was imagining there would still be some stock – wrapped cakes and things, staff who already know how to bake and run the business. We haven't even decided what to call this place and we don't have any experience in running a tea shop!"

"That," Felicity said coolly, "is the challenge we face. We can't afford to employ anyone to help so we must just be grateful for the lifeline Peter's thrown us. I'm trying not to blame Reggie for being such a fool, landing me in this situation. Surely the man knew he couldn't keep taking money that wasn't his . . . We must simply buckle down and get on with it – there's no other choice."

Diane nodded, secretly resenting the fact she'd have to cut her long fingernails. They were her pride and joy – thanks to the quantity of cheese she ate. Foregoing her favoured scarlet varnish in future in case it chipped off into the buns was a major sacrifice.

"But far worse than that, we'll have to get our skates on because Peter expects us to run the cake stall at the village fayre. We haven't even got a name for the shop yet, Felicity. *And* I won't even mention that I still have terrible nightmares about Frank – how he lost his life at the Hall because of that dreadful fig tea. Have they thought of that? No, they have not. If you ask me–"

"It will be a steep learning curve, as they say," Felicity interrupted.

"I can't see how calling it, 'THE MANNERS-GORE & PARGITTER TEA ROOMS' will get the customers rolling in. Hasn't got much of a ring to it. We need something snappy and perhaps a bit clever, so people will remember it."

Felicity thought for a long moment before the answer seemed to trip off her tongue. "What about *All Buns Glazing*? It's a Spoonerism, but it fits our purposes nicely."

"What?" Diane asked ignorantly.

"A Spoonerism. The Reverend Spooner used to periodically transpose the first letters of words without meaning to, so he ended up saying something funny. He was giving a sermon once and said, 'The Lord is a shoving leopard' instead of a 'loving shepherd'. Do you see?"

Diane nodded, hating it when other people were so much cleverer than her. "I suppose it'll have to do," she muttered.

♥

Inside the kitchen at *All Buns Glazing*, things were not going to plan. In the throes of making a coffee and walnut cake for the fayre, Diane had encountered some problems. Felicity unwittingly entered the scene to find Diane muttering, poking at the two halves of sponge in tins just removed from the oven.

"It's a complete disaster," Diane wailed pitifully. "I followed the recipe carefully, but just look at it!"

Felicity regarded the two cooling sandwich tins critically, making the damning observation, "It's lopsided – you had the oven too hot. On the collapsed side, it's got a burnt edge."

"Maybe when it's a bit cooler, I can prize it out of the tins?" Diane ventured, her thin, pencilled eyebrows rising with unstinting hope as she urged the cake not to lose the will to live.

Felicity shook her head, sensibly remaining mute as Diane whipped a carving knife out of the nearby drawer. Not stopping to consider the consequences, she plunged it into the cake, hacking off the burnt edge like cleaving into a rock face. This action was speedily followed by slicing the bulging, risen top off the still-too-hot to handle better half. It protested in the strongest terms, breaking open so that the proposed top layer now sported a wide chasm, akin to a leering grin.

Diane and Felicity stood back to assess the situation in full. "I'll glue it back together with icing," Diane suggested. "You won't even know the difference."

Felicity shot her a look confirming that she begged to differ and she left the kitchen, shaking her head.

Setting about her task with a hope and a prayer, Diane took a palette knife to the seemingly healthier of the two cake halves, running it around the edge of the tin. Turning the still-molten sandwich tin over with strong conviction she tapped gently, fully expecting the contents to flop elegantly out onto the cooling rack, strategically positioned on the work surface.

Much of the cake obliged, but a stubborn quarter remained stuck firm. *What should I do?* Diane thought with desperation. *Start again? Head to the village shop tomorrow before the fayre opens?* Too late, Diane recalled Nella's instruction to always properly grease and line the tins in order to lift the perfectly-risen, golden-brown sponge halves out with joyful expectation of another winner. *Maybe next time . . .*

"Butter cream!" Diane squealed out loud to no one in particular. With the knowledge that there was no butter lurking in the fridge, only a concocted, primrose-coloured margarine, she did her best with the materials available to her. The yellow spread mixed well with the icing sugar but separated violently with the addition of a few drops of instant black coffee for colour and taste.

Panicking anew, she poured in half a bag of icing sugar to thicken the mixture, which stubbornly remained the consistency of lumpy, runny porridge. The colour and smell were good though, Diane assessed, brightening. Sticking the jigsaw slowly back together, she gained confidence and loftily announced, "It's looking fine now – presentation isn't everything."

To her horror, Felicity appeared back in the kitchen to watch the sad scene. Gathering as many cake crumbs as she could muster, Diane carefully spooned them into the gaping abyss, pressing the edges of the sponge firmly together, willing them to retain a vague cake shape.

"The butter cream wasn't altogether a success either, but I'm sure it'll taste good," Diane assured her audience, trying hard to convince herself.

Felicity gave Diane one of her knowing looks, the kind that indicated she was virtually Mrs Beeton by comparison. "I can't see many walnuts. Did you chop them up really finely?" she interrogated.

Diane's hand shot to her mouth, making it all too obvious there had been a complete oversight in the nuts department. In an attempt to salvage the cake, Diane made what she thought was a perfectly legitimate suggestion. "I could shape it like a heart, cutting that wonky bit off that I've stuck on the side – it will look better once it's iced."

Felicity shot her another look, mumbling, "There's no need to provide a running commentary. Your impediment is that you often have to pause for breath." With this, Felicity returned to her task of looking over the business accounts in the sitting room. As a parting shot she observed candidly, "I wouldn't bother with the icing, it's beyond help."

But Diane was unwilling to give up quite so easily. She emptied the remaining icing sugar into a glass bowl. A cloud rose up, making her choke as the atmosphere filled with sweet little white specks.

"How much water do you add to icing?" Diane muttered to herself, denying Felicity the pleasure of denouncing her efforts.

With tenacity, Diane resolved it was possible to turn this ugly duckling into a swan, (and then Felicity would literally have to eat her words, forced to try a slice of the calamitous coffee cake).

She continued to mumble sarcastically, waving her head from side to side. "I'm now adding the remains of the coffee for colour and flavour," she informed no one in particular. Diane added a prayer that she kept to herself: *For what I am about to do, may the Lord make me truly accurate . . .*

Without any particular skill, she proceeded to hack and whittle each half into a vague heart shape. This achieved, Diane nervously confronted the bowl of icing, hoping the sticky substance would cover a multitude of sins.

The disastrous icing mixture was still too runny and Diane abandoned it to stiffen in private, turning her attention to slavering on the sumptuous buttercream to sandwich the sponge heart halves together. The ailing filling remained in a state of separation following the earlier addition of hot, liquid coffee.

Having hastily applied the brown, fatty mixture to the bottom layer of sponge and carefully positioning the top layer, Diane quickly sandbagged whole walnuts around the edge to prevent leakage. This also (she prided herself generously) made up for not showing the cake even a whiff of walnut until this point. *No one would ever know . . .*

Of the opinion that she had cunningly gotten away with her walnut-and-runny-icing sandbagging technique, Diane turned to find Felicity behind her, scaring Diane to the extent that she almost dropped her remaining walnuts.

"Ooh!" Felicity commented, evidently not approving of the ingenuity, "It really isn't looking good, is it?"

Diane did not respond positively to the constructive criticism, inserting more emergency walnuts around the sandwiched edges of the two tiers – or *tears*, as it had almost descended to. Filling oozed menacingly ever-nearer the tipping point, threatening to flood out like an overly-sweet pyroclastic flow of magma. In one swift movement of which Diane was immensely proud, she pushed the unstable top storey into a better position on its shaky walnut foundations, sustaining only a slight fracture to the ego in the process.

Felicity remained in the kitchen with harassment in mind. "Isn't adding icing just compounding the fiasco?" She pointed a well-manicured finger at the oozing, heart-shaped failure on the counter top.

Diane ignored her, continuing the task – no one could accuse Diane Pargitter of lacking tenacity as she dripped coffee icing over the uneven craters of sponge.

"See?" she cried with jubilation, "It's really sticky now – I'm having a job spreading it." Diane gesticulated with her spatula and an unhealthy amount of smugness.

Proceeding without caution, Diane wielded a palette knife like a trowel, filling gaps and gluing chunks in situ when they were lifted out of place by the probing, sticky blade.

"I've run out of icing now," she exclaimed, peering into the bag, doubting there was enough to finish the job. She mixed the sparse remainder (hidden in the folds of the bag of icing sugar), with a few more teaspoons of freshly made coffee.

"It's not even the same colour!" Felicity blurted, causing Diane to marvel at the woman's excellent observational skills. The icing now uniformly covered the structure, hiding a multitude of sins, although the cake still looked as though it had been unexpectedly involved in a derailment which had startled it severely.

Despite the fact that the icing refused to spread, a new calamity was now in progress. "Help – it's running down the sides!" Diane cried, looking on sadly as the whole uneven mess became alive with dripping icing.

As the cake continued to seep dangerously, Diane roughly inserted more emergency walnuts between the two layers, a desperate effort to heighten the shorter side and stem the flow. A ring of walnuts around the top of the cake slowed the seepage and overflow.

"What do we do now?" Diane asked, standing back in a surveying manoeuvre with the expectation of being told that, all things considered, it didn't look too bad.

"Stick it in the fridge so we don't have to look at it," came the savage reply. Shoving Diane's creation unceremoniously onto the bottom shelf at the back of the large fridge, Felicity declared that she would rather not have the pleasure, if it was all the same.

An hour passed with Diane completely miserable, fighting a growing hatred of all things baking-related. Needing a very large dollop of cheering up, she ventured into the *All Buns Glazing* kitchen, opening the fridge door to peer in.

The cake appeared to have firmed up a lot and Diane brightened, telling herself this was just a dry run. Convinced she could not possibly sell it at the fayre, Diane bravely brought the cake out of its confinement and cut a slice. She was delighted to see that the innards looked quite tempting and moist.

She took a generous bite, surprised by the result. The icing sweetness was offset by the fact that Diane had used less than the required amount of sugar in the recipe, as well as one less egg because she'd forgotten to order more and only had two. With Diane's rounded cheeks extended like a gutsy gerbil as her jaws tackled the generous proportion of whole walnuts, Felicity entered the kitchen, catching her at it.

"What *are* you doing, Mrs Pargitter?" she asked with incredulity, using the other woman's full name as Felicity did when she wanted to emphasise something especially well.

Diane stopped chewing for a brief moment, then spoke, spraying Felicity with crumbs. "It's really rather good," she cried. "We couldn't sell it, obviously, because it doesn't look right, but the coffee flavour is marvellous!" She continued to chew with an expression of sheer ecstasy, proffering the remainder on her plate towards Felicity.

Her business partner gave a disgusted look, brushing the projected crumbs from her pale pink twinset. Clearing her throat, Felicity enunciated carefully, "Obviously you feel it's your duty to test any baking failures – which have been many. Evidently you were compelled to wolf down a third of this latest creation." She shook her head, adding a pitying look. "At this rate, we won't have a thing for the cake stall, or to open the shop with next week, as you're eating all the profits!"

Finishing her mouthful, Diane belligerently placed both hands on her hips as she countered, "Well, I don't see *you* doing any cooking, and I hate to see anything go to waste."

Felicity sighed, leaving Diane to finish her wedge of cake. She bit her tongue, stopping herself from adding, "More like going to *waist*."

In the pristine foyer of The Crown Hotel, a tall man in a smart grey suit cleared his throat to attract the attention of the receptionist. The younger man turned from his task, regarding the newcomer. The visitor smiled briefly, placing both hands flat on the desk; immediately, the receptionist noticed the pale band of skin on the third finger of the man's left hand where a wedding ring had recently been.

"How can I help you, sir?" the receptionist asked politely.

A rich, smooth voice responded with an American accent, informing the receptionist that he would like to book in.

"Certainly. Single or double?"

The man smiled again, although it did not reach his eyes. "I believe my wife is already staying here . . ."

The receptionist became instantly wary. "And what name would that be, sir?"

The stranger looked momentarily shifty. "Barbara Andrews. I think she booked for the whole week."

Instantly recalling the glamorous American woman with startling green eyes, he wondered who this man was to her. *It's obvious he's an American, but what if she's booked herself in here because she doesn't want to see him?*

At that moment, the lift doors opened and Barbara Andrews strolled confidently out into the foyer. She stopped dead when she saw who was at the desk and the receptionist felt a surge of excitement, expecting some kind of fireworks.

"*Darling*!" Barbara cried, crossing the floor to greet the man with enthusiasm. "I didn't know you'd be here so soon."

The visitor gave his full attention to the gushing blonde. "My bit of business finished early, so I took a flight and here I am!" He smiled broadly, his cornflower blue eyes sparkling. But the receptionist suspected it was all for show.

"Have you booked in? I got us a double room, number 24."

He continued to smile at his wife while the receptionist tried to hide his irritation at having neither the man's name nor intention. Trained to be discreet and not to interrupt when guests were in conversation, he decided he was within his rights to demand a name – if this gentleman was planning to stay at The Crown.

Mustering courage, the receptionist cleared his throat loudly. "Could I just take some details? The manager will fire me if I don't have a record of who's staying in each room!" The joke sounded hollow, the voice tinny in his own ears. He bowed his head and waited.

Taking his time and holding Barbara Andrews' left hand firmly as if she were more precious to him than rubies, her husband turned to the receptionist. "I'm Charles Andrews, and I'll be staying with my wife in room 24."

The receptionist cringed inwardly, irritated by the complacency. He glanced at the bookings register, attempting to look busy while the American couple chatted on, regardless of his presence.

"So, now you're here, you can join me in a little trip to the village library," Barbara said with marked enthusiasm.

"Sounds interminably dull," her husband replied in a bored voice. "Wouldn't you rather we find a nice restaurant for lunch?"

Barbara Andrews shook her head fiercely. "No! There's something I have to do before I can even think about food. Here's the room key – take your bag up and I'll wait for you here."

Charles headed for the lift without another word. His wife gave a quick glance at the receptionist – who had been about to offer Andrews his own key and the services of the hotel porter. He caught her look and smiled, busying himself unnecessarily at the pigeon-holes. *Is it my imagination, or is she looking rather furtive?* he assessed.

At lunchtime on a Friday, Milford village library was dead. The wall clock ticked loudly and dust motes jostled one another in a bright beam of May sunshine spilling through the window.

Lily peered around the empty cathedral of silence, wishing it was time to catch her bus to Fig Tree Hall. Even the elderly Mr Lucas was absent, having departed to the local park to eat his spam sandwich, the same thing he had every day.

As she daydreamed of getting back into the re-cataloguing of the flora and fauna section in the Fig Tree Hall library, the door creaked open revealing a startling sight. A couple made their way towards the enquiry desk, although the man appeared to be holding back. The woman smiled pleasantly but Lily faltered, feeling she needed to sit down rather quickly. Instead, she gripped the desk in front of her until her knuckles went white.

Just take some deep breaths, she told herself. *It can't possibly be her . . .*

The woman arrived directly in front of Lily to enquire, "Are you all right? You're so pale, your freckles are standing out."

Horrified by the personal nature of the woman's comment, delivered in a smooth American drawl, Lily merely nodded. Her mind darted back to the previous autumn when she had met a virtually identical creature who said she was schooled in America. *But Cecelia Morris is in prison for attempted fraud and blackmail . . .*

"Quiet as the grave in here," the woman observed, peering around the empty library and catching her companion's eye as he stood nearby, examining a bulging shelf of art books.

"Y-yes. Err, how can I help you?" Lily finally managed, her mind going ten to the dozen.

"Well, I've just arrived in Milford after many years abroad – took a stroll down here from The Crown Hotel as it's such a fine day." The woman paused to pat her already immaculate hair into place before continuing with her request. "I wonder, do you have anything on the big manor house up the road – Fig Tree Hall, I think it's called?"

Lily's mouth began to form a perfect 'O' as she stared openly at the smartly dressed blonde. *This is like déja vu.* Suddenly shaken back to her senses, Lily resumed her usual professional air, announcing, "I'll just check for you."

Knowing only too well what information the library kept on Fig Tree Hall, she bent to pull out a drawer of index cards, mercifully breaking eye contact with the woman's piercingly vivid green stare. Lily rummaged loudly in the drawer for what she considered was a suitable time, straightening to meet the unrelenting emerald gaze once more.

"Well?" the woman demanded impatiently, "Do you have anything or not?"

Lily was taken aback by her brusque tone but tried not to let it show. *Remarkable! This creature even has a similar temperament to her jailed counterpart,* she decided, significantly unnerved.

"We do have this short pamphlet on the history of the Hall, recently produced by the current owner, so it happens," Lily provided evenly.

"Oh, is that all? I was hoping for some proper background," the woman said, snatching the pamphlet from Lily's grasp. "You see, I absolutely *love* anything to do with architecture and history. The Hall looks so beautifully gothic, I've decided I just have to go and visit it while I'm here."

Lily suspected a red hue was creeping up her neck as she took personal responsibility for the lack of information. "I don't think the current owner accepts visitors as the Hall isn't a public attraction locally, but there is a village fayre in the grounds tomorrow, if you're interested. . ."

The woman gave Lily a direct look, cupping her beautifully manicured hands on the enquiry desk in a dominant fashion. "Oh yes, I'm interested. Do you have a leaflet about that too?"

Lily handed her a leaflet taken from the pile provided by Mrs Doris Weaver, village organiser and all-round clever-clogs with a clipboard.

"The resident's association provided us with these, giving the time and place. This also tells you about some of the stalls and attractions to expect." She watched the woman's attractive face harden as she greedily took possession of the leaflet.

"Do you know anything about the new owner," the visitor suddenly asked.

Lily paused for a long moment before saying, "A little. Why, what is it that you wanted to know?" Her heart quickened, sensing there was more to the intense interest than mere tourist curiosity.

The American woman drew in a sharp breath. "Well, I heard the new owner came by the Hall in very unusual circumstances."

Lily felt panic surge inside her and she struggled to remain calm. "Where did you hear that? You mentioned you've only just arrived in Milford."

"Oh, I can't recall . . . Perhaps it was someone talking in the hotel bar before lunch."

Eyeing the blonde visitor warily, Lily carefully chose her words. "I'm afraid I don't know any of the details – I'm just the local librarian."

Tossing her head with superiority, the woman replied, "Oh, don't do yourself down! Granted, you have red hair and freckles, but with a bit of make-up, you could be quite acceptable."

Stunned, Lily could do no more than stutter, "T-thank-you. I hope we see you at the fayre tomorrow."

Sashaying away, the woman nodded, throwing over her shoulder, "You surely will."

In the kitchen at Fig Tree Hall, Nella Barnes, Seb Treadmill, Kitty Walker and Peter were seated around the table.

"Well, we're certainly ready for an early start tomorrow, but I doubt those two at the tea shop are," Nella announced with scorn.

"Why, what's happened now?" Peter asked his mother, almost afraid to hear the answer.

Nella chuckled. "That pair haven't got a clue about baking, and after all the training I've given them! They both turned up here earlier like two hungry orphans pleading for cake, so I said I'd bake an extra four Victoria sandwiches so they can have them on their stall!"

As the chortling continued, Lily burst through the back door, sending Kitty shooting from her chair. "Blimey!" she cried, clutching her chest, "I nearly had heart failure!"

"Sorry, sorry," Lily said, pulling up a kitchen chair to join them. "I've just had the most extraordinary experience! You'll never guess who I just had in at the library, or thought I had in . . ."

Kitty looked confused as Seb made a stab at a guess. "Film star?" he asked hopefully.

"Not quite," Lily replied. "A blonde woman who looked the absolute spit of Cecelia Morris, you know – the one who was imprisoned for trying to defraud and blackmail the Manners-Gores last year?"

"What did she want?" asked Peter with interest.

"She asked for information about the Hall, said she'd heard the new owner inherited under unusual circumstances!"

Nella looked horrified. "Well I hope you sent the nosey baggage away with a flea in her ear! It's nobody else's business."

"Not exactly," Lily said, biting her lip.

"What then?" Treadmill asked, keen for some juicy gossip.

"I told her the village fayre was being held here tomorrow and she asked for a leaflet.

Unforeseen Circumstances

Saturday 20th May, 1958

Positioned behind a trestle table that sagged in the middle, Lily carefully re-arranged a brace of books across the hazardous space. *This is not what I imagined*, she told herself, peering around to see other stall-holders similarly trying to create an eye-catching display as they set out their wares.

To her left, Diane Pargitter and Felicity Manners-Gore prominently displayed the four donated Victoria sponges to be the first thing any hopeful cake-purchaser saw. Plates of uneven pastry creations and some aptly-named rock cakes also lurked with intent further back on the table.

On Lily's right, Arthur Hodges, the local antiques 'expert' set out a selection of china cups and saucers that did not appear to match, along with a large clock with no mechanism inside, and a chipped Willow pattern tureen. He caught her gaze and grinned to reveal a missing front tooth.

To Lily's horror, Arthur made his way casually over to her stall. He stood surveying the book titles she had just unpacked from the two boxes at her feet. Some of the spines sported library tags – Mr Lucas had kindly agreed she could have a few less popular titles for the village fayre. Many books were acquired – dog-eared and well-thumbed, with yellowing pages or obscure titles, placed in a box in the library by well-meaning patrons as a donation.

Arthur Hodges picked a worse-for-wear paperback out of one of the boxes at Lily's feet, invading her space by stepping behind the trestle table barrier denoting customer and seller.

"*How to Deal with Annoying People* by Patricia Frobisher-Wright," he read, grinning again to reveal the black chasm in his dentition. "If her name's anything to go by, the annoying people she probably means are tradesmen at the door, when her servants are too busy to answer the bell."

How apt that he should chose a book about annoying people, thought Lily, smiling politely. "Do you want to buy it, Mr Hodges? It's for a good cause – all proceeds go to Milford cottage hospital."

"Not to your boyfriend, then?" he leered in an over-friendly way, getting even closer.

"Certainly not! Peter offered the grounds of the Hall for the fayre, that's all. *And*, strictly speaking, we're not open to the public until nine o'clock – I haven't finished laying out my stall yet."

"I'm not *the public,* dear," Arthur Hodges said belligerently, fingering a large cookbook laying across the dip where the two halves of the table met. "Other stallholders always get first dibs on the good stuff before the public streams in." He rummaged carelessly through the second box of books, giving Lily a perfect view of his shiny scalp at the back of his head. "Have you got that Agatha Crispy novel, *A Thwack Across the Noggin?*" he asked hopefully, straightening up to face her.

Lily gave him the full benefit of her librarian's stare. "Are you just being silly, or is there something you actually want to buy?"

He looked perplexed, venturing, "Maybe I've got the title wrong. Maybe I meant, *Murder on the Orient Express . . .*"

"There's no Agatha Christie. Her books are very popular at the library and none were donated – people like to keep her books and read them again and again." *If there were any Agatha Christie novels going begging,* Lily thought, *I'd have got there first.* Smiling benevolently, she said, "If that's what you're after, I'm afraid I can't help you."

Arthur Hodges shuffled back to his own stall muttering, "Not much point having a book stall then, specially if you've got nothing popular."

♥

When the flood gates opened at nine o'clock there was a steady trickle of visitors, keen to inspect the permitted section of the grounds for the first time. As Lily made her first sale of the day, *Build Your Own Light Aircraft* to Ivor Mugg who, she mused, lived in a flat on the outskirts of the village, Diane Pargitter's penetrating voice met her ears.

"All I'm saying is, why did they put the refreshment tent so near?" She assumed her trademark hands on hips posture. "Puts people off buying *our* cakes if they can have a sit down and a cup of tea at the same time just over there." Her pencilled eyebrows rose as she posed the question to Felicity Manners-Gore, seated behind the cake stall in a stripey blue and white deckchair.

Distracted by gazing at the Hall that had once been her home, Felicity shook her head, coming out of her daydream. "Does it really matter? People will buy ours to take home with them, and eat Nella's while they're here."

Diane tutted loudly, refusing to let the subject drop. "I've only sold two rock cakes and a scone from a packet I got at the shop, but there's been a constant stream of customers to *that* tent. You'd think people wouldn't need topping up so soon after breakfast!" To emphasise her point, Diane took a scone from the plate in front of her, cramming it into her mouth. She chewed briefly, swallowing it in five seconds flat.

Felicity looked suitably revolted and closed her eyes, letting the May sunshine warm her face.

"*And,*" Diane continued doggedly, pointing a pudgy finger at a plate of brown triangles in various unappealing states, some bursting open, others verging on cremated, "you haven't even mentioned my peach and apple turnovers!"

Felicity raised one sleepy eyelid, squinting at her demanding business partner. "I thought it kinder not to, dear."

Diane turned away, her face doing a good impression of a boiling kettle. She contented herself with re-arranging the table display, helping herself to a generous slice of Victoria sponge to assist her concentration while gentle snores came from the deckchair. Interchanging a plate of shop-bought fondant fancies with her home-made rock cakes, Diane glanced up and gave a shrill scream.

"*What on earth!?*" Felicity spluttered, catapulted awake by a noise akin to a hippo breaking wind. She came rapidly to her senses, staring in astonishment.

"I thought that nasty piece of work was locked up," Diane hissed, aptly summing up what Felicity was thinking. No holds barred, Diane continued with her observation. "I suppose she could be out by now . . . But what sort of person returns to the place they committed fraud and blackmail? She's got the cheek of the devil, that one. I see she's now got some poor sap in tow!"

Felicity said nothing, unable to believe Cecelia Morris would return to the Hall under any circumstances after her former disgraceful behaviour.

"Oh, sweet Jesus, *they're getting closer!*" Diane exclaimed, rather too loudly. Lily looked up from the book she was perusing to follow the line of Diane's open-mouthed stare.

"Good morning to you," the smart woman said, arriving directly in front of Diane and Felicity's stall with her male companion.

"What on earth are you even doing here!?" Diane cried, refusing to believe the audacity of the brazen female.

"*I beg your pardon?*" the woman replied haughtily, her friendliness turning on a dime.

"You've got a damned cheek, Cecelia. That's all I have to say!" Diane moved away, refusing to make eye contact as the unscrupulous bitch stood bold as brass in front of her Victoria sandwiches.

The woman removed her tortoiseshell sunglasses, green eyes glinting with bewilderment. "I think you've made a mistake," she said in an even tone. "I'm not this Cecelia person – my name is Barbara Andrews."

"Whatever you're calling yourself now," Diane blurted harshly, "you're not welcome at the Hall. Poor Felicity here has lost her husband and her home because of the secrets you stirred up–"

"Show her your passport, honey," the man said, looking bored with this example of English eccentricity.

Diane glared at the couple in a way she had been practising for difficult customers in the shop. *Come opening day, anyone being difficult with me will be given short shrift . . .*

The astonished female rummaged in her black, patent leather handbag, waving an American passport under Diane's nose.

"See? I'm exactly who I say I am! I know you English can be odd at times, but I didn't think I'd have to show my passport to buy a pastry!" The woman's Cupid's bow lips formed a bemused smile, annoying Diane further.

"I'm prepared to sell you one of my peach and apple turnovers – although you're lucky I have any left, them being so popular. *But* that doesn't mean I believe you – anyone can have a passport made up in a false name these days. It's a trick played in all the good detective novels." She glanced over at Lily for clarification. Diane then chose an unfortunate-looking turnover, placed it in a bag and thrust it at the woman.

"How much?" she asked, keen to get away from the mad person seemingly entrusted to be in charge of the cake stall.

"A penny, or just put a donation in the biscuit tin," Diane indicated, tapping the receptacle she had personally emptied earlier that week. "That is," she added scornfully, "if you've got any *English* coinage."

The woman opened her bag, withdrew a red suede purse and threw a couple of coins into the tin so they clattered on the metal like bullet shots. Clutching the brown paper bag now sporting numerous greasy smudges, Barbara Andrews turned to leave with her companion. "Have a nice day!" she drawled tightly as a parting comment.

Peter Beresford bounded over to the book stall with a grin on his face. "Sorry, it's been non-stop, answering questions and people congratulating me on how lovely the grounds look. It's almost as if I'd mowed them myself!" he said jovially.

Lily placed another book on her table from the boxes. *Forgotten Foods: Enjoying How They Used to Cook,* had been sold to Bert Buttermere, who had lingered unpleasantly.

"Well things haven't been quite so jolly here, I'm afraid. That woman turned up again, the one I told you about who looks the exact spit of Cecelia Morris. Says her name's Barbara Andrews – even whipped out her passport to prove it!" Lily recounted.

Peter raised a dark eyebrow. "So where is she now, this *doppelganger*?"

Lily shrugged. "Don't know. I heard the man she was with mention he was heading back to the hotel. She went off in the direction of the fortune teller's tent clutching a bag containing one of Diane's cakes." Lowering her voice conspiratorially, Lily whispered, "Poor thing's probably succumbed in the shrubbery!"

Peter laughed. "Or Madame Lazonga, a.k.a. Flossie Draper from the fish shop, foresaw something in her crystal ball and Barbara's gone trotting off to seek her fortune!"

Peter suddenly caught Diane Pargitter's eyes on him as she attempted to listen in to the conversation. He turned away, lowering his voice as Lily's mouth formed a straight line.

"Seriously though, I expect she's just one of those blonde women who looks exactly the same as another because she has the same hairstyle or similar clothes. There can't be two Cecelia Morris's in this world!"

Lily looked thoughtful for a long moment. "But it's not just that. They also have similar mannerisms and the same vivid green eyes. This Barbara person is American, and Cecelia said she went to school over there. *And*, as I told you, the woman was asking about the Hall, saying she'd heard you came by it in an unusual way."

Peter Beresford shrugged. "I particularly love how you're so good at piecing together throwaway facts, as demonstrated at the murder mystery last year. It's probably just a rather weird coincidence that an American tourist looks like someone we know."

Refusing to accept it was that simple, Lily concluded, "But with your policeman's intuition, I'd have thought you'd instantly see why I'm suspicious. There are some very odd people out there . . ."

Light-heartedly, Peter replied, "There sure are, but I'm not going to worry about it at the moment. Shall I take over the stall while you visit Flossie the Fortune Teller? I know there's always a whiff of haddock about her, but I hear she's pretty good."

Smiling, Lily came around to the front of her trestle table. "Think I'll do just that!"

Peter searched in vain to find a brief summary of the book Ida Pritchard had declared she wanted to buy. Turning a few pages then flicking to the back cover, he quickly read the short paragraph. "Well, as the title suggests, *Hot Muffins!* is about the history of bread baking, from ancient times to present day–"

"Ohhh!" Ida exclaimed, her face falling. "I think I'll leave it then." She scuttled away, gripping her wicker basket tightly, heading for the cake stall with hope in her eyes.

"Are you Peter, by any chance?" an exasperated man said, pulling a harness attached to two donkeys that lagged behind him.

"I am. You must be the man who does the donkey rides, unless you've just brought them to the fayre for a day out." Peter chuckled as one of the animals stretched its long grey neck, taking a muzzle-full of one of Diane's Victoria sponges.

"Rufus! Stop that!" the man cried as the donkey snatched a peach and apple turnover, knocking the plate to the floor. The animal chewed determinedly.

Diane glared angrily at the mess, her round face magenta and critical. "I can't sell those now – they'll have to be thrown away!" *He'll pay dearly for that!* she decided, placing both hands on her ample hips to demonstrate her displeasure at the creature's indiscretion. Felicity chortled from her deckchair, then dozed off again.

"Shouldn't be allowed," Diane muttered menacingly, "letting wild animals roam around, helping themselves to the cakes!"

"Sorry lady. He's already had two teacakes and a scone in the refreshment tent. I only went in to ask where I could set up the rides. A grey-haired woman in there said I should come and find Peter, as she wasn't sure."

Diane was not impressed.

The man stroked the ears of the better-behaved donkey as Rufus looked on belligerently. "Wingnut here is as good as gold, but this one! I had to give the refreshments lady both a shilling and an apology – he's costing me more than he'll make giving rides." Rufus brayed loudly while Wingnut looked smug.

"I'm not really sure where you should put them, as I'm not in charge of organising the fayre," Peter told the harassed man. "It was just decided by the villagers to each do something, make a bit of money for the hospital. And they've all shown up – fantastic really." Peter watched Rufus eyeing up the plate of rock cakes. "Mrs Doris Weaver is in charge, overseeing things, but I couldn't tell you where she is at the moment. Maybe back at the refreshment tent?"

The donkey owner looked doubtful. "I'm not taking him back in there! Took ages to coax him away from the individual apple pies – he's got a whiff of them now and he'll clear the lot, if you let him."

Peter nodded, catching sight of Lily making her way back to her stall. She had an ice-cream cornet in each hand and licked at one that was beginning to drip, holding the other out to him.

Without skipping a beat, Rufus extended his neck, clamping his muzzle firmly around the proffered cornet. He sucked it from Lily's grasp before she knew what was happening. The stubborn animal then chewed thoughtfully, his eyes widening as he got to grips with the freezing cold mouthful.

"Ohhh!" Lily cried in disbelief, "That was full-cream vanilla!"

The donkey owner bowed his head in contrition. "He prefers chocolate, but he'll eat anything."

"So, what did you learn from Flossie?" Peter asked Lily, grateful to see Mrs Weaver leading the donkey-owner towards a small patch of grass where Rufus and Wingnut could give their rides.

Lily's eyes shone as she recounted her experience. "You were right, there was an aroma of haddock about her, but she was spot on with what she told me."

"Really?" Peter replied, having little time for such mumbo-jumbo. As a policeman, he believed only in solid facts.

"Flossie said she could see a forthcoming wedding and happiness for me. She also saw books and said I'd have a long career in a job that I loved and was very suited to."

"But," Peter scoffed, "that's hardly a revelation! I should think everyone in the village knows we're engaged, so a wedding is the next step. And the fact that you love books and work in the local library is no secret!"

"Yes," Lily agreed, "but it's the *way* she said it that mattered. You had to really be there to appreciate it fully."

Peter paused for a moment before telling her, "Ahhh, but I was here, fending off a greedy donkey and Mrs Pritchard–"

"Did she actually buy anything?" Lily interrupted.

"No. She almost did, until I explained what the book was about."

"She loves a racy romance novel, does Ida Pritchard. *Anyway*, that's what Flossie said about me, but she also predicted that something terrible would happen here at the fayre before the day was out."

"A severe outbreak of indigestion brought on by rock cake consumption?" Peter joked.

"Well," said Lily, her face grave, "she did sound very convincing. I hope that whatever it is, it's as simple to put right as a bout of stomach ache."

♥

In the refreshment tent, calm had just about been restored after the donkey incident. Nella Barnes manned a huge tea urn, guarding it like a surly bulldog while Kitty Walker waited on tables, providing slices of cake and buns for visitors to take to an indoor seating area.

Nudging two custard tarts onto a plate for Ida Pritchard, Kitty continually fidgeted until Nella instructed her to go and have a look around the fayre.

"I won't be long," Kitty said excitedly. "I just want to have my fortune told and enjoy a donkey ride!"

"I wouldn't bother, horrible smelly old thing," Nella replied, pouring tea for another visitor as she spoke.

"Who, Flossie the fortune teller?" Kitty asked, confused.

"*No*, the donkey, you silly article."

"Wonder how Seb's getting on with the parking and security?" Kitty asked, genuinely impressed that Peter had shown such faith in the butler-cum-valet.

"Probably having a long doze under a tree as far away from the fayre as possible so he doesn't get disturbed, if I know that lazy devil! Now off you go – the sooner you leave, the sooner you'll be back to help me here."

Kitty skipped off out of the tent and made her way to see Flossie Draper. The fortune teller's tent, adorned with a hastily painted banner sporting the words, *Madame Lazonga* in bold red letters, was pitched just past the hydrangea bush. Kitty eagerly pushed open the tent flap, noticing the faint odour of the sea accompanying the inhabitant.

Seated at a little table covered in purple velvet that looked suspiciously like an old skirt Flossie regularly wore, the mystic sat waiting with a black veil covering her hair and the bottom half of her face. A pile of Tarot cards sat to her left, although there was no attempt to shuffle them to lay out a spread for a reading. When Kitty took a seat opposite, Flossie grabbed her hand roughly and the beady dark little eyes that peered out over the black veil shone.

"What is it that you want to know?" Flossie asked mysteriously.

"Well, err, I suppose, just the usual sort of thing – am I going to meet a tall, dark stranger soon?!" Kitty giggled nervously. The pressure of Flossie's hand grew and Kitty could feel the roughness of calloused skin, well-used to gutting fish.

Flossie inhaled deeply, emitting an ethereal moan that startled Kitty somewhat as the grip grew tighter still. "I see . . . I see grey hair. He is stubborn and you must be careful. The fragrance is strong . . . You will regret your decision . . ."

"What does that mean?" Kitty wailed with frustration, her eyes widening. "Can't you tell me any more – what's his name?"

"The vision is fading," Flossie announced, rolling her eyes for effect. "And now, it is gone." Madame Lazonga sat upright, fixing Kitty with a hard stare. "Put your sixpence in the saucer on your way out, duck."

Completely disillusioned that Flossie Draper had not foretold the arrival of a good-looking young man in her life, Kitty crossed the grass to an area where a harassed man stood with two donkeys.

"Hello!" she exclaimed, trying to overcome her former disappointment.

"Hello Miss, fancy a donkey ride?" the man replied, looking hopeful.

"I do," Kitty agreed, approaching a reluctant-looking Rufus as Wingnut hoofed the ground with anticipation.

"You'd probably be better off with Wingnut here," the man said quickly. "You'll find Rufus can be a bit of trouble." He patted Wingnut on the flank and the animal thrust its head forward, giving a wide grin.

"Oh, I don't know," Kitty said, closing in on Rufus, "I think he's rather lovely. I've never got this close to a donkey before – can I ride him?"

The man looked doubtful. "You can try. I think he's worn himself out already." He helped Kitty up onto Rufus's back, handing her the reins. "Hold on very tight and tap your heels against his sides."

Kitty did as she was instructed, skirt hitched up and perched atop a creature whose coat felt bristly on the insides of her bare knees. She tapped her heels gently, fearing she might hurt the animal, but it had no effect.

"Come on now Rufus, don't be naughty!" The man tried pulling the donkey's harness forward to encourage it, but the creature merely yanked its head backwards.

"He's lazy in the short-term, and tired on a long-term basis," the man explained to Kitty, who was starting to feel silly as people looked on and smiled. The man then resumed his attempts, shoving the defiant beast so it twisted this way and that. "Try another kick with your heels," he suggested.

Kitty bravely did so. The donkey broke wind very loudly, shooting off so fast, she almost flew from his back. The man ran excitedly behind, waving his arms for the animal to stop. Wingnut looked on, bemused, taking another mouthful of hay from the bale he was tethered to.

Abruptly, Rufus inevitably stalled, leaving skid marks in the grass. His owner caught up and placed a steadying hand on the donkey's harness. In response, Rufus lifted his tail and emitted a series of thunderous farts.

"It might be best if I help you down," the man said. "He's had a lot of cake and I don't think it agrees with him . . ."

Kitty nodded, taking the man's hand as she jumped down from Rufus's back.

"No need to make a donation – you haven't had a proper ride," the owner told Kitty, embarrassed as Rufus let rip again.

She fished for a coin anyway. *What had Flossie said? Grey hair, stubborn, fragrant, something she'd regret?* Kitty marvelled at her accuracy.

A Fête Worse Than Death

As the day drew on, Diane Pargitter's mood did not improve. Turning on Felicity, happily still dozing and dreaming in the deck chair, Diane glared, hissing her displeasure loudly.

"Am I going to be on my feet *all* day? You haven't done a hand's turn all morning, *and* we're running out of things to sell."

Felicity squinted at the woman who would not have been her first choice of business partner, replying candidly, "Well, perhaps you should have brought some emergency cakes and pastries, just in case."

Diane took the comment as a personal slight. "It's hardly *my fault* that people flocked to buy my pastries – I expect word got around." She placed a hand on her chest, emphasising that blame had been wrongly cast.

Deciding it was better to remove herself from the line of fire, Felicity levered her back end carefully from the deckchair's low seat, straightened up stiffly and made her way to the refreshment tent.

"Turncoat!" Diane yelled after her for all to hear. A single rock cake sat lonely on a plate and Diane considered it looked bad for business if the stall wasn't completely sold out. Lifting it to her mouth she took a bite, almost breaking a tooth on a baked-hard currant. She chewed on regardless with Peter hovering again.

With a devil-may-care attitude, Diane threw herself bodily into the deckchair, simultaneously toppling and destroying it in one swift manoeuvre.

"Mrs Pargitter! Are you all right?" Peter exclaimed, watching with horror.

Diane sprawled in an unladylike fashion on the grass behind her trestle table, the collapsed deckchair resting in a heap next to her.

"I'm fine, I'm fine! These things aren't built properly nowadays – could have had my eye out!"

Peter offered Diane his hand to help her up. She eagerly took it, anchoring herself and pulling upwards to make her full weight Peter's sole responsibility. He grunted loudly, staggering forwards with the burden of trying to raise more than his own bodyweight from the ground.

Witnessing the scene, Lily shouted over, "Try and put a bit of effort in to help him, Diane, or poor Peter will slip a couple of discs and he'll be bed-bound for the next month!"

With a face resembled a sweating beetroot as she finally managed to get one hefty knee bent under her, Peter hauled Diane upright.

"I told Felicity I'd absolutely kill for a sit down!" she announced breathlessly. "I can't believe she's been so selfish – letting me do all the hard work, then swanning off to get herself a nice cup of tea!"

Just then, Lily spotted Felicity exiting the refreshment tent with a tall pile of tins that almost covered her face. Lily ran to help the older woman, who gratefully unloaded three tins into her arms, avoiding a painful collision with the tombola stall. As the pair returned to their posts, Lily caught a snatch of the heated conversation between Diane and Peter.

"I'm not convinced – it's definitely her!"

"What are we talking about?" Lily asked, depositing the three tins she held onto the cake stall trestle.

Peter continued, knowing Lily would get the gist. "Don't forget, it's a good eight months since you last saw Cecelia Morris – the memory plays tricks."

Lily nodded. "She wouldn't come back here–"

"Well, so you say, but I think we have to do away with her before she can cause any more damage!" Diane blurted.

"What are you driving at, Mrs Pargitter?" Peter asked with concern.

"I think she means that we should convince the woman to leave," Felicity provided. She emptied the tins of fairy cakes, a caraway seed cake, and a quantity of coconut macaroons, kindly provided by Nella who had clearly had more foresight.

Diane was in no mood to have her thoughts interpreted, bitterly resenting Felicity for not bringing her a cup of tea.

"Don't put words into my mouth!" she cried, biting down hard on a macaroon, temporarily forgetting that she hated coconut. She spat the mouthful hurriedly into a lace hanky produced from the sleeve of her floral summer frock, making Felicity wince. Peter exchanged a look with Lily and both remained quietly out of the argument.

"What I *actually* meant," Diane continued, "is we should persuade her to go home, wherever that might be . . ."

"That's exactly what I just said," Felicity murmured darkly.

Diane fixed her business partner with a glare. "The thing about actresses," she declared in a carrying voice, referring to Felicity's former career, "is they know how to deceive us. You've certainly deceived me today – I thought you were going to help out. We're supposed to be in a partnership, yet you've left me to do all the selling and arranging."

Felicity assumed the look of a slapped kipper.

Giving a resentful glare, Diane tossed her head. "I'm going to pin the tail on the donkey!" she announced, marching away.

In her position as fayre organiser, Mrs Doris Weaver had decided all donkey-related items should be positioned side by side. With this finalised on her clip-board, the donkey owner had the go-ahead to operate his rides next to the Pin-the-Tail-on-the-Donkey attraction.

Rufus was now lying on his side behind a hay bale, having been violently sick. His owner fretted as he decided the best course of action – Rufus was clearly rather ill and not up to giving rides. *Perhaps*, the man hoped, *he'll just sleep it off.*

Diane appeared suddenly next to the troubled man, having almost knocked young Patricia Spencer flying at the Pin-the-Tail-on-the-Donkey attraction, determined to get a break from the cake stall. Apologising insignificantly, Diane saw there was something occurring over by the donkey rides and changed course, heading over to satisfy her curiosity.

"What's the matter with him?" she asked the owner, who knelt beside Rufus, stroking his ears. A still-tethered Wingnut stood by, looking concerned.

The owner shook his head, rising to his feet. "Don't know. He's been a bit funny all day – probably had too much cake!" he said this with an air of embarrassment, recalling Diane's earlier anger after Rufus had helped himself to the contents of her stall.

"I hope you're not suggesting his being unwell is anything to do with my cooking!"

The man held up both hands in surrender, registering her indignation. "No, no, not at all! He also had several buns in the tea tent and–"

"Probably something to do with them then," Diane interrupted, recalling she'd vowed the animal's actions would cost him dearly. But she felt no guilt on seeing that her wish appeared to have come true.

"Not sure what to do about him really," the owner continued bravely. "He knows I love him dearly – despite the fact I always have to tell him off."

"Get the vet to him!" Diane blurted.

"*I beg your pardon*?" The man exclaimed, horrified that the bad-tempered fat woman from the cake stall now appeared to be suggesting Rufus should be executed for his crimes.

Diane pointed in disgust. "He's just been sick all over the rhododendron!"

♥

The vet shook his head. "This won't come cheap!"

"I feared you were going to say that," the donkey owner muttered. "What do you think is making him so sick?"

"You tell me," the veterinarian replied, arms crossed over his chest as he peered down at a stricken Rufus. Sensing the presence of the hated vet, Rufus groaned miserably.

"Well, I thought it might be because he's eaten so much ice cream and cake today – probably doesn't agree with him, but it's never taken him like this before . . ."

The vet gave the owner a direct look, an expression of disbelief crossing his face. "You feed the animal on ice cream and cake? You do know that a donkey's digestive system is only meant for hay and things like apples?"

The man suppressed his annoyance at being told the obvious. "Yes, but you try stopping him! He's had several buns, a peach and apple turnover – so that's fruit of a kind – and a vanilla ice cream today."

The vet gave a loud tut. "Well, no wonder the poor creature's ill. Give him plenty of water so he doesn't become dehydrated and let him rest. If he doesn't improve by tomorrow, give the surgery a call and I'll come out to him again. I'll put this on your bill."

The vet turned and strode away, leaving the owner to wonder how on earth he was going to relocate Rufus back to his field to lay down in peace.

In the foyer of The Crown Hotel, Mr Charles Andrews greeted a beautiful, dark-haired young woman. The receptionist noticed that Andrews appeared very pleased to see her, lingering far too long over their welcoming peck on the cheek.

The woman, in turn, brushed at his lapel in a very intimate gesture – the kind reserved for lovers and conscientious wives who wanted their husbands to look smart.

"We'd better book you in, honey," the receptionist heard Andrews say. Immediately busying himself with some paperwork, the receptionist made it look as though he'd not been paying attention to their presence or conversation.

"My secretary here would like a room, if you can tear yourself away from what you're doing," Charles Andrews announced in a commanding voice.

No doubt designed to intimidate me and impress the girl, the receptionist thought. He assumed a wide, friendly smile. "Certainly, sir. We have a single room available on the floor above you."

"Nothing closer to number 24? We have work to do, so I can't keep asking Madeleine to come downstairs every time we need to liaise."

Madeleine, is it? the receptionist mused. *And what does Mrs Andrews think of that, I wonder?* "I'm afraid that's the only room available at present, sir – but there are a few guests checking out on Wednesday, if that helps?" The receptionist maintained his benign expression, hoping to convey displeasure at being unable to comply with Andrews' request.

Madeleine giggled. "There's no need to worry, Charles. Just call, and I can pop down when you need me!"

Charles Andrews conceded defeat. "Well, it'll have to do. Book her in and she can get settled – Madeleine Turner."

Complying with the command, the receptionist offered Madeleine Turner the key to room number 35. She took it without thanks, giggling again. Without waiting for the porter, Charles Andrews picked up her luggage and escorted Madeleine to the lift.

I'm like the three wise monkeys, the receptionist mused. *I see and hear everything, but I say nothing . . .*

At half-past twelve, the crowds thinned slightly at Milford village fayre as lunch became a priority. Some people entered the refreshment tent for a sausage roll or a pasty, others left altogether, having had their fill of excitement for the day.

The St John's ambulance kindly escorted Rufus home to his field, with much hilarity that he was not their usual sort of patient. The day remained warm and pleasant, and all was right with the world as villagers enjoyed the company of their neighbours and friends.

Even Diane Pargitter appeared to have lost some of her venom when she arrived back at the cake stall. To her amazement, Felicity was in full swing, handing out bagged macaroons and slices of seed cake like a professional.

"How much have we made for the hospital?" Diane mumbled, taking her place behind the trestle. She carefully stepped around the pile that was formerly Felicity's favourite deckchair.

Diane watched as a brazen blackbird landed close to her feet, pecking greedily at the remains of the peach and apple turnovers trodden into the grass. She bent to gather some chunks oozing with fruit filling, throwing them as far as she could manage to land under a secluded tree. Multiple birds suddenly gathered, eating quickly before flying off.

Felicity looked up briefly from the lunch-time rush to respond. "Don't know, dear – haven't had time to count it, but the tin is getting quite full!"

Diane nodded, but instead of assisting on the cake stall, she sloped away to engage in idle conversation with Lily.

"I've been accused before of not letting things drop," Diane said, examining a book on water divining, "but that's really unnerved me, seeing Cecelia Morris here like that. . ."

Allowing herself a calming breath, Lily said, "But it's not Cecelia, it's a woman called Barbara Andrews, if the passport she showed you can be believed. If you remember back to the murder mystery, Cecelia didn't have an American accent. Never mentioned having a husband either – she certainly wasn't wearing a wedding ring if she was married."

Diane stopped distractedly flipping the book pages to give Lily her full attention. "She could have acquired the husband since coming out of prison, adopting the American accent just for show. I should imagine it'd be quite easy for her to mimic it, having been at an American boarding school for all those years."

Lily thought for a long moment, realising what Diane was getting at. "You're right, of course. She could well have reappeared in Milford for some reason – but I think that would be a very foolish move, trying to pretend she's someone entirely different!"

"But confidence-tricksters are bold as brass! They think they can easily fool other people into believing just what they want them to. Well, I'm not that naïve! Pargitters have a nose for trickery. You mark my words, she'll bring us all more trouble before the day's out!" Diane declared prophetically. She then moved back to her own stall, judging that the lunchtime rush was now over, leaving Lily to muse on what had been said.

Seb Treadmill opened his eyes, stretched his back against the wide tree trunk and yawned. Studying his watch, he realised he'd been asleep for several hours; all in all, it had been a good day's work.

His stomach told him it was time to seek sustenance, preferably free on account of him being staff. Seb rose lazily to his feet, brushing off his trousers that had become rather rumpled as he slept. He looked around the grounds of Fig Tree Hall but saw no one, and that was the way he liked it.

Seb judged that the shortest way back through the trees to the front of the Hall and the refreshment tent would only take him a couple of minutes. As he walked, the noise of the fayre grew louder. He looked to his left to see the white stone chapel nestling in the grounds. *Should have gone in there for a kip on one of the pews,* he mused.

Without warning, Seb tripped almost full-length over a woman's black boot. On his hands and knees, he discovered that the black boot in question was at the end of an outstretched leg. To his horror, he saw the body of a woman, face down under an oak tree, her skirt hitched to reveal bare skin; the woman's other leg bent sharply at the knee.

Pushing himself slowly upright, Seb made his way around to the woman's blonde head where he found her face was hidden. The woman's jacketed arms were bent at the elbow and sprawled in front of her, the strap of a black patent leather handbag clutched tightly in the left fist.

Seb gazed around him, wondering what to do next, knowing it was unlikely that anyone would come looking for him. *This has to be handled very carefully indeed*, he told himself. *I should go and alert Peter . . .*

He set off at a pace until the sight of the thronging fayre came into view, continuing onward, breathless and anxious until he spotted Peter talking to Lily behind her book stall. Seb saw that the obnoxious fat woman, Diane Pargitter, was close by. *Have to be careful and make it look as though nothing's wrong*, he decided quickly. Closing the gap between them, Seb fixed a smile on his face, slowing his breathing.

"Hello, sir, could I perhaps have a word, if it's not too much trouble?" Seb enquired.

Peter turned from his conversation with Lily, bemused at being called 'sir' by a member of staff who didn't usually bother with such formalities. "What is it, *Treadmill*?" he said jovially, with intonation in his voice.

Seb faltered slightly, but continued, "There's something I'd like you to see, *sir*."

Peter grinned, glancing at Lily and tilting his head towards the butler-cum-valet as his behaviour amused him. "If it's how fast a donkey can wolf down a plate of apple and peach turnovers, we've already witnessed that this morning!"

Diane scowled, catching Peter's reference to the earlier loss of her home baking to the opportunist quadruped. Her bat-like ears strained for further pertinent information; she busied herself re-arranging the plate of macaroons nearest to the conversation.

"It's a matter of urgency, sir," Seb persisted.

"Oh, all right then," Peter said light-heartedly. "Do you fancy a bit of a stroll, Lily?"

To Seb's horror, Lily Green nodded with enthusiasm. He saw he had little option other than to go along with it, deciding to explain fully when they had some privacy from the Pargitter woman.

"Diane," Lily said in her most amiable voice, "could you do me a huge favour and look after my stall for five minutes?" She hoped that by asking politely, the other woman would not see any reason to refuse her request.

After a long moment, Diane Pargitter barked, "Oh, go on then. I'm always doing things for other people, but they never do anything for me–"

"You're an absolute star!" Lily beamed, nipping quickly from behind her trestle to join Peter and Seb. The three walked side by side, with Seb indicating this was a private problem that he would disclose in due course. With his mind otherwise engaged, Seb almost collided with Nella, taking her first break of the day from behind the tea urn.

"Watch yourself, you clumsy oaf! You almost had my tea over!"

For the first time, Seb saw that Nella carried a cup of tea in one hand and a fondant fancy in the other. "Sorry, can't stop – emergency business," he announced importantly, hoping for a quick escape.

"What sort of emergency?" Nella asked with suspicious eyes, huge behind her owlish glasses.

"I can't say."

"Well, I'll come along anyway – I could do with stretching my legs. Kitty's manning the urn and I think the lunchtime rush is just about over. She can cope on her own for a bit."

Seb looked irritated beyond belief. "It's not really something I want broadcasting – it's a matter of a very sensitive nature!" he hissed, adopting a grave expression.

"Don't be daft!" Nella said, taking a slurp of tea and placing her cup on the edge of a trestle table containing toys that had seen better days. "Let's get on with it then!" she urged.

Unable to shake off the unwanted bystanders, Seb had no choice but to usher Peter, Lily and Nella to a spot where he would not be overheard.

"The thing is . . . I was patrolling the grounds to see if any of the villagers were having a nose around, and I came across something unexpected."

"Like what?" Nella scoffed' "A courting couple?"

"Not exactly . . ."

"What on earth is it, Seb?" Peter asked, growing tired of having the enjoyable afternoon interrupted.

"Tell us what's wrong," Lily said kindly.

Nella quickly swallowed the last of her fondant fancy and shook her head, knowing Seb's gossip and tales of old.

"I found a woman's body," Seb blurted, uncomfortable under Nella's scrutiny. "It's just over here, behind the large oak . . ."

Nella and Lily gasped simultaneously. Peter, instantly assuming a policeman's demeanour, asked, "Have you touched the body at all?"

"Of course not! What do you think I am?" Seb exclaimed, offended.

"I meant, did you check whether the woman was still breathing? Let's have a look."

They approached the huge oak and Lily cried out, seeing the body there as Seb had reported. Peter stepped forward, bending to clutch the woman's right wrist with his fingertips. "No pulse," he announced.

"She looks vaguely familiar," Nella muttered quietly.

"That's the woman I was telling you about," Lily confirmed with displeasure. "Her name's Barbara Andrews. I think you'll find she carries her passport with her." She pointed to Barbara's handbag.

Having witnessed the argument between Barbara and Diane earlier that day, Lily marvelled that the woman was forced to produce her passport to prove she wasn't Cecelia Morris.

"I'm going to roll her over, just so we can make sure," Peter said.

"Should you be doing that?" Seb asked nervously. "You just said it was the right thing *not* to touch anyone found dead."

"Well," said Peter darkly, "she apparently died on my property and I *am* a policeman, so I think that gives me the right."

Seb considered himself told. He watched as Peter gently rolled Barbara Andrews' body over so she was prone on her back, her arms flopping above her head on the grass; the leather handbag – strap still tightly clenched in her fist – moved with Barbara. Lily and Nella gasped, catching their first sight of the woman's bloody nose and deathly pale face.

"How long do you think she's been here?" Lily asked.

"Who knows?" Peter replied. "That's a question for the police pathologist. But you mentioned you saw her this morning, at the cake stall?"

"Yes," Lily recalled the argument again and the woman's movements afterwards. "As far as I know, that was about half-past ten. I think she headed over to the fortune teller's tent . . . Oh, but that was after the man she was with – I don't know for sure if he's her husband – told Barbara he was heading back to the hotel."

"What do we do now then – as the police are already here?" Seb asked belligerently.

Peter ignored him. "I'll go up to the house and call the pathologist to report a suspicious death."

"Is it suspicious?" Nella pointed out. "Looks like she just might have tripped over a branch and fallen face-first, smacking her nose badly."

"But why is she even in this part of the grounds?" Lily asked. "Look, she's landed under the tree Cecelia found last year – when she thought these carved initials were one of the murder mystery clues."

Peter pursed his lips. "Maybe the initials D.A. meant something to her so she stopped at this tree for a reason. Maybe she fancied a stroll away from the beaten track to walk off Diane's indigestible pastry. Then she had a nasty fall, like Mum says . . ."

"That locket she's wearing is worth a bit," Seb observed candidly.

"Trust you to eye up the jewellery of a dead woman!" Nella scolded.

Seb hung his head and muttered, "Just saying . . ."

"Now you come to mention it," Nella said, "that locket does look familiar. Perhaps we should open it, see if there's a picture inside?" Lily shivered at the thought of touching the dead woman's necklace as Nella bent to press the little clasp on the edge of the gold locket, engraved with

scrolling hearts and flowers. It sprang open
to reveal an image.
　　And Nella screamed.

The Burden of Truth

Nella's hands rose to her face as she muttered repeatedly, "Oh dear, oh dear. . ."

Peter led his mother away from the scene that had clearly upset her. "I know it's not nice to see someone dead," he soothed, "but don't let it–"

"It's Evelyn Ambrose!" Nella whispered, loud enough for Lily to hear. "You know – the wife of Professor Ambrose?"

"You mean that picture in the locket is my father's wife?"

"Exactly that. I don't know what this young woman has to do with it all, although she does look remarkably like Dorcas Ambrose. If it's her, come back to the Hall after all these years, that could explain things . . ."

Lily moved nearer to Peter, leaving Seb gazing forlornly on the prone female, wondering what would happen next.

"Sorry to intrude, but did you just say this woman is Dorcas Ambrose, as in the Professor's missing daughter?" Lily's inquisitive blue eyes became wide as she stared in disbelief.

Nella nodded. "That's what I think. She was given her mother's locket when Evelyn

Ambrose died of a heart compliant in 1934, so Dorcas would have only been about ten years old at the time."

Lily nodded, stunned as Nella continued.

"I remember how she was cruelly packed off to a boarding school in America by her uncle when he took over Fig Tree Hall. That was after the Professor went missing that same year."

Peter pursed his lips, not wishing to revisit the events surrounding finding his father's mummified body during the murder mystery weekend the previous autumn.

"But why would she come back here, where there are so many terrible memories?" Lily asked, bewildered. "Last year, we discovered that Dorcas's younger brother died of scarlet fever when he was only six. Her mother died, then her father disappeared. That's surely enough family tragedy for anyone to cope with."

"Perhaps she had a score to settle," Nella muttered darkly.

"Why do you say that?" Peter's eyebrows arched with the question as he looked directly at his mother.

"Well . . . Lily saw her going into the fortune teller's tent, so she was obviously keen to learn what might happen in her life."

"Isn't everyone though? It's all part of coming to the fayre, having your fortune read," Lily blurted without thinking.

"What I'm getting at," Nella added patiently, "is that she had a purpose. Ezra Ambrose changed Dorcas's name before he packed her off to America, so that it was less distinctive. He could easily have changed to . . . what was it?"

"Barbara, and whatever the new surname was before her marriage," Lily supplied.

"She came back here after twenty-five years for the same reason any sane person would return to a house that has caused so much misery," Nella continued in hushed tones to exclude Seb from the conversation. "She's got wind of your inheritance – thought she'd come and have it out with you in person."

Peter's cornflower blue eyes widened with shock. "Don't be ridiculous! The professor's will left me the Hall and all the income from his invention patents. No mention was made of Dorcas, as far as I know. You said he was delighted when I was born, it gave him a male heir to pass everything on to."

"Now don't get upset," Nella chided, knowing Seb was all ears, missing none of the drama. "But don't forget, you didn't actually see the will . . ."

"I'm not *getting upset*," Peter hissed under his breath. "I just think it's a bit far-fetched as explanations go. Let's just deal with this properly. I'm going inside to make that call. We can't leave a dead body out on the lawn." Peter then strode away, leaving Lily and Nella staring after him.

"What can you tell me?" the pathologist quizzed.

Seb gave a bewildered look, brought on by the enormity of the situation. He'd never been questioned by the police, or anyone official, for that matter, and was feeling cautious about how he should respond.

"I err . . . well I just sort of found her here . . ."

"And what time was that?"

"Oh, err, now, let me see . . ."

"Just roughly. It sometimes helps to establish the time of death."

"Well, it was around lunchtime-ish."

"Right." The man scribbled something into his notebook with a stubby pencil and continued to examine the dead woman's neck area. "And you haven't moved her or wiped any blood away from her face?"

Seb's jaw hung open, his throat seizing up. *He thinks it was me who killed her!* "I-I, err . . . I just found the body."

"I'll take that as a no then," the pathologist summed up, jotting something else down in his notebook before moving to examine the clenched fist wrapped around the woman's handbag strap.

Seb nodded, feeling under scrutiny.

"Well, it's a warm day, so that won't have helped the decomposition process. And she was found face-down, so that probably explains things."

The man smiled at Seb and indicated to his two assistants that the body could now be escorted to the hospital morgue.

Seb stood frozen and worried. *Can I go back to my duties now? Surely this calls for a sit down and a strong cup of tea in the kitchen, or maybe even a whisky for the shock?*

Peter approached from behind, placing a hand on his shoulder. In response, Seb almost shot two feet into the air with a yelp of surprise. He spun around, clutching at his chest to show his heart was racing ten to the dozen, only just managing to stop it from jumping out of his body completely.

"Sorry, sorry," Peter said, doing his best not to form a faint smile. "Mum and Lily are in the kitchen making tea, if you'd like some. I expect it's all been a bit of a shock for you."

Understatement of the year, Seb thought, but he said nothing, following Peter across the lawn to the back entrance of Fig Tree Hall.

Swinging open the door, Peter indicated Seb should go first, before pulling the door firmly shut after him; briefly, he peered out through the smeared glass panel into the grounds. He watched as the police pathologist and his staff headed away with the body of Barbara Andrews, wondering what the post mortem findings would reveal. Peter then made his way to the kitchen table, his thoughts turning back to the fayre.

"I really ought to get back to my stall," Lily told Nella as Peter took in the kitchen scene to see that Seb had already flopped listlessly into one of the wooden chairs. "Heaven only knows what that woman will have done to my display of books. . ."

"It's always best to keep busy at a time like this. You go my duck," Nella reassured her. "If it's anything like her cake stall, Mrs Pargitter's probably let your stock run out by now."

With Nella's words ringing in her ears, Lily hurried away, concern growing that Diane might have abandoned the stall altogether in favour of the refreshment tent and a cup of tea.

"So, what are we going to do about all this then?" Nella asked sharply, aware that although his voice was muted by shock, Seb's ears missed nothing. As he'd discovered the body, she was prepared to make allowances, letting him stay put.

"There's nothing we can do until the police finish their investigations, the inquest is held and the coroner's findings are available," said Peter stoically. "I rang the station to let them know what happened after I informed the pathologist. The police will probably treat it as an accident until they know more, although there are no witnesses for them to question."

Seb heaved a deep sigh, shooting a pitiful look at the teapot.

"I suppose you'll be wanting a cup of tea, and to be waited on hand and foot, rather than pouring it for yourself?" Nella addressed her workmate with sarcasm.

She filled a cup from the huge brown pot and pushed the steaming beverage towards Seb, making the liquid slop dangerously to and fro. "Add your own milk – I know how fussy you are."

Seb accepted the offering without thanks, adding a splash of milk from an earthenware jug on the kitchen table. He took a sip – conveying that it was all such an effort in his dreadfully weakened state – before choosing a custard cream from the tin his employer offered him to keep his strength up.

Nella ignored Seb's attention-seeking, keen to voice her thoughts on the presence of Dorcas Ambrose at the Hall.

"I know you think I'm talking rubbish, but it wouldn't surprise me if Dorcas had heard your news. I expect her nose has been put out of joint because she's not the new Lady of the Manor."

Peter shook his head, giving a huge sigh to show the subject was not up for discussion. He poured himself a cup of tea and held it between both hands, peering down into it to avoid his mother's penetrating, magnified stare.

"But you must admit," Nella persisted, "there's no other reason why she would come back here. Like you say, after such sadness, and the will–"

Peter placed his cup down and pushed back his chair. "I don't want today ruined by that woman. There's probably a perfectly innocent explanation – we just have to be patient." He fixed his mother with a look that told her this was the end of the matter. Heading back outside, Peter went to find Lily and a degree of normality, leaving his tea untouched.

"That's the second one this afternoon," Lily told Peter with a nod towards the dead blackbird under the nearby tree. Her moss-green, A-line summer frock swished as she turned back to her stall and grinned. "I've made a nice amount to donate to the hospital."

"Oh, that *is* good," Peter agreed, lowering his voice so the ever-present Diane Pargitter couldn't hear him. "So, she didn't totally ruin everything then?" He gave a nod towards Diane's large floral print bottom as she bent over to retrieve the last of Nella's tins of fairy cakes, roughly emptying them onto a dainty plate.

Lily shook her head and looked embarrassed. "I feel a bit bad for doubting her, actually . . . She was really good and got top price for everything she sold. Felicity said she intimidated Mr Wiseman into parting with half a crown for *Creating the Perfect Rose Garden*, and he's only got a window box!"

Peter chuckled, imagining just how that sales pitch would have gone. "Good for her. Now, are you just about done here, or do you want to keep going for a bit longer?"

Lily looked doubtfully into the box at her feet, knowing she had little hope of selling the remaining three titles: a tatty copy of *Cooking with Powdered Egg*, something everyone was trying to forget; *Entertaining with Offal*, something no one wanted to do; and *What Your Friends are Afraid to Tell You: A Personal Hygiene Manual*, a subject no one wanted to imagine could relate to them. Shaking her head, Lily said, "I think I'll call it a day." She would donate the three books to the local Oxfam shop and hope they had better luck.

"Let's go and have a final look around before things start running down," Peter said with a hint of false enthusiasm. The appearance of the body of Barbara Andrews had shaken him more than he liked to admit.

As a police officer, he told himself, *I ought to have more backbone about these things.* But it was more than just a dead body – it was the body of a woman who had once lived here at the Hall, who'd shared the same father as Peter and who may well have intended to challenge him for coming out of nowhere, having been left everything.

"Let's go then," Lily said brightly. As they walked, she pointed to a pigeon carcass laying a few yards short of the tree where two dead blackbirds had also ended their days. "Ugg! More dead birds – it can't be a coincidence!" Looking puzzled she headed over to one of the stiff little bodies, staring directly into the cold, dead eyes of a blackbird.

"Don't go near them!" Peter shouted, hurrying across the lawn after her. "I'll ask Seb to get rid of them."

"Perhaps I should take them away for examination!" said a deep voice behind Peter, making him spin around to see a large, florid man with his sleeves rolled up. The man produced a hessian bag from his trouser pocket, carefully manoeuvring the bag inside out so that he could grasp the first of the deceased blackbirds without touching it. He did the same with the second body, desperately trying to prevent the seized birds from falling back onto the grass again as he struggled to collect the last.

Lily was shocked by the man's interest in the feathered beasts. She shied away as he came to stand close to them, proffering the open bag in their direction so they could gaze inside.

"Are you interested in taxidermy?" Peter asked, intrigued to know why the man was so keen. He linked arms with Lily as she pushed closer to him, sensing peculiarity.

The man held out his free hand to Peter, his face breaking into a wide grin showing uneven teeth. "Oswald Hawke's the name. I'm president of the Milford branch of the RSPB – the Royal Society for the Protection of Birds, in case you haven't heard of it."

Lily nodded and eyed the open bag, wishing that both Mr Hawke and his finds would disappear.

"I was wandering around the fayre and went to the cake stall to get a nice apple and peach turnover. The lady said they'd sold out, then I saw bits of pastry on the grass. A blackbird seemed very interested, and he gobbled up what he could find. Don't know if this is him."

Mr Hawke waved the bag even closer under Lily's nose and she stepped back hastily, almost colliding with a small child brandishing a dripping ice cream.

"Well," said Peter in an amused voice, "you're very welcome to him, and his friends. What will you do with the, err, bodies?"

"Oh, haven't decided yet. Might send them for a post mortem, see what killed 'em!"

Peter was unsure how to reply until he realised Mr Hawke was joking, making reference to the fact that Peter was a local police constable.

"Righto!" Peter replied jovially. "You be sure to let me know whether it was a stabbing or a strangulation!" He led Lily away quickly before Mr Hawke could wave his morbid hessian bag again.

"That was all rather horrible," Lily said, feeling slightly sick at the thought of an avian assassin active in the village. "What do you fancy doing now – coconut shy?"

"Are they?"

"What?" Lily was bewildered for a moment until she realised it was a joke. "Oh, ha, ha! Yes. Well, let's do something normal for goodness sake – I feel that what with Barbara Andrews and now these blessed birds, there's been far too much death at the fayre."

"And that would make a good title for a book! You should write that one down. Coconuts it is then," Peter replied. They set off just in time to see the man running the attraction furtively gluing a large hairy coconut onto its podium so that no one would stand a chance of knocking it off.

The telephone rang early on Sunday evening and Seb rushed to answer it. "Fig Tree Hall – to whom am I speaking?"

Seb's telephone voice was a cause of hilarity and Kitty waltzed past him on her way to the kitchen, her forefinger holding the tip of her nose in the air.

"The name's Hawke. I'd like to speak to Constable Beresford, if it's not too much trouble to you."

Seb Treadmill placed the telephone receiver back on the hall table without another word, leaving Mr Hawke at a loss. The butler-cum-valet beetled off towards the kitchen to relay the message. He burst into the room, making Kitty, Nella and Peter jump.

"Got a phone call for you . . . A Mr Hall. No, wait . . . something about a bird . . ."

Peter pushed back his chair from the kitchen table, rising to take the call. "Thank you Seb, most helpful, as always." Seb nodded graciously as Peter passed him, taking his seat at the table, oblivious to the sarcasm.

"Hello, Mr Hawke?" Peter said into the receiver, having worked out that the caller must be the RSPB man.

"Ah, yes. Wasn't sure whether your man had heard me or not. The thing is . . . I've had those birds tested, as three dying in one hit is rather peculiar . . ."

"And?"

"And the whole thing is very strange indeed. All three – the two blackbirds and the pigeon – died of arsenic poisoning. I'm going to have to inform the authorities, old man–"

"Just a minute . . . Are you sure about this?"

"Completely sure. The arsenic levels are very high indeed. As they were found on your property, an investigation will have to be carried out."

"But, they're only birds!"

A blast of silence erupted down the telephone line. After a long moment, Mr Hawke's seething voice came back on.

"I will overlook that ignorant comment, *Constable* Beresford. You may think it's perfectly acceptable not to view avian deaths as important. However, there could be a serious health issue locally, to wit, dangerous levels of arsenic in the grounds of your home. If birds are dying, I have no choice other than to take action to–"

"My apologies, Mr Hawke. I didn't mean to make light of this situation . . . I'm shocked to hear what you've told me."

"Very well then," Hawke replied gruffly. "I'll bid you good day." As the dialling tone buzzed indicating that Mr Hawke had hung up, Peter stared into the receiver in his hand. He recalled his police training in poisons. *Arsenic – the inheritance powder . . . But how did three birds in my garden end up dead because of it?*

An hour after Peter had spoken to Oswald Hawke, he realised that the man was as good as his word. Glancing out of the drawing room window into the fading sunshine of the early evening, Peter observed a number of villagers with placards, determinedly making their way up the long Fig Tree Hall driveway. As the leaders drew closer still, Peter clearly saw the hastily painted signs being waved in anger. One particularly irate protester, whom Peter recognised as Mr Blewitt, the local ironmonger, brandished a sign that read 'BIRD MURDERER!'

Nella crept up behind her son to comment in Peter's ear. "Oh dear! Mr Blewitt seems to have done a roaring trade, if this business is anything to go by . . ."

Starting badly, Peter turned to his mother, exasperated at her stealth tactics. "It seems that word has gotten around. What do you mean, *a roaring trade*?"

Nella smiled, moving past him to draw the curtains. "He's sold everyone the nails to construct their placards."

"Do you think I should go out there, try to reason with them?" Peter asked nervously.

Stoically, Nella shook her head. "I thought I saw more of 'em coming up the driveway. It could get out of hand – people are very protective of their animals."

"It was a pigeon and two blackbirds!" Peter scoffed.

"Don't let *them* hear you saying that!" Nella advised, turning on her heel to return to the kitchen.

"Mum, wait. Mr Hawke told me those birds died from arsenic poisoning. How can that be my fault?"

Nella considered the problem, biting her lower lip in concentration. "Perhaps it was something they ate . . ."

"Yes, that's probably it. I once heard of a case where a farmer's delivery of grain was tainted with arsenic pesticide. Wild birds could easily pick that up from a farmyard. Perhaps I should point that out to the very diligent Mr Hawke?"

"Probably wouldn't do much good. I know him from the village and he doesn't take any prisoners, ex-army you see. You'll never get an apology from that one–"

"I don't want an apology," Peter blurted. "I just want these people to go away."

Nella nodded. "They'll get bored eventually, given time."

After dinner, Peter tweaked the drawing room curtains to find that more protesters had gathered. They seemed fairly quiet, although when they caught sight of him, they shouted and chanted their slogans.

Feeling trapped, Peter turned sadly away, deciding to telephone Lily at home, warning her not to come over. Knowing some of the bristly characters in the mob, they would go out of their way to make Lily feel intimidated. He dialled and the telephone was answered by Mrs Forbes, Lily's eccentric, somewhat deaf mother.

"Hello Elizabeth, it's Peter. Is Lily at home?" he asked loudly into the receiver, knowing that it was probably fruitless.

"Have I been to *Rome*?" Elizabeth replied, louder still.

"It's Peter!" he shouted. "Is Lily there?"

"Who is this? I've got a whistle – I'll blow it!" Peter sighed heavily, ready to give up until he realised that Lily had coaxed the telephone receiver away from her mother and that she was now talking.

"I was just coming into the hallway and I heard you shout, 'It's Peter!' from about five feet away! Sorry – you know what mother's like. I've told her not to answer if the telephone rings, but it's force of habit, I'm afraid. She can hear the ring but not the speaker . . ."

Peter sighed. "Not to worry. I wanted to warn you not to come over. It seems that those birds died of arsenic poisoning – Hawke's got people waving placards outside my window."

Lily gasped in surprise. "Why on earth are you being held responsible for some dead birds? I thought Mr Hawke was a bit strange, but to organise a protest–"

"Mum says he's ex-army. Anyway, I didn't want them harassing you if you came over," Peter interrupted, not wanting to think about the horrible Mr Hawke and his dead birds longer than was necessary. "I could come over to you, sneak out the back way, but that would mean you can't do any work in the library here. What do you think?"

"How on earth do garden birds get poisoned with arsenic? I mean, people, yes, but not birds. Do you think that a certain blackbird had left one of his relatives some berries in his will, and the other birds just couldn't wait to get at them?!" Lily giggled merrily to herself, pleased at her own joke and ignoring Peter's question entirely.

Not in the mood for frivolity, Peter said, "Ha, ha," grumpily into the telephone receiver.

"I mean," Lily continued, "it's not like you've been outside, deliberately feeding the birds arsenic pellets! Hang on a minute . . . I remember reading that apple pips contain arsenic. Only a tiny amount that wouldn't affect a human if swallowed, but maybe a bird, being smaller–"

"I really couldn't care less at the moment – I feel like a prisoner in my own home."

"Did you *want* to go outside then?" Lily asked, candidly.

Peter considered the question briefly. "Not particularly. It's just that with them all out there looking in if I go to the window, I feel . . ."

"Persecuted?" Lily provided helpfully.

"Yes. It's not my fault, but I'm somehow being blamed as though it is."

"It's the way of the world," Lily said philosophically.

"Well anyway, hopefully they'll just go and that'll be an end to it all."

"You can but hope."

Where There's a Will

Sunday evening seemed to drag for Peter. He avoided the drawing room, not even peeking around the curtains at the mob, if indeed they were still there. He now realised the plight of the innocent when faced with a wrongful arrest, the finger of blame cast where there was none.

As he pushed away his unfinished evening meal with a deep sigh, Peter decided he only had one course of action. He would prove the arsenic had not originated from either him or his garden. *But where to start the investigation?*

An answer began to formulate as Nella cleared away the dishes with much clattering. Her mind had settled on the pressing problem of Barbara Andrews.

"I was thinking," she said to Peter as Kitty worked the dishmop over a gravy-coated plate, "you should get onto that pathologist first thing tomorrow, see if you can find out how she died."

"I assume," Peter replied, eyeing his mother, who was now busily drying as Kitty washed, "you're talking about *that woman* again? I expect I'll find out what there is to know in due course, as she died in the back garden."

"They're *grounds*, not just a garden." Nella sniffed, irritated that Peter wanted to ignore the subject.

"Don't be a snob, mother. Anyway, I've got this bird thing to deal with first."

"Maybe the two are connected in some way." Nella turned to her son, eyes huge.

"Don't be ridiculous. Barbara Andrews obviously tripped and fell, but we'll wait and see. As I always tell Lily, the pieces of the jigsaw don't give the full picture until the end."

"But what if they think there's foul play?"

"By whom?" Peter demanded. "There *is* no one else–"

"Correction," Nella interrupted sharply. "There's that husband of hers who went back to the hotel, leaving her here to die. They say it's usually the husband or wife that does away with the spouse, nine times out of ten."

Peter sighed heavily, deciding the weekend had started well, then rapidly deteriorated. "But she had no wounds, so the pathologist said. No marks around her neck, no blow to the back of the head. Short of the husband bringing a pillow from the hotel and smothering her with it, I can't see it somehow."

"Odd,' Nella said, holding the dripping milk jug but making no attempt to dry it. "Normally you policemen are very suspicious and it's the public who have to convince you otherwise."

"Not now it's happened on my own doorstep! I've told you, just let it be."

"And then, of course – there's you . . ." Nella persisted.

Peter's bull-like head thrust forward as he demanded, "What do you mean by that?"

"Well, the police will wonder if you didn't try to shut her up, get rid of her because she was back here with a purpose."

Peter stared at his mother in disbelief. "You can't seriously believe that? I didn't even know she was coming here – it was a complete surprise when you said the woman was Dorcas Ambrose!"

"Ah, yes. But you have to look at it from her point of view. Did she want to speak to you about the inheritance? Did she feel it was unfair, not to get her fair share?"

"How on earth should I know what she was thinking?" Peter shouted, making Kitty cringe and wish she could disappear.

"Well, she *was* mentioned in the will . . . You never saw it, but I did, if you remember? You got the Hall and the professor's patents income. But Dorcas was left something that's at the solicitors for safekeeping."

Peter was struck dumb by the news. Nella had never mentioned it before. He wondered why she'd chosen this moment to spring it on him. Remaining silent for a suitable length of time, Peter breathed deeply in an effort to become calmer. He gathered his thoughts, forming a suitable reply.

"What was it that she inherited?"

Nella looked furtive, suddenly not wanting Kitty to be privy to family business. "I don't know exactly, but now that she's dead, there's nothing stopping you going to the solicitor to ask about it . . . as the next of kin, so to speak."

After a morning of run-of-the-mill police business, and some unreadable looks from Sergeant Whittaker – potentially linked to the body in the garden – Peter made a decision. He telephoned Darius, Cummings and Bennett, the solicitors who had dealt with his father's will, arranging a visit in his lunch break.

Mr Darius greeted him in a perfunctory fashion and invited him into his office, possibly because Peter was dressed in his police uniform. Peter stepped into a quintessentially Victorian study. It had flock green wallpaper, a huge oak desk with a green studded leather top, and an overwhelming aspidistra plant by the fireplace. Bookshelves covered the far wall, framing a round window. Mr Darius gestured that Peter shout sit.

"You do know that your wallpaper is green because of arsenic?" Peter provided as an opening comment.

"I'm sorry?"

"The colour. Arsenic makes it green, then they discovered it was poisonous. Apparently, that's what happened to Napoleon on St Helena."

"Did you come here today to discuss the colour of my office wallpaper?"

"Not exactly, but it is vaguely relevant. You see," Peter said, not really knowing where to start, I've just been informed that it was my half-sister, Dorcas Ambrose, who was found dead in the grounds of Fig Tree Hall on Saturday. Apparently, our father, Professor Thaddeus Ambrose, left her something in his will."

Darius shuffled forward in his seat, showing Peter a concerned expression. "I see."

"So," Peter added with caution, "I wondered if you could let me know what she's been left, as I'm sort off her family. . ."

Mr Darius remained quiet for a long moment, steepling his fingers in thought. "I'm able to divulge what the item is, although I fail to see what that has to do with arsenic," he said bluntly.

Unsure whether to even mention it, Peter gave a faint laugh. "Just some dead birds in the grounds, found to have arsenic poisoning. The two are not related."

"I see," Mr Darius said again, making no effort to locate Professor Ambrose's paperwork.

"So, how do I go about getting that information?"

"Well, I can tell you now. Professor Ambrose left his daughter a key."

Bewildered, Peter shook his head, imagining that Dorcas had been left a spare key to Fig Tree Hall. He remained silent as a sea of emotions washed over him and he felt betrayed, cheated, angry.

"It's a key to a safety-deposit box, and I can let you have it . . . in due course."

What was so important that Dorcas needed to be left a key to a safety-deposit box? Peter wondered distractedly.

Darius slid open a drawer in his desk, rummaging in one of the internal compartments. He produced a small silver-coloured key, waiving it at Peter.

"You'll find that this fits a box number, but first, we must have the inquest into Dorcas Ambrose's death."

Peter raised his eyebrows in surprise. "Do you know, I hadn't thought of that!? Of course, the inquest has to happen to release any possessions."

"And when will the inquest be, do you know?" Darius asked.

Peter shook his head, realising that he was no further forward. "I'll contact the coroner and find out, then I'll get back to you."

Rising from the hard chair designed to keep attention sharp, Peter bid Mr Darius farewell and headed back to the police station.

"Chief Inspector Reed wants to see you," Detective Constable Brian Cribbens informed Peter as soon as he walked through the door of Milford police station.

Nodding and not bothering to ask Cribbens why, Peter headed to Chief Inspector Thomas Reed's office. He knocked and waited.

"Come," a gruff voice said after a long moment. Peter placed his hand on the door knob with trepidation, a feeling of foreboding washing over him as he entered the room.

"Ah, Beresford . . . I have something to tell you." There was much shuffling of papers on the desk to make the workspace look just so before he continued. "This investigation into the death of Barbara Andrews – It hasn't escaped my attention that the sorry business occurred on your doorstep."

Peter nodded, not wanting to say the wrong thing or mention that Barbara was, in fact, his half-sister, Dorcas. Reed fixed him with the stare of an iced halibut.

"It's unfortunate, but I need to warn you off the case. Take this as official notice that you'll not be involved with any aspect of police business concerning the death of Barbara Andrews."

Nodding again, Peter's head swam with thoughts. *That means I won't be able to find out what's going on . . . Will I be invited to attend the inquest? What secret is buried in that safety-deposit box?*

"That'll be all, Beresford!"

Peter turned, closing the door quietly after him, wondering what he should do next. He would talk to Lily that evening. In the meantime, a visit to The Crown Hotel was in order to ask a few questions of his own.

As the station was quiet, he took a huge risk and telephoned the coroner, but the line was constantly engaged. Conducting a private investigation was going to be difficult, but he was not about to let that put him off.

After an afternoon spent logging details of a missing cat, and telling two boys off for dropping litter – after their harassed mother hauled them into the police station to teach them a lesson – Peter could finally give his attention to detection. The Crown Hotel stood beautifully positioned on the side of the road, painted white and festooned with hanging baskets of colourful cerise-pink petunias and blue lobelia. The façade looked welcoming and Peter entered without rehearsing what he wanted to ask.

As he stood by the hotel noticeboard, a large yellow poster with bold black print screamed for attention. It announced, without ceremony, an emergency meeting of the Milford Residents' Association the following evening, held on account of the recently poisoned birds. Peter was horrified to see that the poster named Fig Tree Hall as the centre of death.

"Can I help you?" said the hotel receptionist, his little eyes gleaming, following Peter's glance to the lurid poster.

Caught off-guard, Peter managed a passable, "I wanted to ask you some questions about Mr and Mrs Andrews – I believe they're staying here?"

The receptionist gave a coy look, peering over his shoulder to check no one was listening.

"Yes, a queer business. I must say . . . The husband is coping very well with his grief – I expect that *Madeleine* helps." The receptionist thinned his lips to pronounce the woman's name. No more than she deserved, he felt.

"Sorry, who?" Peter asked, still reeling from the news there was to be a village meeting about the dead birds that kept plaguing his life.

"Mr Andrews' secretary," the receptionist replied with vigour. "There's more to that little relationship than meets the eye, if you get my drift?"

"So, you think the husband is at it with the secretary?" Peter said, hushing his voice as a couple drifted past on their way to the hotel restaurant.

The receptionist leaned in closer. "I most certainly do. Mr Andrews *demanded* I put her in a room nearer to his own – and with his wife right there with him!" A proud hand went to his chest. "Of course, I did my best. Gave her a room on the next floor so he couldn't be sneaking along there so easily."

"Very interesting indeed," said Peter, all thoughts of the Residents' Association bird agenda gone from his mind as new information took hold. "And what about the wife's things, are they still here?"

"They are!" the little gossip said brightly. "I can show you up to the room if you'd like. Mr Andrews and his secretary are out to dinner at the moment – they've handed their keys in. You see," he leaned in conspiratorially, "I shall know when they're back, so I can tip you off by telephoning up to the room. I'll delay them by chatting about their day and their meal – people always like to talk about themselves!"

Peter nodded eagerly, not having expected such a turn of luck. The receptionist grew more animated, crossing the room quickly and reaching behind the reception desk to a row of hooks. He retrieved a key before nipping back to where Peter stood.

"Or I could come up with you! Room number 24 – shall we?" The receptionist gestured towards the lift, making Peter feel distinctly uncomfortable.

Turning to the eager-faced young man, who seemed only too willing to please, Peter said gravely, "It might be better if you keep a look out here. I don't want you getting into trouble for abandoning your post."

With disappointment in his brown, puppy-dog eyes, the receptionist nodded. "Righto, probably for the best. Don't do anything I would!"

Peter smiled politely as he was given the Crown Hotel fob, wondering if the receptionist was this free and easy with everyone's keys. He was grateful though for the ideal opportunity to have a snoop into Dorcas's possessions, searching out any clues to why the woman had arrived in Milford.

Peter took the stairs to the second floor and found number 24; the key slid easily into the lock. He glanced down at the gold crown on its black background, placing the sturdy key fob on a chest of drawers by the door – a reminder to take it back down with him. He crossed to one of the bedside cabinets. It contained a map of Milford and a watch inscribed: 'To Charles – yours always – Barbara'. Peter headed past the neatly made-up king-size to its twin bedside cabinet, yanking the drawer open. Inside, he saw a new jar of face cream, a pretty green enamelled powder compact, and an envelope addressed to him.

Amazing, Peter thought, snatching up the envelope bearing his name and address. *But if I remove it, the husband will know it's missing and it might come out that I've been here . . .*

Deciding he couldn't possibly leave the envelope behind, Peter tucked it inside the jacket of his police uniform. He closed the drawer, taking a final glance around to ensure everything was as it should be. He saw, for the first time, the floral wallpaper sporting small, vibrant pink and purple flowers, the over-zealous attempt to keep the busy pattern going with the matching curtains and bedspread.

Having seen enough, he exited and locked the room to make his descent via the stairs. In the empty foyer, Peter carefully handed back the key, making sure that nobody from the lounge beyond saw him. He gave a nod to the hopeful young man behind the reception desk, leaving without a word.

Ha, ha – see no evil, hear no evil, but gossip like there's no tomorrow, the receptionist thought with a grin, watching the really rather handsome policeman go.

That evening, Lily was full of stories about her day at Milford library, so much so that Peter kept the news about Dorcas's letter to himself. He nodded attentively as Lily continued, completely oblivious that he had something important to tell her.

"*So then*, after Mrs Pearce fell, Mr Lucas tripped over her outstretched walking cane and broke his ankle! He was rushed to the cottage hospital and it's very nasty, apparently, so he'll be in plaster for at least eight weeks! That leaves me running the library on my own, but I'll go and visit him regularly. He'll be wanting a good read to pass the time, so I'll have to find him something . . ." She finally took a breath, peering at him.

Peter smiled wearily. "Sounds like you've had a very eventful day. Who'd have thought a quiet little village library could host so much excitement?"

Lily looked at him oddly. "I don't think Mr Lucas sees it that way. He's been Head Librarian there since William the Conqueror commissioned the Doomsday Book. He sees himself as a calming rudder, negotiating the library's way through the stormy seas of literature. It'll all come as a horrible shock, now that he has to hobble aside – so to speak – letting me take the reins."

"Good for you, though," Peter encouraged. "Might mean a promotion at some stage, after you've had this experience with the rudder and reins." He said this with humour, his mind flitting to his own, longed-for promotion. The untimely death of Dorcas Ambrose on his property would not help the cause.

"True – I hadn't really thought about that aspect of things," Lily lied, knowing full-well the thought had more than crossed her mind earlier that day, giving her a warm glow and a sense of hope. "Anyway, that's enough about my exciting exploits for the time being – what about yours?"

Peter gave her a bewildered look. "What, my exploits or my day?"

"Your day, silly!" Lily giggled. "You haven't had chance to say what you've been doing, with me going ten-to-the-dozen. Any more information about–"

The door of Fig Tree Hall library swung open without warning, revealing Seb standing there. "Telephone call for you, Peter. It's the *pathologist.*" He mouthed the last word as though some terrible fate would befall him if he said it aloud.

Peter smiled apologetically at Lily, heading off to answer the call. He noted, with some irritation, that Seb lurked with intent in the hallway, trying to overhear details of Dorcas Ambrose's death by default. Peter lifted the receiver, turning his back on the butler-cum-valet, although he knew it wouldn't deter him. He said "hello" into the receiver, listening to what the pathologist had to say.

"I'm afraid it's bad news," the highly efficient man summed up. "I thought, initially, that the mucosal lining of the nose had broken down. It was a hot day and she was found face-down, explaining the bleeding from that area – it's quite common. But after I examined the stomach contents, it was quite a different story . . . ."

Peter nodded, aware the pathologist at the other end of the line was left with no response. He saw that Seb had whipped out a cleaning cloth, taking the opportunity to run the rag unnecessarily between the bannisters next to the telephone table as an excuse to remain in the hallway.

Although it was petty, knowing he'd not given anything away to the nosey article that was Seb Treadmill was a strange sort of victory for Peter. He replaced the telephone receiver, striding back into the library without a word.

Lily looked up from the newspaper she was reading but remained quiet, letting him speak when he was ready. He stood for a long moment by the mullioned window with his back to her. Just when she thought he would say nothing at all, Peter cleared his throat.

"Well, now we know the truth about Barbara Andrews, a.k.a. Dorcas Ambrose," he said finally.

Standing to stretch her legs, Lily wheeled around. "So, what *did* happen – does Seb know anything about it?"

Peter braced an outstretched hand against the mullioned window frame, peering out into the darkness. "I have no idea what Seb knows, but I assume he's told the police everything."

"Don't you know?"

Peter shook his head, still facing away as if somehow, things were not quite so real if he examined the intricate, colourful design on the old stained glass and the roughness of the cut grey stone.

"Inspector Reed's taken me off the case, as it happened here. It's the right thing to do."

"But to exclude you from the information so you can't keep track of what happens . . . Does this mean they think you have something to do with that woman's death?"

Peter turned to face her, knowing that the time had come. "There's been a few developments . . ."

Lily waited, wide-eyed.

"I don't really know where I stand, or what to do for the best at the moment," Peter said, sweeping his free hand backwards over his hair in a calming gesture. "One minute, I was enjoying a lovely day at the fayre, or was it a fête? The next, and excuse the terrible pun, it's a fête worse than death!"

"What do you mean – what's happened for goodness sake?" Lily exclaimed, growing more concerned.

"So much seems to have happened in such a short space of time. Let's see, I went to The Crown Hotel on my way home to have a word with the receptionist. But before I even got to the desk, a huge poster on the noticeboard declared an emergency meeting of the Milford Residents' Association – on account of the bird deaths that occurred here!"

Lily gasped, horrified that the whole thing had been blown out of all proportion by some of the small-minded residents of Milford. "So, when is this so-called meeting?" she demanded.

"Not so-called. It's taking place tomorrow evening at seven-thirty in the church hall. Refreshments will be provided, apparently."

"Right then, we're going!" Lily cried, her anger boiling to a crescendo. "I shall give them all a piece of my mind, and you know how annoyed I must feel if I'm thinking like that!"

Watching her fume, Peter guided Lily into a chair as explosion was imminent. "I don't know if that's a good idea – they're not going to change their minds, just because we're there. Maybe it would be best if we–"

"I want to know what's being said!" Lily interrupted. "They can't go around waving placards and holding meetings like this – it's not right!"

"Perhaps you'd better hear the rest of my news before you make up your mind. . ."

Lily gazed up at him from her seat, having forgotten that the birds were just the beginning of the problem. "Sorry," she said, meaning it. "Do go on."

Sighing as he tried to marshal the events, Peter paused for a moment until he caught sight of Lily's irritated expression. "This lunchtime, I visited Mr Darius, the solicitor who dealt with Professor Ambrose's estate."

"You mean, *your father's* will?"

"Well yes," Peter said with some distance in his voice, "although you know I don't really regard him that way, as I didn't know him. Anyway," he shot her a look, warning against interruption, "he told me the professor left his daughter the key to a safety-deposit box in his will–"

"Oh, how thrilling," Lily squealed, curling her laced fingers into a tight, excited ball.

"The old man told me I can have the key – as I'm sort of next of kin – once an inquest into the cause of death has taken place. So, it'll be really interesting to see what's hidden in that box."

Lily nodded and gave an inquisitive look. "And is there anything else you want to tell me – the telephone call from the pathologist?"

"I was just coming to that . . ."

Suspicious Minds

Outside the library door, Seb listened with interest. He filed the overheard titbits away for later use in The Gassy Herring public house, concluding that it was Peter the police were interested in.

They don't need to question me, and that has to be a good thing. Yes, Seb reassured himself, *they suspect Peter of doing away with the woman. No one's wondering why I didn't tackle the killer in the grounds. They say that eavesdroppers never hear any good of themselves,* Seb mused, *but in this case, it's put me in the clear . . .*

The Milford Resident's Association emergency meeting was brought to order by the terrifying Mrs Wilberforce. Dressed in a brown, hound's-tooth suit covering her bulk like an over-tight picnic rug, the look was completed with a pair of stout brogues.

She scowled around the room in an attempt to install some quiet into proceedings. The very sturdily pinned bun on the top of her head failed to move with her on account of the amount of hair lacquer holding it in place.

Ironmonger, Mr Blewitt, stood up with the intention of calling for a bit of hush. Oswald Hawke beat him to it, much to the annoyance of Mrs Wilberforce.

"Order! Order! Can we get this meeting underway please? I will now pass you over to Mrs Wilberforce to raise the first item on the agenda." Hawke bowed sycophantically then sat down, seeing the vinegar expression across Mrs Wilberforce's Elizabeth Arden, fuchsia-pink mouth.

"Thank-you Mr Hawke," she said graciously, still retaining the lip pucker. "Firstly, I would like to raise the issue of the poisoned birds in the grounds at Fig Tree Hall. I've conducted extensive research. This has also happened on a previous occasion, although," she looked around to ensure eye contact was made with every single member of the audience, "it was found to be the result of tainted grain up at Duke's Farm."

A long moment of silence passed during which the incident was recalled by those with good memories. The door creaked open and Lily slid in. A sea of curious heads turned to acknowledge her, making Lily feel horribly exposed. Some of the crowd immediately faced front, others scowled and tutted. Someone even loudly hissed, "What's she doing here?" from a far corner.

Lily wondered if she'd done the right thing by attending the meeting, but pushed her way along a row of reluctant feet and knees to a spare seat. *It's a public event and I'm perfectly entitled to be here, if anyone challenges me.* She hoped desperately that no one would.

"It's a disgrace!" shouted Ida Pritchard, the villager who, according to Peter, had decided against buying *Hot Muffins!* from Lily's book stall. "Killing innocent animals just because he feels like it. . ." she petered out, catching the look that Lily shot her.

"It's undoubtedly a travesty," Mrs Wilberforce agreed. "The facts are plain to see. Those birds have been tested, and they each died with a high level of arsenic in their systems. Now the question is . . . how did that arsenic get there?"

"Well, to my mind," interjected Hamish Bodkin, a keen local angler, "it's the same as when those fish died. It's pollutants, that's what it is – and I bet I can tell you who put them there!"

"That was also a very unfortunate incident," agreed Mrs Wilberforce, happy to include any tenuous data to back up her evidence. "The birds at Fig Tree Hall were brutally–"

Lily could keep quiet no longer, the insinuation that Peter has poisoned the birds on purpose hanging heavily in the air.

"And how, do you propose, were the birds encouraged to eat said arsenic?" Lily blurted. "I certainly didn't see anybody force-feeding them poison pellets." She delivered her verdict in a raised voice so no one could miss it.

Mrs Wilberforce took it all in her stride, fixing Lily with a gimlet stare.

"Well, that's just the kind of devil-may-care attitude that lets animals go unprotected. It's clear that some of us care more for our feathered friends than others. Poison must have been put down before the fayre began in order to dispatch the beasts, keeping them away from the food stalls – it's nothing short of bird murder!"

Oswald Hawke nodded fervently.

Spluttering with disbelief, Lily straightened in her seat, staring blatantly back at the formidable Mrs Wilberforce.

"Firstly, what has happened is clearly an accident – the birds could have eaten poison anywhere, then flown on to Fig Tree Hall. Secondly, I think we need to get this into some sort of proportion as it was three birds that died, not a villager, and thirdly–"

"Ahhh!" Mrs Wilberforce interrupted, living up to her name. "But there is more on this meeting's agenda than you know!"

She stood with arms crossed defiantly over her chest, pushing up her ample bosom and continuing the unrelenting glare as Lily was held up as the villain of the peace for daring to show her face. With a bold look directed at the harridan, Lily matched her pose, only with considerably less frontage.

Giving a patronising shake of her head, Mrs Wilberforce moved on to a further item on her meeting agenda. "Although I was keeping this news until the end, now seems as good a time as any to let everyone know that the poisoning was not restricted to *just birds.*" Her voice became sharper as she built up the tension to deliver her bulletin.

Lily's eyes narrowed.

"I spoke to our local vet about the implications of the bird deaths . . ." Mrs Wilberforce imparted. "I was informed that the donkey who became ill at the fayre also suffered arsenic poisoning, only thankfully, it didn't kill him. Being a much bigger animal with a larger metabolism, his system was just about able to cope with it. The arsenic made him extremely ill and it was touch and go, apparently . . ."

"How do you know the animal had consumed arsenic?" Lily asked suspiciously.

Mrs Wilberforce shook her head at the temerity of someone who would question the word of the vet – a highly respected community member.

"After the animal left here in the St John's ambulance, he was transported back to his field. When they tried to unload him, he vomited rather badly – the owner called the vet out again as the poor creature was at death's door. He took a sample of the. . ." she waived her hand to indicate that she was referring to vomit, but would not say the word again.

"I see," said Lily, worried that the issue wasn't going to go away in a hurry. "But how can I reassure everyone that this was an accident? There was no plan, no desire to take the lives of birds, or donkeys . . ." Lily added.

Mrs Wilberforce arched her eyebrows. "Well, you say that, but what can be done to prevent it happening again?" she asked directly.

Shaking her head and rising from the uncomfortable wooden seat that had succeeded in making her backside numb, Lily continued calmly. "Animals can't be watched twenty-four hours a day. That donkey was apparently eating things all over the show, so who knows what upset him?"

"But *arsenic* is the common denominator!" Mrs Wilberforce screeched.

Having heard enough, Lily made her way past the begrudging feet and knees to the door, turning as she left. "Just an unfortunate coincidence, I'm afraid," she said as her parting shot.

♥

As her head buzzed with images of the stern Mrs Wilberforce and her convictions, Lily walked quickly to Fig Tree Hall. The evening was glorious, but she failed to notice in her search for answers. *There's no doubt that those birds ate the arsenic,* Lily decided. *But how?*

The first thought that struck her was to look up the digestive system of birds in a book. Books had never failed her and Lily knew she could rely on them, much more so than she could on people. Books were constant, steady, always there in times of need. They never had a hidden agenda, only that on their pages. Yes, the answer would be in a book. Lily reached the driveway of Fig Tree Hall and began the convoluted walk up to the house. All was peaceful, the nasty accusations a mile up the road in complete contrast with the beautiful building and its grounds.

Peter, seeing her coming from the drawing room window, rushed to open the front door. "Is the meeting over already? That was quick!" He stood back so Lily could enter the hallway, following as she gestured they should go into the library. Without speaking, Lily located a thick, leather-bound book from the shelves and sat on the window seat, totally absorbed.

"I thought as much!" she exclaimed, flicking the front cover over her thumb so

Peter could see she was reading from *Arkwright's Book of British Birds.* "It says here that seeds and pips pass straight through a bird's digestive system untouched."

"Right," Peter nodded, unsure where this was leading.

"So, if you'd poisoned the birds with fruit pips, presumably they would have passed through, although I suppose the arsenic might have been absorbed in transit, so to speak. . ."

Peter took a seat next to her. "Can I assume that they all think I poisoned those birds?"

With a sad look, Lily nodded. "And, apparently, that donkey who was a bit of a handful."

"Oh!" cried Peter, throwing up his hands, "That's just perfect! No one told me the donkey was dead too."

"He's not, but I found out the vet tested him. Apparently, it was also arsenic that upset him, although being a larger creature, he survived. That's where my bird argument failed – shot down in flames with the news about the donkey. . ."

Peter stood abruptly and began to pace the room. Coming to a halt in front of her, he felt the time was right to share some news.

"So, we have the birds – a worry at the moment, but it will pass. Then we have the donkey – I think he's called Rufus – who's miraculously survived. But what can't be ignored is Barbara Andrews. I kept this quiet the other night, but she was poisoned with arsenic too. The pathologist found traces in her stomach and he thinks it was enough to kill her."

Lily shook her head from side to side. "I don't believe it! How?" She ran her fingers through her red curls in distress. "Who on earth's doing this? It's horrible!"

Peter pulled Lily to her feet. "We'll get to the bottom of it, don't worry."

In the kitchen, Seb took the opportunity to gossip whilst Nella was out in the garden, gathering over-ripe tomatoes.

"So, then he told her that that woman in the grounds was poisoned as well – the pathologist told him that, so it's straight from the horse's mouth."

Kitty's amber eyes flared like burning coals. "Cor! So, someone was going around the fayre poisoning on Saturday? It could have been any of us who was killed!"

Seb nodded and muttered darkly, "You never hear death coming, that's for sure."

"So, what happens now then?" Kitty asked, her inquisitive little face tilted with the question.

"Well, can you believe, the copper told his bookworm he's been taken off the case – he's not allowed to investigate it. They're carrying on without him! I'll bet it's because they suspect that he–"

"Haven't you got any work to do, Seb Treadmill?" Nella said sharply, entering the kitchen via the door from the garden. She carried a trug full of tomatoes she'd wanted to select herself, rather than trusting Kitty with the task. Nella's tread had been so light, Seb failed to hear her coming.

"I have, yes. I was just–"

"I know what you were just . . . No one's saying Peter is a suspect – there's no evidence to show he's done anything wrong. He didn't even know that woman was coming back here. So, if you were thinking of spreading a nasty tale that arsenic did for her, think again."

"Who said anything about arsenic killing the woman?" Seb said with interest.

Nella bit her lip, realising she'd just let the cat out of the bag. "The pathologist confirmed that's what killed the poor creature," she said evenly.

Not wanting to let the subject drop, Seb became animated. "Well then, anyone could have done it. Arsenic's freely available to everyone," he suggested. "It's on fly paper, in weed and rat killer, used to colour green dye for hats, soap, fake plants, all sorts. And they do call it *the inheritance powder . . .*" He trailed off under the intense scrutiny of Nella's gaze.

"You seem to know a lot about it. Who's to say it wasn't *you* who poisoned the birds, and the woman in the grounds?"

"And that donkey!" blurted Kitty, trying to be helpful.

Seb shot Kitty a hurt look for betraying what he'd told her, hanging his head for Nella's benefit.

"We've worked together too many years to remember. I like a gossip and I'm not everyone's cup of tea, but to murder another living soul! How could you think that of me, Nella Barnes?"

Realising she had overstepped the mark, Nella emitted a loud harrumph, turning away to blanch the glut of tomatoes picked to make mock crab.

Peter stared out of the mullioned window in the library, aware of the heightened tension in the air. Lily was expecting him to come up with a plan, but his brain just felt foggy. Ideas swam in and out, but nothing gelled together. He sighed deeply, his head heavy with thoughts.

"It's not so much the events, it's the fact that people I've known for years seem to think that I killed those birds. *And* a woman who wandered around the grounds of the Hall. Because they know I'm a policeman, you'd think that would count for something, wouldn't you?"

Lily dutifully nodded. "We need to formulate a plan. Have you got any paper in here?"

Pointing to the library table, Peter said, "There's some in that drawer underneath, and a pen too."

Silently, Lily retrieved the pen and paper and came to sit back down, holding both as a secretary would when preparing to take dictation. She jotted down the facts, then held up the sheet of paper.

"So, what do we have? Arsenic in the birds, donkey and Dorcas. What about motive? Why would anyone want to kill Dorcas?" Lily exclaimed.

"Ah, I forget to say. The receptionist at The Crown told me that Charles Andrews was definitely having a relationship with his secretary, or so he reckoned."

Lily scribbled the information down. "Good, good. So, the husband might have wanted the wife out of the way, is that what we're thinking?"

"I don't know – are we? What we need to establish is a motive, an opportunity and the evidence. I suppose it's one of the oldest motives in the book if the husband killed her to be with his secretary. But why bother to come over to England with the wife to do it – why not just stay in America?"

Lily shrugged.

"And then there's the fact Andrews brought his secretary over here too. He could have made it easier for himself by staying in the States *with* the secretary, if he wanted time alone with her. So, the opportunity had to be to kill the wife here."

Lily tutted loudly. "It's so annoying that you can't question him about that."

"The receptionist *did* say the husband wanted his secretary moved to a nearer room. That implies the wife knew, or had a strong suspicion. Surely he wouldn't carry on an affair under the wife's nose otherwise?"

"So, the wife suggested he accompany her to Milford, to keep an eye on him!"

"Something like that. I find it hard to believe he couldn't take a couple of days off without having his secretary in tow. That reminds me – I had an opportunity to search the room occupied by Mr and Mrs Andrews . . ."

"And?"

"And I came across something very interesting. In the bedside cabinet, I found a letter addressed to me–"

"What! Where is it? Have you read it – what does it say?"

Taking a calming breath, Peter waited a moment before answering. "I haven't opened it yet. I think it's from Dorcas – Mrs Andrews, as I can't imagine that Mr Andrews would want to write to me."

"So, where is it then?" exclaimed Lily with irritation.

Peter gave her a grave look. "I decided to keep it safe in my locker at work – in case I mislaid it, what with Seb and everything. I can just imagine him steaming the envelope open with a kettle in the kitchen."

With a hurt expression, Lily said, "You didn't think it was such an important turn of events, you should bring it home and we read it together? Or even," she added to cover her anger, "that you read it in private, then tell me about it . . ."

"I honesty haven't had the opportunity to open it. I'll bring it home tomorrow, I promise. It probably just says I'm lucky to have got the Hall, and I already know that."

"But, surely that letter is the evidence we're looking for?" exclaimed Lily with dismay. "It's something Dorcas might not have wanted you to see until a later date. What if the husband realises it's gone and tells the police? What if the hotel receptionist blabs and it comes out that you've been there?"

"It was a spur of the moment thing. I shouldn't have taken it, but couldn't just leave it once I'd seen it. And I think the husband's so caught up with his secretary and the inconvenient death of his wife, he won't even notice."

"Let's hope! We could go down to the station and fetch it now, before it gets dark."

Feeling bullish, Peter didn't move. "It's fine where it is, for now. Whatever the contents, it won't change anything – Dorcas will still be dead, and the villagers will still blame me for those birds." A thought suddenly struck him. "Did you get the impression that the villagers at that meeting knew about Dorcas being poisoned as well?"

Lily shook her head. "No, just the birds and the donkey. If Mrs Wilberforce had known, there would've been an explosion of bile when she was flinging her accusations about."

"Well, that's something at least." Peter gave a hunted look. "Do you mind – that I'm in no rush over this letter, I mean? In some strange way, keeping it unopened means I don't have to deal with the contents right now."

"Of course not," Lily replied, forgiving him instantly. "But don't leave it too long before you read it. You never know – it could be of some use."

♥

A sharp knock came at the library door and Seb appeared without waiting to be invited in. Peter looked him up and down. *At least this time, he's seen fit to knock, rather than just barging straight in, completely unannounced.*

"What is it Seb?" Peter asked in a tired voice.

"A Sergeant Whittaker is here to see you." Having delivered the news, Seb then turned sharply, flinging open the library door that had obediently shut itself. He ushered the bemused policeman forwards.

"Thank you Seb, you can go now," Peter instructed, knowing full well he would probably listen outside the door. With a disgruntled expression, Seb beetled away without a word.

"Peter," began Whittaker, "I'm here on official business . . . Reed wants me to question you and Miss Green about the incident at the fayre involving Mrs Andrews."

"Dor–" Lily blurted, snapping her mouth shut halfway on catching a warning look from Peter. She quickly realised that the police were unaware of the woman's real identity.

Peter nodded and Whittaker continued. "Are you aware of anyone who might have wanted to hurt Mrs Andrews?" he said stiffly, his bovine features showing clear discomfort at his task.

"Not really," said Peter, taking charge. "We were just saying it's odd the husband didn't stay with her. Lily saw them together at the fayre, but then he went back to the hotel."

Lily nodded to back Peter up.

"She bought a pastry at the cake stall next to Lily's, then went off to have her fortune told," Peter continued. "That's all we know until Seb informed me he'd found the body."

"Shame Flossie Draper couldn't have seen this coming and warned her," Whittaker said dryly. "So, you didn't see the woman eating the pastry in question?"

Lily shook her head like a little girl caught stealing biscuits, protesting she wasn't to blame. Peter pursed his lips before saying, "Well, as you know, I'm not allowed to be involved in the case. Are you saying it was the pastry that poisoned her?" His eyes were wide and innocent.

"Err, well," Whittaker mumbled awkwardly, "strictly speaking, the pathologist thinks she might have eaten something that didn't agree with her."

"Surely it didn't agree with her a great deal if it killed her?" Lily blurted, seeing no harm in it.

"Well, yes. But keep it to yourself mind. If Reed finds out I let slip the woman was poisoned, and I've told you the coroner found the pastry in her stomach, he'll have my guts for garters!"

"You didn't say a word, we just put two and two together . . . Is that all you want to know?"

Whittaker looked suspicious. "You're taking this all very calmly. Doesn't it bother you that someone died out there in the grounds of your big house?"

Peter raised his chin, clasping his hands behind his back. "I wish there was something I could do to turn the clock back, but I can't. I don't know anything, other than what I've told you, and neither does Lily. Getting angry isn't going to do me any good. Neither is feeling I'm being accused because Reed's banned me from the investigation."

"Just standard practice though, but difficult when it's a fellow member of the force. I wish it wasn't like that, but it is. We want to find out who killed Barbara Andrews, although Reed insists the county police will take over. There are no witnesses – the husband's the only other person we're questioning. . ."

Eyes wide, Peter said, "So you think he might have done it, killed her, I mean?"

"You know I can't divulge any more information, but I don't think the husband choked her to death with a peach and apple turnover! I'll leave you in peace and see you at work tomorrow afternoon – got me doing the late shift."

"I'll see you out," Peter said amiably.

Lily caught Whittaker saying, "Nice place you have here. . ." before his voice faded and the front door opened and closed again.

Peter was back in an instant, his eyes shining. "Did you hear that?"

A Nasty Business

Lily stared at her betrothed with hope in her eyes. "Does this mean they think the husband did it?"

"They do," Peter replied with a huge sigh of relief. "I thought, for a moment that Whittaker was going to ask lots of difficult questions about my inheritance – that woman having obviously come here to stake her claim to the Hall."

"But," Lily nodded to show her understanding, "the police don't actually know that Barbara Andrews was formerly Dorcas Ambrose, do they? Otherwise they'd be going with that line of enquiry."

"Get you," Peter said proudly, "using police terminology!" He saw a blush form on Lily's neck that swept quickly up to her cheeks. "That's thankfully private knowledge and hopefully, the police won't ever make the connection. Let's hope Seb keeps his mouth shut in the pub."

"Doesn't that make you feel rather naughty?"

"What about?" he asked, raising a hand innocently to his chest. "I know I haven't done anything wrong – I certainly didn't kill her. It was Mum who recognised the locket around her neck, realised it could only be Dorcas who had that picture of Eileen Ambrose."

Lily nodded.

"And from what Whittaker just said, they've come to the conclusion that the arsenic was somehow in the pastry Dorcas ate, unless she ingested it another way. The main thing is, it takes the suspicion away from my door!"

Lily looked worried, taking a long moment to respond. "I think we still need to investigate for ourselves, just so we know. There's the bird deaths and the poisoning of that donkey, as well as this business with Dorcas." She tried to sound hopeful as Peter flopped into a leather armchair. "I was reading a book on poisons at work today," Lily continued. "It said that in small quantities, arsenic can be beneficial, but it depends how much is swallowed. As they all had arsenic in their systems, it can't just be coincidence!'

Peter smiled generously. "I'll go on looking into it as far as I can, if it makes you happy."

"You should want to do it to clear suspicion away from you and the Hall. . ."

Peter gave her a direct look and said, "Of course, you're right."

♥

In the back room of *All Buns Glazing*, Felicity sat opposite Diane. Reflecting on the stressful first day it had to be said, all had not gone well for several reasons.

As the tea shop was about to open for the very first time under new ownership, Diane had pulled back the net curtain at the window to see five hopeful patrons, waiting for the grand unveiling. She responded with a scowl, grudgingly turning the sign to 'OPEN'. Diane ushered the bewildered customers inside, retaining her expression.

"Sit where you like," she had instructed in a not altogether friendly tone. Looks were exchanged between customers as Diane disappeared into the kitchen.

Felicity fortunately then bustled out from behind the counter, her mood charm personified in complete contrast to her business partner. She made a careful note of each individual requirement, assuring the four hopeful ladies and one gentleman that their order would be promptly dealt with.

She had scribbled the list onto a single sheet of paper from a pristine pad kept in her frilly apron pocket. The list being duly passed to Diane to organise and deliver. As the orders were prepared, Felicity conversed politely with the five patrons, extolling the benefits of her choice of blue gingham tablecloths to the curious audience.

In the kitchen, Diane was flustered. She'd snatched at the small sheet of paper, immediately slamming it down on the counter with her pudgy hand, deciding she could not, under any circumstances, read Felicity's spidery scrawl.

Instead of going back into the tea shop to confirm the orders with some vague attempt at accuracy, Diane made a wild stab at each item deciding that this would just have to do.

After an unexpectedly long wait for hot water as she had forgotten to put the urn on to heat up, Diane filled a huge tray with a pot of coffee and one of tea, adding a jug of milk. She recalled that a small china bowl of sugar cubes already adorned each table, along with a single pink carnation in a tiny white porcelain vase.

Staggering out under the weight of the beverage pots, Diane made it to the counter, plonking the tray down heavily with a loud, unceremonious crash. She then turned on her black stiletto heels, avoiding eye contact with Felicity, returning to her task of deciphering the cake orders.

In the tea shop the conversation was jovial, despite a prolonged wait for cake, as plentiful tea and coffee had finally arrived. Felicity reaffirmed the order, and two coffees and three teas were carefully poured. Felicity looked towards the door connecting with the kitchen in desperation, her jaw aching with the effort of maintaining a welcoming smile.

"I'll just go and hurry along your cake orders, so sorry . . ." Felicity apologised, scuttling out of the shop and through the swing doors, rubbing her jaw muscles as she went.

Once in the kitchen, she found Diane peering intently at the sheet of paper, a fist braced on either side of the work surface to support her ample upper body. To Felicity's horror, there was no evidence of any kitchen industry, with no plates or cakes to be seen.

"What on earth are you doing, Mrs Pargitter? The customers want to have their drinks *and* their cake at the same time!" She grabbed four side plates and placed them on a tray, searching for two teacakes, a coconut macaroon and a fruit cake to slice. "One of them is on a diet, but the rest want cake! Where have you put them?" Felicity raised her hands in desperation.

"Didn't have time to make any, so I bought a fruit loaf and some tea cakes from the local shop. They're over there, in the bread bin." Diane pointed vaguely to the far corner and continued to peer at the page. "I can't even read this! We don't sell fish cakes!"

Rapidly slicing two teacakes for toasting, Felicity snapped back in a voice loud enough for the customers to hear, "It says *fruit cake*, you stupid woman!". She waited impatiently for the grill to heat and thrust the tea cakes under, then hunted in the refrigerator. "Butter?" Felicity enquired, already knowing the answer.

"Need to get some of that too," Diane replied belligerently. "In fact, we probably need to do a proper shop. I just haven't had time to think about that, what with all the work involved with the fayre and setting up here."

Felicity fixed her business partner with an ice-cold stare. "You knew we were opening today! I would have thought you'd have got the basics in – like a pound or two of butter."

"Don't shout at me!" Diane pointed a fat finger at the grill. "Your buns are burning."

Whipping around to face the semi-cremation, Felicity caught the odour of burnt currants, grabbing the grill handle in an effort to salvage them.

"Oh, not too bad!" Felicity cried, plucking the buns from the wire mesh and dropping the too hot to handle specimens onto a cool china plate. She prized out several shrivelled currants resembling dead flies from the top of each tea cake, leaving a telling crater.

"There's some marg in the fridge," Diane suggested, with no attempt to make up the rest of the order as she observed Felicity panicking.

Grabbing the primrose-yellow margarine, Felicity generously spread some onto the darker side of each bun. She watched it shimmer, realising she'd only toasted the bottoms. Felicity thrust the two plates at Diane with the instruction, "Take these through – man in the checked shirt with the malodorous breath and the woman with the funny eye."

Diane didn't move. "What do you mean – *funny eye*?"

"Oh, for goodness sake!" Felicity's voice rose again before adding, "she's got a stye in the corner!"

"Well, everyone knows about it now!" Diane reprimanded, marching through to the tea shop.

Felicity hacked a piece of crumbly fruit loaf from the shop-bought packet, wondered what on earth she was going to say to the woman with the huge bosom who'd ordered the coconut macaroon.

After the morning rush where the customers had politely thanked Felicity (whilst Diane lurked in the kitchen), the look in their eyes confirming they would never return, *All Buns Glazing* experienced a quiet period that included the lunch hour.

At two in the afternoon, the doorbell jingled enticingly and Felicity was out of her starting blocks to descend on the new customer, having gained much experience that morning. She shot through the door to confront the peckish newcomer, waving a hand at Diane to signal she should get the water boiling for tea.

"Welcome!" Felicity said, arms spread expansively. It was a long moment before her eyes registered fully.

"Mrs Manners-Gore?" the policeman enquired.

Felicity bristled awkwardly. It had been a great come down to drop her self-appointed title of Lady. Being referred to as 'Mrs' sounded insultingly ordinary to her ears. "Err, Felicity, please," she managed, grinning widely and regretting it as her jaw muscles protested in the strongest terms.

"My name is Detective Constable Cribbens from Milford police. I'd like to ask you some questions."

Felicity's hand shot to her bare throat, eyes widening in shock. "What on earth for?" she blurted, wondering what a Milford policeman was doing in Wenham.

Fixing the twittering woman with a detached glare, DC Cribbens continued. "A woman was found dead during the Milford village fayre on Saturday. The post mortem shows she consumed a fruit pastry shortly before she died. We have reason to believe she purchased that pastry from a stall run by yourself and Mrs Diane Pargitter."

Turning white with shock, Felicity yelled for Diane to join them, her eyes not leaving the policeman's face. A crash came from the kitchen, followed by a shout and some muttering. Diane arrived, red-faced in the tea shop. She stood stock-still, catching sight of DC Cribbens.

"It seems a woman has died after eating one of your peach and apple turnovers, Mrs Pargitter," Felicity said sharply, turning a look of utter contempt on her business partner. "What on earth have you done now?!"

Diane fixed DC Cribbens with her piggy stare, pencilled eyebrows rising as she asked, "Who says so?"

"The pathologist says so, Mrs Pargitter," Cribbens informed her. "We'll need samples of all foods in your kitchen, and for you to tell us exactly how you made the pastries so we can determine when the arsenic was added."

"Arsenic!" Diane blurted, her eyebrows remaining unnaturally high on her forehead. "I suppose you think I added poison on purpose? Unbelievable! Coming in here on our first day of opening and throwing accusations like that about. It'll send the customers running for the hills, that's what it'll do!"

"I'm afraid I've another bit of bad news for you," said DC Cribbens in an even tone. "Until your premises are searched and the tests are carried out, this business won't be able to operate. We need to ensure arsenic isn't getting into the food."

"I beg your pardon?" Felicity squawked, hand still at her throat for comfort.

"But the pastries were sold at the fayre!" Diane protested. "They weren't sold or consumed here."

"Yes," replied DC Cribbens patiently. "But the kitchen here was used to prepare the food you sold – do you see?"

"I see perfectly well," exclaimed Diane angrily. "There's opposition to us opening in Wenham. Because there's also Pearson's Tea Rooms in the village, they don't like the competition. They want us closed down with rumours about poisoned cakes!" She stood belligerently, hands on hips, refuting the news.

"I can assure you, Mrs Pargitter, I'm not here because of some business rivalry. A woman has died, poisoned with arsenic after eating a pastry from your stall at the fayre. She definitely bought it from you. I have it on good authority that the refreshment tent wasn't selling," he glanced at his notebook for confirmation, "peach and apple turnovers on Saturday."

"Pah!" said Diane, turning on her heel and storming back out to the kitchen.

"So, we're no longer able to operate," Felicity whispered.

"That's correct. Samples will be taken later today and I'll need a statement about how the pastries were made. Then we'll take it from there." DC Cribbens nodded.

"Thank you," Felicity managed meekly, sitting down heavily at one of the gingham-clad tables and stroking out an invisible crease in the cloth.

Lily rang the brass bell outside Fig Tree Hall and waited. The weather that evening was extremely good. Her thoughts turned towards summer, although with flaming red hair and freckles, she didn't like the weather too hot. Lily always joked that she never tanned, only going a darker shade of white.

As she started to wonder if anyone had heard the bell, the thick oak door opened a crack and Seb peered out at her. He made no attempt to invite her in.

"Is something wrong?" she enquired.

"Not that I know of," Seb muttered, finally moving so she could get inside. Ignoring the butler-cum-valet's odd behaviour, Lily made her way to the kitchen where a familiar raised voice dominated.

"I'm only saying you should do more about it, otherwise it might just catch you out! Lily heard Nella exclaim as she pushed open the door, finding Peter sitting at the kitchen table. His mother stood, holding a wooden spoon mid-air like a conductor's baton.

"What's happened?" Lily asked, taking a seat and peering at Peter's tired expression.

"One of his workmates has said something," Nella supplied. "I was just telling him that he should report it."

"Was it Whittaker?" Lily asked with annoyance. "Because if it was, you *should* say something. He made out everything was just routine when he was here yesterday evening!"

Peter shook his head. "It wasn't Whittaker. Cribbens went to question Felicity and Diane at the tea shop. He asked how they'd made the pastries for the fayre. Naturally, Diane said she'd used Mum's recipe, so that brings the suspicion over Dorcas's death back here again!"

Lily stood, open-mouthed at the news as Seb entered the kitchen sullen-faced, plonking himself down in a chair. Without warning, he began to mutter mournfully.

"They probably think we plotted to get rid of the woman because she could have made trouble for us . . . the facts speak for themselves. Nella gave Mrs Pargitter the turnover recipe, Peter wanted the American out of the way because he's inherited the Hall, and I found the body in the grounds. It looks like we planned it!"

"Don't be ridiculous!" Nella snapped. "And Peter didn't *want her out of the way*, he had no idea she was coming here!" She wiped her hands roughly on a frayed red and white striped tea towel, turning to Lily with a forced smile. "Now, are you staying to dinner, my duck?"

"I didn't say I was blaming you . . . I just said it was your fault," Seb explained to no one in particular.

"If I agreed with you," Nella said coolly, fixing Seb with a sharp look, "then we'd both be wrong."

Lily glanced at Peter and he shook his head. "I'm taking Lily out to dinner at The Crown Hotel tonight. Thought it would make a nice change." He pushed back his chair and walked over to Lily, not making eye contact with Seb as he passed. Lily flashed an apologetic smile at Nella as they left the room.

Peter headed to the front door, ushering Lily back outside. When they'd walked several yards down the gravelled driveway, he said in a hushed voice, "I hope that's all right with you?"

"What?" Lily smiled, linking arms and falling into step with him. "Going out to dinner, you mean? I think it's a lovely idea, although I look a fright. I've been on my feet all day at work – it's surprising how much Mr Lucas does behind the scenes."

"I wanted to get out of there – it can be a bit overpowering at times. When it was just me in my own little flat, I could please myself. Now I've got my mother nagging, as well as Seb spending a lot of time with his ear at the keyhole."

As they reached the main road, Lily trotted towards The Crown Hotel with anticipation. "She means well – Nella. Do you think Seb is spying on you then?" she asked with surprise.

"I do wonder sometimes," Peter muttered darkly. "He seemed to know about Dorcas being poisoned before anyone actually told him, and he's got an unfortunate habit of bursting into rooms without knocking."

Lily nodded with concern.

"Anyway," Peter continued, relaxing a little now he was able to speak freely, "I've got that letter from my locker with me. Plus, I thought we could keep an eye out at The Crown for Andrews and his secretary."

Lily nodded again, feeling somewhat deflated that his intention was not purely to have the pleasure of her company. As they entered the foyer of the hotel, she caught sight of the yellow poster that, although now out of date, still advertised the meeting about the dead birds at the Hall. Lily turned her back and ignored it, hoping Peter would too. If he'd seen it, he said nothing as they made their way towards the restaurant.

"Hello, sir – have you booked a table?" a moustachioed maître de in black trousers, a white shirt and a cherry-red waistcoat enquired cheerily.

Peter shook his head. "I didn't. Do you have a table for two available?"

The man nodded, showing them to a secluded little spot by the window. He pulled out a chair for Lily, then did the same for Peter.

"Can I get you some menus or would you like to hear the special we have this evening?"

Glancing at Lily, Peter caught her almost imperceptible shrug of the shoulders. He asked, "What's special tonight?"

"We have–"

"Just a minute," Peter said, raising his hand. He glanced past the bewildered man to where he'd spotted a smartly dressed customer entering the restaurant with a beautiful girl on his arm.

Lily shot him a quizzical look.

"I think that's them," he hissed. "Just bring us a couple of specials, would you?" he asked the maître de, who nodded briefly, leaving them to it. Peter watched intently as the couple were shown to the table next to theirs.

Lily tried to see what was going on without being too obvious. "What luck!" she chirped, spotting Charles Andrews with his companion. She turned to Peter, a look of concern crossing her face. "Do we actually know what the special is? Perhaps we should have asked . . ."

Peter cast a glance at Andrews and his secretary. "It said on the board as we came in that tonight's special is beef Wellington."

"Oh," said Lily, who had missed this. "Well, I could certainly eat some–" Her mouth snapped shut as she was interrupted by a sharp giggle from the next table.

". . . She had the nerve to say that she'd found me out!" Madeleine Turner conveyed in a carrying voice for interested restaurant patrons to hear. Lily dipped her head forward, giving Peter a wide blue stare.

With an awareness of his surroundings that did not occur to Madeleine, Charles Andrews merely nodded before the next juicy titbit was delivered.

"I couldn't leave it at that, could I? I took her to task and said, *What do you mean, you found me out?* The cheeky bitch just replied, *You should know.* I think she was trying to be clever with word-play. She'd telephoned when I was at lunch, so, 'I found you *out*' meant I wasn't there. But it said it like she knew more than she was letting on."

Inconveniently, two steaming plates of beef Wellington then arrived before Lily and Peter, with accompanying vegetables and roast potatoes. The interruption annoyed Lily, gripped by the unfolding saga at the next table. She shrugged to show Peter it wasn't important, but secretly, Lily wanted to know more. Fortunately, the appearance of two more specials in front of Charles Andrews and Madeleine did nothing to quell her enthusiasm for chatter.

"So, I said to her, 'I've got nothing to hide!' And she replied that I was no better than I ought to be, because I knew exactly what I was doing!"

Throughout the almost packed restaurant, a multitude of forks – or spoons for those who had reached the dessert course – remained frozen between plate and mouth. Listeners concentrated on Madeleine's voice cleaving through the air.

Hearing the woman in full torrent, Peter watched as Charles Andrews made a discreet gesture, suggesting Madeleine might possibly tone it down slightly. She ignored him.

"I couldn't believe the bare-faced cheek of the creature! It's hardly my fault, is it Pooky?"

Peter witnessed Charles Andrews cringe, the man's squat neck turning a startling corned beef shade before it was masked by his stiff collar. Lily utilised her peripheral vision, knowing it was out of the question to turn around.

"Is everything to your satisfaction?" asked the maître de, materialising by Lily's side without her noticing. She started badly and tutted, wiping a splash of gravy from her skirt with the crisp white serviette provided. With irritation as the beginnings of a stain formed, Lily cursed that she hadn't thought to protect her clothing with the serviette over her lap. She glanced past Peter to a large woman in furs and a tiara, chewing a mouthful of beef Wellington with the determination of a ruminant.

For the first time since Madeleine Turner sat down, she paused to take breath, staring at her untouched plate. Charles Andrews continued his meal, relishing the sudden silence. The maître de asked the same question as he hovered close, viewing Madeleine's poor enthusiasm for the Wellington with displeasure. Andrews nodded without making eye contact and the little man in the robin red-breast waistcoat beetled away.

As silence erupted at the next table, Lily shot Peter a look conveying she didn't want dessert. What she wanted was to talk.

As if by thought transference, the maître de was back. Peter asked for the bill, earning him an unhappy look that they weren't staying longer. Moments later the bill was delivered on a small china saucer and Peter reached into his jacket for his cheque book.

The smooth Basildon Bond envelope containing Dorcas's letter reminded him it was there.

A Dead Letter

The bright yellow poster still loomed in the foyer. Lily considered – given the angry discussion that had ensued at the Milford Resident's Association meeting about the avian inhabitants of the village – that it had all come to nothing. She waited patiently until Peter had paid the bill and they were both standing outside The Crown Hotel before excitement got the better of her.

"What do you think of that then?" she blurted, her eyes shining. Peter shrugged noncommittally as they began their slow walk back to Fig Tree Hall. The evening was still pleasant, although there was a distinct chill in the air. Lily hugged her arms across her chest, wishing she'd worn something more substantial than a white blouse, olive green skirt and sandals that morning. *But then*, she considered, *I had no idea we'd be dining out . . .*

"The secretary didn't really say anything helpful to the case. It might just be an innocent comment – *I found you out*. I've been trained to only look at snippets of conversation in context. You can read all sorts of things into the most innocent of remarks."

Lily stopped in her tracks, turning to look at him with an expression full of incredulity. "Oh, come on," she said far too loudly. Walking on the opposite side of the street, Ida Prichard turned to gaze intently at them both. Lily smiled and waved and Peter gave a gracious nod. With an irritated scowl, Ida pulled her coat tightly around her ample bosom and walked on. Waiting until she was well out of earshot, Lily continued, "You know as well as I do, she was talking about their affair!"

Pulling her close as they linked arms, Peter said, "But we can't be sure. Granted, it sounded like that was the topic of conversation, and she did her best not to name names, but still. . ."

"Oh, you are hopeless sometimes! I'll bet you a pound to a penny that's exactly what she meant – that the woman was challenging her for having an affair with Dorcas's husband."

"If you say so," Peter mumbled compliantly.

"It's woman's intuition. Women know women. Now, when are you going to open that letter? If it was me, it would be burning a hole in my pocket by now."

Peter gave her a hunted look, preferring to deal with the matter in his own time. "If only it was as simple as just opening the damn thing! It's the reasoning behind it that worries me. The longer I leave it, the longer I'm protected by oblivion."

"Well," said Lily matter-of-factly as they reached Fig Tree Hall, "it's best to bite the bullet, get it over with. It might be a nice letter saying she's happy you're living here."

"I very much doubt it, but we'll look at it properly when we're inside. Come on!" Still holding Lily's arm, he jostled her up the driveway and they yelled and giggled like a pair of teenagers.

Once inside, all appeared quiet and Peter pushed open the library door, switching on the light. He turned to scan the hallway, just in case Seb was lurking with intent in the shadows.

"Let's get settled in here – do you want a drink before we start?"

Lily shook her head, the prospect of finally having the secret of the letter revealed being too tempting. "No, I'm fine. Sit down and get that envelope open!"

Sitting in a comfortable emerald leather armchair, Peter made a great show of delaying tactics to annoy her. Withdrawing the quality envelope from his pocket, he experienced another stab of dread. He tore the sealed flap open, revealing the equally fine writing paper within, folded precisely to fit its confines perfectly. Peter's stomach tightened, gripped by an iron fist as his mouth grew arid, heart beating a loud tattoo inside his rib cage. With shaking fingers, he drew the folded letter from its casing and stared upon it. He was reluctant to unfold it, unwilling to see the ink on the page.

"Go on then, what are you waiting for!" Lily chided, not altogether sympathetically as she sat eagerly forward in her chair opposite him. Snapping back to the present after his brief sojourn into semi-oblivion, Peter unfolded the letter, keeping his gaze firmly on Lily. Nodding her encouragement, he forced his eyes to the page.

Peter read the document in complete silence, a vague perception of irritation radiating from Lily's chair. Awareness of her was insubstantial as he became gripped by the content. He slowly placed it back in the envelope, laid the envelope in his lap and folded his hands over it as if to protect the delicate news.

Lily waited in expectation, eyebrows raised, saying nothing. After an inordinate amount of time had passed, Peter finally looked up and met her gaze.

"Well . . . . it's what I expected, really." He glanced down at his lap and seemed surprised to find the letter nestled there. "She's full of blame and hatred for me."

Lily rose silently, crossing to his side and seating herself on the arm of the chair to give Peter a concerned look. She felt it best not speak as the atmosphere was highly charged, knowing he would continue in his own time.

"She says it's unfair that I got the house. I'm only the son of a cook who took advantage of her father in a moment of weakness, following the death of her mother. Obviously, she was very angry when she wrote this, feeling I did her out of what was rightfully hers. It's a shame I never had the opportunity to talk to her, prove I didn't know that her father and my mother had a–"

Placing a gentle hand on his shoulder, Lily nodded her understanding as Peter continued.

"Dorcas clearly wasn't content with merely telling me how she felt. She says here," Peter tapped the letter with the back of his hand, dismissively trying to brush it away, "that she intended to contest her father's will. She was about to take legal action against me when she died."

"But that's ridiculous!" Lily blurted, her gentleness gone as anger took its place. Peter merely nodded. "So where does that leave us?" she asked in a tone that was more challenging than she would have liked.

Peter shook his head. "Technically, it's not actually your problem, is it? It's mine."

Lily looked suitably reprimanded, redoubling her efforts to be understanding. "What I mean is, we're a partnership.

Whatever affects you also affects me. I'm just concerned about where this is all leading."

A deep sigh came in return, telling Lily all she needed to know. Silence filled the room but eventually, Peter said, "I've been thinking . . . . There are several major implications arising from the existence of this letter, but of course, we don't know—"

"We don't know what?" Lily interrupted with what she hoped was a winning smile.

"Well . . . firstly, does anyone else knows about this letter. Did she give her lawyer in the States a copy, tell him her intention? Does her husband know what she was planning and how she felt? Don't forget, I took this from the bedside cabinet at The Crown – Andrews might now have realised it's missing. . ."

"I'd be surprised if he's concerned himself with the contents of the drawer on his wife's side of the bed," Lily exclaimed. "But I'll bet she had a good rant about the contents of the will," she added.

Although his train of thought had now been derailed, Peter explained what he'd learned from his police work.

"I've seen many a couple who don't actually talk to one another, don't share their intentions, hopes or dreams. It's astonishing, but some couples just rub along as if they're two independent units, not telling one another about what goes on in their life."

Lily nodded, pursing her lips.

"I remember," Peter said, losing himself in recollection to illustrate his point, "I met one couple where the wife was totally blind all her life, but she never told her husband. It turned out, he never even knew! How amazing is that, that you could keep something so important to yourself and not share it with a loved one?"

Lily's mouth gaped open with incredulity. Knowing it was unattractive, she snapped it shut under his gaze, shaking her head with disbelief. "That's what I like about us," she said. "The fact that we share everything and talk to one another. That's what I meant by, 'How does this affect *us*.' I can't believe people can be so secretive . . . I wouldn't be able to contain myself if I was planning to contest a will."

"Well believe me, people do keep the most important of secrets quiet. Anyway, worrying about who she might have told isn't my only concern. Dorcas died before she could give me this letter, and she met her end here at the Hall, which is now under my ownership . . . It makes it look more and more like I wanted her dead – so she didn't stir up any trouble. Maybe Dorcas was planning to get the Hall back."

"But . . . why? She was obviously comfortably settled in America with her husband. Albeit a cheating, lying husband who seems to prefer the attentions of his flighty secretary, but you know what I mean."

Peter nodded.

"Granted, she was peeved the Hall was left to you," Lily went on, "but Professor Ambrose wanted a son because little Nathaniel died of scarlet fever. He wanted a *male* heir to look after the Hall, probably because he knew Dorcas would marry and move away from her childhood home."

"From the tone of her letter, I don't think Dorcas considered that angle. Whether her father wanted it or not, she obviously felt unfairly usurped by my entitlement to this place. She had a right to be aggrieved – I wouldn't be too happy if the boot was on the other foot."

"Oh, come on!" Lily said, amazed he was being so magnanimous about it all. "Dorcas was just bitter that all she was left was a key by her father, while you ended up with his home and a regular income from his invention patents! It was the professor's choice and she just couldn't live with that!"

Peter stared at her for a second. "But she didn't live with it, did she? She died in my back garden after eating a pastry from the fayre I foolishly agreed to host here. She wasn't run over by the number 32 bus from

Milford to Wenham. She didn't drown in the pond in Milford Park–"

Lily put her hand over his in an effort to calm him, but Peter continued.

"She didn't even take her own life with sleeping pills in a fit of jealousy because she discovered her husband was having an affair . . . It wasn't her intention to die before she could see this through!" He snatched up the letter with disgust, waving it in the air for emphasis.

"OK, OK. You'll have Seb outside the door!" Lily hissed. "Obviously, she didn't know she was going to die after eating that turnover, but from what I've heard, it's amazing more people haven't succumbed to Diane's cooking!"

The misplaced humour was met with an eye flash, telling her to be serious. Lily continued. "But no one's been in touch from the States, saying you need to take action, no fancy lawyers she might have told. If her husband's antics are anything to go by, he seems utterly indifferent to the fact his wife has just died in a rather horrible way."

Peter nodded. "Seems that way, doesn't it? It's so frustrating that I can't look into the case, see what he's up to. Perhaps Dorcas didn't know about the affair. Or perhaps she did, and was planning on leaving Charles Andrews to come back to England and the Hall after all these years."

"Perhaps that's what she was up to," Lily agreed.

"The station seems to think Mr Andrews is coping well with his loss, that the whole thing was just a terrible accident. I know these things take time, but I hate being out of the loop. Samples were taken from the kitchen at *All Buns Glazing* – that I know, but as for the results or any further investigation, I'm completely in the dark."

"We can only do what we can do . . . What can we do exactly?" Lily screwed up her face unattractively as she tried to formulate a plan of action, a primordial soup of facts swimming in her head.

"Not much really. We could do some questioning of folk around the village, see what they've got to say. But that could be risky if they get to hear about it at the station."

"How would they?" Lily asked naïvely.

A sharp guffaw from Peter shocked her. "You'd be surprised. A sergeant questions so-and-so and they say, 'Oh officer, I've already told that other policeman all I know about the woman who died." It's happened before when an officer was moved off a case. Turned out he knew the victim – conflict of interests, they call it."

"But it's only a small risk someone might innocently spill the beans, right?"

Peter knotted his eyebrows, knowing what was coming. "Well, yes. But–"

"Then let's make a list of all the people we think might have seen something at the fayre, have a casual chat with them," Lily cried excitedly. "It's Saturday tomorrow and we're not working. I'll start the list." She shot away to fetch paper and a pen from the drawer in the library table. "Have a think who might have seen something useful."

Lily gave a keen knock on the faded yellow door of Bert Buttermere's little cottage. She smiled widely at Peter as they waited impatiently for the door to open. Irritated grumbling could be heard inside, accompanied by muffled shuffling footsteps that gradually grew nearer.

After some time, the front door flew open to reveal Bert in all his glory. He stood, unashamed in only tartan carpet slippers and a pair of baggy white underpants, the elastic having long since given up any hope of holding said pants in place. Instead, Bert had utilised a pair of cherry-red braces fixed on either side of the gaping waistband. The excess of stretched material billowed freely on the outskirts of his hips.

Lily gasped and tried to avert her eyes, but it was too late – the image was already firmly imprinted on her retinas. "Mr

Buttermere," she managed, having little idea of how to respond to such a vision. "Is it OK if we ask you some questions about the fayre last Saturday?"

"What about it?" Bert grumbled, sucking his teeth, his concave and startlingly white chest beginning to develop goose bumps before their eyes. "Come in before you let all the warm air out – I can't afford to heat the whole street!"

They followed Bert into his untidy, stiflingly hot sitting room, the back view of the underpants and braces combo proving similarly unpleasing to the eye. There was no obvious place to sit, the shabby settee strewn with objects that should have had a home elsewhere.

"Tea?" Bert enquired with a low mutter, which could equally have been any other short word in the English language. He made no attempt to cover himself with the moth-eaten brown cardigan slung haphazardly across a squat little footstool.

"Err, we won't, thanks. Not long had breakfast," Peter supplied, taking in the cobwebby corners of the room. The floor appeared to have at least one full packet of biscuits crumbled into the busy faded carpet.

Bert shrugged thin bony shoulders, his unwashed armpits emitting a powerful odour. "Suit yerself. Got no milk anyways."

"We'd like to ask what you remember about the fayre last week," Lily ventured, having never been so close to the old man before as there was usually a library counter between them. Several large pieces of dark furniture did little to help the rabbit hutch of a front room.

Bert placed a gnarled forefinger to his cracked, pale lips. "Well now, I got there about nine, or was it ten? Had a wander round and came to see you, if I remember rightly. Bought that book on forgotten foods . . ."

Lily nodded, remembering the encounter well.

"Very useful it is too. Found a recipe for pigeon pie and as it happened, there was a few of 'em just lying about on the grass. I put a couple in my pockets to try it out – not that I'm any good at pastry mind, so I got 'er next door to do me some."

Horrified, Peter stepped forward, instantly regretting it as a waft of unwashed body hit him fully in the face. "You mean you asked Ida Pritchard to make you some pastry and you *ate* the pigeons in a pie?" His eyes were wide with shock, imagining Bert dropping down dead in front of them from arsenic poisoning and having to explain himself at the station.

"Aint a crime now, is it? Very nice it was too – lasted me a good three days that pie

did. Reminded me of my younger years –
when I used to go shooting with my father.
We'd bag ourselves some pigeons or a
couple of pheasant if the time was right, and
mother would cook 'em up."

"So, the book allowed you to re-visit old
memories," Lily supplied unnecessarily.
"That must have been nice."

Bert nodded. "Twas. I asked Ida if she
wanted to share the pie but she turned her
nose up, so I had it all myself. Felt a bit iffy
afterwards mind, but I get a lot of bad
stomachs these days. Doctor says it's my
age, but what does he know? Could have
been the giblet gravy . . ."

"What sort of bad stomach?" Peter asked
to Lily's surprise as she wondered if Bert's
bowels were pertinent to the investigation.
Pausing to recall the vivid details, Bert then
gave a full and frank description of the
diahorrea he had suffered, which was of
Biblical proportions.

Shuddering with disgust, Lily turned to
Peter, pleading with her eyes that they
should leave. "And that wasn't all," Bert
continued with relish. "Told the doctor I'd
been very tired lately, with pins and needles
in my hands and feet, but he wasn't
interested. Puts everything down to age,
that one. Said it was probably poor
circulation and that I should put more clothes
on."

"Have you eaten all of the pigeons you found?" Peter asked, thinking that the doctor had a point.

Nodding, Bert placed his hands on bony hips, resting them on the excess material of his underpants as the braces strained, upholding their end of the bargain. "Shame, as it was free. And 'er next door didn't ask any money for the pastry, so that was another win. Pension doesn't go far these days."

"We'll leave you to it then, Mr Buttermere. I'll see you next week," Lily said.

"What?" the old man replied with surprise.

"The book you borrowed about ballroom dancing is due back next week. I've got to be extra diligent now Mr Lucas is in hospital with his leg."

"Good job too," said Bert, who failed to get along with Mr Lucas, the Head Librarian with a quiet, unassuming manner. "Book was no good anyway – I haven't got any ballroom shoes."

Lily nodded, backing away to make an escape. Once outside she took several deep breaths, marvelling at how anyone could live like that. She turned to Peter, who seemed to have coped better with the overwhelming stench.

"What do you make of that then? How can the arsenic have killed Dorcas, but only affected Mr Buttermere . . . as it did?" She shuddered again as the graphic image threatened to invade her thoughts.

"Don't know. We should see if Ida Prichard will talk to us, as we're here." Peter knocked on Ida's dark green front door, but it appeared that the lady was not at home to visitors.

Lily and Peter walked slowly towards the bus stop, intending to catch the next one to Wenham. The street was almost deserted for a Saturday morning and all was quiet, enabling them to talk in private.

"I can only assume Mr Buttermere ingested a much smaller quantity of arsenic after eating the pigeons than Dorcas did from eating the turnover. He'll be back to normal in a couple of days, once it's left his system. Plus, we don't know how much the pigeons actually got, although it was enough to kill them. What he told us implies that the arsenic came from different sources though, doesn't it?"

Lily looked thoughtful. "I suppose it does. I mean, Mrs Pargitter wasn't making pigeon pasties in the *All Buns Glazing* kitchen, was she? No arsenic residue could have been transferred into what she made for the fayre, plus that was before the bird deaths."

"Did the arsenic that killed Dorcas even come from the pastry, or was it some other source?"

"You see?" Lily said with excitement. "Now things are getting interesting. There's also the fact that Bert Buttermere used to work in a timber yard when he was younger – so he once told me. I'm sure at some time or other, I read that they use an arsenic compound as a wood preservative, to stop it rotting."

"So maybe Bert has built up some sort of tolerance to it over the years – that's why it only gave him the runs and pins and needles."

"Could be," Lily agreed as the bus finally came into view. "Let's go and have a word with Diane Pargitter, see what she's got to say."

A is for Arsenic

"I hope you're not implying I had anything to do with that woman's death!" Diane Pargitter screeched at the top of her voice, her thin, pencilled eyebrows rising rapidly to her hairline. She stood, fists clenched on wide hips, glaring at Lily and Peter who sat on wooden chairs in the tea shop. They'd been ignored for some time by Diane after knocking on the front door – although they were sure she'd seen them. Now inside, there was no sign of being offered a beverage.

"Not at all," Peter said in his best policeman's timbre. "I just thought I'd get far more sense from you than talking to anyone at the station about all this." He sincerely hoped the buttering up wasn't too obvious, quickly realising he'd judged the situation perfectly.

Diane's countenance changed immediately, her face becoming all smiles as she patted her hair into place, heading towards a chair at the same table. Plonking herself down so the four slim wooden legs supporting the seat were severely tested, Diane began to pull the petals from a pink carnation in the vase on the table.

"Now, what would you like to know exactly?" The remaining petals fell into the sugar bowl by way of protest and Diane tutted loudly. "Oh well, it's not as though anyone will be wanting sugar in their tea for a while," she muttered stoically.

"What have the police said to you, about when you can re-open here?" Peter asked gently.

"Absolutely nothing!" Diane exploded. "They don't seem to realise they closed us down on our first day, barely a shilling in the till. Now we have to sit around losing business, waiting for them to say I'm not poisoning people with my cooking. It beggars belief, it really does!"

"It must be awful, not knowing–" Lily began, being rudely interrupted by Diane, who failed to recognise or appreciate the gift of empathy.

"–Of course, Felicity is taking it all in her stride with a, 'Yes sir, no sir' attitude. That's only because her Reggie's in prison for fraud and she doesn't want to go the same way."

Lily nodded sympathetically as Diane ranted on.

"I possess the sort of mind that requires constant stimulation. I don't have the money to entertain myself since Frank died, so I have to be content with baking to release my creative energies."

Peter tried to control his eyebrows as they threatened to rise in complete disbelief at Diane's self-delusion.

The street outside appeared deserted as Lily peered past the swathe of blue gingham curtain to the vista beyond. The shop was rather quaint, she decided, with its charming little tables and matching gingham cloths, the white ceramic vases holding a single carnation. The blackboard affixed to the wall detailed what was on offer and the price of each item. Even though the circumstances were unexpected, Lily was glad they'd come to see Peter's investment in person.

"So, we just have to wait," Diane continued, delighted to have someone familiar with the details so she could complain at full throttle – and a policeman at that. Felicity had been most uncharitable in this respect, Diane decided – her business partner suggesting that what was done was done. "They've taken lots of samples from absolutely *everywhere* – goodness only knows why. They even took the hair off my comb!"

"Probably so they can test it for arsenic!" Lily blurted, before considering the full implications.

To a complete hypochondriac drama queen like Diane, that sort of information could be dined out on for months. Peter imagined the conversation between Diane and the poor, unsuspecting Post Office counter clerk. She would inform the defenceless man – who had nowhere to run – that the police considered she might only be alive for a few more months as she slowly succumbed to the evils of arsenic too.

Lily received an eye flash by way of a warning as Peter continued in vain, trying to smooth the way now that the seed was firmly planted. "It's just a precaution, in case the arsenic is environmental. It's in all sorts of products, and pesticides have been used widely on local farmland."

Wondering if this had just made everything a whole lot worse, Lily soon found she was right. Diane took in a deep breath like a steaming bull, about to charge and let rip at Peter.

"Do you mean to say, you bought us a property with dangerous levels of arsenic coming across from neighbouring fields?" Diane fumed.

Peter was too stunned to speak, and Diane raged on, paying it no heed.

"No wonder the former owners couldn't get away quick enough! You leased this place to salve your own conscience about Frank dying at the Hall, and Felicity losing her home. Granted, Felicity's much older than me, so she probably isn't long for this world anyway, but I," Diane drew a pudgy hand to her ample bosom, "am in my prime!"

Lily couldn't stop a sharp laugh escaping in response to the over-the-top reaction, earning her the icy glare Diane threw her. Lily cleared her throat before exclaiming, "Felicity is only in her early sixties! She's got years left in her yet!"

"Glad to hear someone still has confidence in me," announced Felicity, sweeping theatrically through the double doors from the kitchen into the shop. Having opted to wear some sort of iridescent ball gown affair, she seemed totally out of place, given the surroundings.

"I thought I heard voices – what can we do for you?" Felicity gave a warm, genuine smile and Diane tutted loudly with contempt.

"They've come to inform us that this property is riddled with arsenic because it blows in from the farmer's fields!" Diane announced loudly.

"Actually," Peter remarked calmly, "I came to ask what the police have said to you."

"Don't you know?" Felicity asked, her glinting sapphire eyes wide with surprise.

"No. You see, because Barbara Andrews died in the grounds of the Hall after eating the–" Peter just managed to stop himself mentioning Diane's tragic turnover that would no doubt have set her ranting again. "I've been taken off the case until the investigation is complete."

Diane gave one of her wildebeest guffaws, snorting unattractively. "So, they think *you* had something to do with it, do they? Your own workmates suspect you of trying to bump that American woman off! Well that's made my day, that has. It's not all about us anymore, ha, ha!"

"Mrs Pargitter, please!" Felicity reprimanded sharply, knowing of old how the insensitive woman trod on other's corns as a hobby.

"Can we just all calm down, please?" Peter asked in an authoritarian tone, directing his request at the indomitable Diane Pargitter. "We just came here hoping to find out some little snippet of information, something the police might have overlooked. I'm sure we can discover how this awful tragedy occurred – I'm also sure it was a terrible accident. *But*," Peter raised his voice, shooting Diane a direct glare, "I need to know what happened from your perspective. So, go on – tell me."

Felicity took a deep breath, aiming a silencing look at Diane. "Mrs Pargitter used your mother's apple turnover recipe, adding her own twist by also involving peach. She made a batch of twelve and when we got to the fayre, they were placed on a plate at the front of the trestle table to display them, although some were overly-done and oozing."

Diane grew mutinous but remained silent.

"Not long after, Barbara Andrews bought one – I remember there was that hoo-ha when Diane suggested she probably hadn't got any English money to pay for it. Diane put the pastry in a brown paper bag and Barbara went away with it. That was the last we saw of her. Then that awful donkey arrived with its owner and ate a pastry from the plate in one gulp, knocking the rest to the floor so we couldn't sell them."

Lily nodded, considering that the account was pretty accurate from what she remembered. But it was more what happened after Barbara left with the pastry that they needed to find out. *I suppose we just have to assume*, thought Lily morbidly, *that after seeing the fortune teller, she went for a wander in the grounds, ate the pastry and died on her own by that tree . . .*

"So, the long and short of it is, the woman died and your colleagues took numerous samples from the kitchen and in here," Diane chimed, in a tone only marginally less accusing than earlier. "I do believe I've already given a full account to the other officers. They wouldn't tell either of us what was going on, or what they suspected."

"It's just routine," Peter confirmed.

"That's what they said!" Diane confirmed. "Obviously a standard reply meaning they don't want us poking our noses in. Which makes it all the more suspicious that you're here, asking questions when they've taken you off the case. News travels fast in a village. If people hear about all this, it could take months before we get any customers again, so shove off, you're not helping."

Peter ignored the jibe. "And was there anything unusual in the way you prepared the fruit for the turnovers? For example, you didn't soak it overnight in alcohol?" He took in Diane's simmering beetroot face, knowing she would undoubtedly continue with her hate-filled rant.

"Alcohol! Do you think we're made of money? I though you knew we were on our uppers. They were lucky to have them at the fayre at all, bloomin' ingrates the lot of them. I didn't get a word of thanks when I handed the money over to that snooty woman, collecting for the hospital."

Lily nervously made eye contact with Diane, looking quickly away.

"Obviously, no one feels it's important to say please, thank you or sorry these days – absolutely no manners! *And* peaches are expensive to buy. Don't know why I bothered, I really don't . . ." Diane sat, deflated and ungracious while everyone ignored her outburst, moving swiftly on.

"So, you can think of nothing at all that might make a difference to the investigation?" Lily asked the question with rapidly fading hope. Her mouth was dry and she was dying for a cup of tea – ironic, she thought, as they were sitting in a tea shop that couldn't come up with the goods.

"Right, well you've both been very helpful," Peter said, rising stiffly from the hard chair. "Telephone me at the Hall if you think of anything else."

He made his way to the door. The dangling 'CLOSED' sign only emphasising further that the two ladies were struggling emotionally and financially with the forced closure.

"Well," said Lily, staring out of the window of the bus as it lumbered down the country lane on its way back to Milford.

"Well indeed," Peter nodded, watching two black-faced sheep in a nearby field. "I've got a bit of an idea though, but it needs to brew for a little longer."

"At least that's something. I didn't get the impression that either of them know anything, although because Felicity was once a celebrated actress, she could be lying."

Peter shook his head. "I don't think that's very likely. Why would Felicity want to poison Barbara Andrews, a.k.a. Dorcas Ambrose, unless she has some wild fantasy about regaining Fig Tree Hall once her husband comes out of prison, knocking off anyone who stands in her way. Perhaps I should watch out!"

"She'll have a long wait – for him to be released, I mean," Lily replied matter-of-factly. "Where to now then, more of the same or do you fancy some lunch? I'm gagging for a cuppa."

"I rather think we can kill two birds with one stone, although killing birds seems to be a rather sensitive subject at the moment. Let's go and talk to Flossie Draper at the fish shop and get some fish and chips afterwards."

"Sounds like a plan."

"I'm only Madame Lazonga when I'm in character," Flossie announced as she expertly coated two large cod with batter and hurled them into the fryer.

"I realise that," replied Peter, "but did Barbara Andrews say anything unusual when she came to see you – in your capacity as Madame Lazonga?"

"Oohh! I'm like a doctor, me. Hypocritical oath and all that. I never reveal what was discussed between me and a client."

Peter resisted the urge to correct her, savouring the smell of frying fish and chipped potatoes. His mouth began to water and for a brief second, he almost forgot his line of questioning.

"We obviously don't expect you to tell us what was said word for word," supplied Lily, stepping in to keep the enquiry on track. "But did you foresee anything important in her reading?"

Flossie seemed to be thinking very hard about the question, although her vexed expression could equally have been trapped wind. Moments passed, leaving Lily and Peter to only imagine what Flossie might be thinking.

"I read her palm and it was really odd. You see, there was nothing there, completely blank. I've never had that happen before and I wasn't quite sure what to do about it."

"So, what *did* you do?" Peter asked in anticipation.

Flossie dipped into the bubbling oil with her wire basket, withdrew the crispy golden catch and liberally applied salt and vinegar. She then wrapped the fish and chips in several pages from the *Milford Advertiser,* placing the hot parcel on the counter. Peter eagerly reached forward with the money and waited for an answer.

"I had to quickly make something up, I'm ashamed to say. Never had to do that before in all my years of reading fortunes. It made me feel like a charlatan, a complete fake. I couldn't exactly admit it, tell her she had no future there on her palm now, could I?"

Lily shuddered. *How creepy, to have no future to predict in a fortune teller's tent. Then to drop down dead that same afternoon . . .*

"What did you make up?" Peter persisted, keen to get at his lunch as the smell of vinegar pervaded the newspaper.

"I told her she was going on a journey and when she arrived, she would finally be happy. . ."

They spent the whole of Sunday piecing together the rather sparse information collected from Bert, Diane and Flossie, trying to come to some conclusion. They failed miserably, getting nowhere. Lily became increasingly frustrated, staring at the few sentences she'd written on a large sheet of white paper as they sat in the Fig Tree Hall library.

"You said you had a glimmer of something manifesting when we were on the bus, so what was it," she asked.

Peter glanced at his betrothed, trying to steadily overlook the fact there was an accusing tone to her voice.

"I don't know yet. I think it has something to do with the variety of arsenic-related deaths and the way it got into each of its victims," he replied in an even tone.

Peter had achieved very little sleep the previous night, wondering if he was regarded as the chief suspect for Dorcas's death. Lily's boundless enthusiasm seemed misplaced, as was her urge to get the case done and dusted, without applying a modicum of patience to the process.

Lily nodded, her red curls bobbing with momentum as she thought over his suggestion. "Yes, first the birds dying, but we don't know if that was from eating some tainted grain they picked up from a farm somewhere, or if it was Diane's pastries. Then the donkey became very ill, which was definitely from eating a turnover after he grabbed it from the plate."

She studied her notes before continuing. "The vet said that being a large animal, the donkey's metabolism managed to cope with the poison. Dorcas died after eating a turnover, but she was a petite woman. And we still don't know if the arsenic came from somewhere else, like a water supply. Then, of course, there's Bert Buttermere. His spectacular stomach problems were due to arsenic from the pigeons he ate," Lily summarised.

"Yes, but surely, all the cases of arsenic poisoning originate from Diane's pastries. Dorcas, the donkey and the birds all ate the peach and apple turnovers, and Bert, in turn, ate the pigeons he found lying dead after they'd eaten the fragments that landed on the grass. If arsenic was in the water supply, more people around the village would be ill."

"What happened to the bag?!" Lily screeched, almost rupturing Peter's eardrums.

"What bag?" he managed to say, rubbing the ear closest to Lily as it rang in protestation.

"The bag containing the bought turnover! Felicity told us that Diane put it in a brown paper bag before giving it to Dorcas. She then saw Flossie Draper in the fortune teller's tent. Dorcas didn't eat it as she walked, with it in her hand . . . She ate the pastry in the grounds behind the Hall, but what happened to the bag afterwards?"

"Who knows?" Peter muttered, wondering if someone helpful, like Seb Treadmill, had plucked it from the grass, screwed it into a ball and tossed it into the kitchen range to be helpful.

"You always say it's the little details that help crack the case. . ." Lily reminded him.

"I don't recall seeing a bag on the grass, although it could have blown away. I'm sure I'd have noticed it.

"Maybe it did blow away," Lily suggested. "Or perhaps Dorcas put it in her handbag to dispose of later. Although if it was horribly greasy and covered with fruit pulp that had oozed from the pastry, I doubt it."

"Wouldn't be much use to us anyway," Peter decided. "We already know there was arsenic in her stomach, so any fruit filling in the bag would be much the same."

"True," Lily agreed, disappointed. They'd failed to crack the case, despite a glimmer of hope, as well as questioning various people around the village. "Tomorrow is another day though, and I firmly believe that something will turn up out of the blue."

"Let's hope you're right."

Lily stood behind the polished wood library counter, nodding while Bert Buttermere, regaled her with more lurid tales of his overactive digestive system. He'd already vividly recounted the problems with his urgency, his long johns, and a particularly tricky lock on his back door, impeding access to the outside privy at a time that would have suited him better.

Giving her most sympathetic look, Lily's mind was elsewhere. *You can barely notice the smell of him in here, as long as he doesn't move about or flail his arms too much. I must be getting used to it, or else my sense of smell is still in shock from Saturday,* she thought.

Bert rattled on about his plans for the afternoon, withdrawing *Ballroom Dancing for Beginners* from his string bag.

Lily quickly date-stamped the book, thrusting it under the counter to be re-shelved later. *When is he going to leave?* Bending to retrieve a card index from a lower shelf, Lily thought she heard the door, assuming Bert had finally tired of his toilet tales. She straightened, finding he was still in exactly the same position, clutching his empty string bag.

"Off to do some shopping now then," he informed her. "Nice bit o' egg custard's what I need to bind me."

Lily nodded with disgust as the image of Bert's loose bowels loomed large once more. "You take care now, Bert," she blurted, after a stab of guilt made her feel ungracious.

The bottle-green telephone rang shrilly, its penetrating sound echoing around the empty expanse of the library. Lily answered the call finding, to her delight, that it was Peter. After preliminary greetings, he made a suggestion.

"I thought you could bring that book about poisons back with you tonight. We can look over it, see if there's anything that might tie this all together."

"Righto, it's really rather good," said Lily, visualising the cover of *Poisons and Their*

Uses as she assumed a more comfortable position. Her bottom stuck out sharply in a way Mr Lucas definitely would not have approved of.

"Well, I'll see you later then–"

"I was thinking, why exactly was Dorcas left nothing by her father, do you think? Maybe, she disgraced herself somehow, so he didn't leave her any money."

"We'll never know now, will we?" Peter replied, having thought along similar lines after leaving the solicitor's office. *Odd that Professor Ambrose didn't leave his only daughter a sum of money. Clearly, Dorcas remained in America, for whatever reason, once she left boarding school . . .*

"What are you thinking?" Lily interrupted.

"Don't forget, Dorcas was left the key to a mysterious safety deposit box – we don't know what's in there," Peter reminded her. "Might be a massive piece of expensive jewellery that belonged to her mother, or the deeds to another property."

"Oh, yes!" Lily exclaimed excitedly. "The safety-deposit box that Mr Darius told you about . . . I'd forgotten all about it! Hopefully there's something good in there when you finally get to open it. Maybe the investigation into Dorcas's death will be over soon and you can finally get that key from Darius's drawer!"

"We can but hope," Peter replied with little interest. This told Lily he now had colleagues buzzing around him at the station, avidly listening in to his conversation. "I'll see you tonight with the book."

Lily replaced the receiver thoughtfully, letting her mind wander to explore all the glorious possibilities of what might be in the mysterious safety-deposit box. It couldn't be anything big, of course, like a piece of antique furniture, but that key held such intrigue, Lily could hardly wait.

Fuelled by the thought of getting to the bottom of Dorcas's death, Lily crossed the room to the exact shelf she needed. As she turned her back, the slim dark-haired secretary to Mr Charles Andrews slipped silently through the library door. It shut gently behind her so as not to alert Lily that Madeleine Turner had heard absolutely every word.

Secrets & Lies

Madeleine Turner burst into room number 24 of The Crown Hotel, ignoring the 'Do Not Disturb' sign hanging on the door handle.

"You'll never guess what I've just heard!" she announced, flouncing towards the occupant of the bed – as far as one could flounce in high black stilettos on thick carpet. Charles Andrews. lay fully clothed on the pink, flowery bedspread, hitched up on one elbow as he read that day's copy of the *Milford Advertiser*.

"What's that honey?" he enquired, his Southern drawl thick with apathy. He didn't lift his eyes from the newspaper, annoying Madeleine greatly.

"That little ginger mouse who works in the library – remember, we saw her the other night in the hotel restaurant? I went in the library to see if they kept any copies of magazines, as I don't have any English money on me. Anyway, she was talking to some smelly old man–"

"So, what? I could have given you some money, if this is a dig about me keeping you short. Why didn't you just borrow a magazine from the hotel lounge? I saw a couple of copies of *The Lady* laying around yesterday. Isn't that what women read over here?"

Madeleine shrugged, irritated that her story had been curtailed by a barrage of unnecessary and unrelated questions.

"*Anyway*," she continued, "because he was there – the smelly old man – I don't think she saw me sneak in through the door. I was standing behind one of the shelving units."

"Why did you hide and not just wait to ask her about the magazines?" Charles Andrews asked with vexation, making eye contact for the first time.

In a tone reminiscent of a waitress at an American diner, Madeleine shouted, "How the hell should I know? It just felt like the right thing to do at the time." She fiddled with one of her hooped earrings, scowling unattractively. Charles wondered – not for the first time – if he should break off the affair as Madeleine had become extremely high maintenance.

"So, as I was saying," Madeleine continued, "she didn't see me come in, so I guess she didn't know I was there. Turns out it was lucky that I went in. After the old man left, she got a call from someone – probably that policeman of hers."

Rapidly losing both patience and interest, Charles Andrews asked, "And this is relevant *how*, exactly?" A further scowl from Madeleine confirmed his intentions. He would dump her at the first available opportunity, after this business with Barbara was over and they'd flown back home to the States.

"If you'd stop interrupting, I could tell you," she said sulkily, not sure that she wanted to share her news with him now he was being so horrible.

Andrews gave a disinterested look.

"They were talking about Barbara and the fact she wasn't left anything in her father's will. But the policeman must have commented because Ginger then said, 'Oh, I'd forgotten about the safety-deposit box key in Mr Darius's drawer!' Sounds as though your wife got this key from her beloved daddy and nothing else, but it's not being released until they complete the investigation into her death."

She turned to go but Charles Andrews had other ideas.

"Wait, I've got a plan hatching . . ."

"That was quick," Madeleine fired back with sarcasm, her tone intending to cause maximum hurt.

Charles ignored it, pushing himself upright from the bed and swinging his legs to the floor. He stood, beginning to pace the room in long strides as his plan came to life. "I think you could come in very useful here, very useful indeed. We're going for a little trip into town to see Mr Darius the solicitor."

He grabbed her hand and she had no choice but to comply, his grip tight and purposeful. Half an hour later, Madeleine found herself standing with Charles in a reception area with sombre dark green walls, chocolate-coloured paint and brooding paintings of non-descript barren landscapes.

A young male clerk sat behind a solid oak desk containing only an open red leather-bound appointments book and a brass ink well. Fuelled by the little bit of importance that came with his position at the prestigious Darius, Cummings and Bennett solicitors, he intentionally did not acknowledge the new arrivals. The clerk continued to write slowly in the book with his spluttering fountain pen.

"Is it possible to see Mr Darius?" Andrews asked the clerk with polite urgency, adding what he hoped was a winning smile to the request.

The solicitor's clerk gazed at them with a slightly startled expression, as though they had arrived directly in front of him without warning. He wore a tight, starched collar under his immaculate dark suit. The former threatened to impede air supply, explaining his blotchy skin tone. The whole effect was capped by a shock of unruly ginger hair, clearly having no discipline as it shot off in many directions.

"Do you have an appointment, *sir*?" asked the clerk in a surprising deep and sensual voice, making Madeleine think of a certain male film star she admired. The clerk's unfaltering hazel gaze fell only on the gentleman before him, not the inconsequential appendage of a woman at his side.

"I don't, I'm afraid. Just dropped in on the off chance," Charles replied as apologetically as he could manage. "You see, my wife was poisoned last Saturday and Mr Darius is familiar with the circumstances. Could I have a word, do you think? It won't take long."

If the charm offensive and mention of poison was meant to elicit a suitable response, both failed miserably. Andrews stared at the unyielding little man who was evidently not going to budge. *This character has clearly heard every excuse in the book – he was probably the author*. Charles had come across this type of officious clerk before: rules were rules. There would be no unscheduled appointment, no free legal advice.

Madeleine stepped forward – as Charles had instructed if circumstances arose – fluttering false eyelashes, adding a luscious red pout for luck. "We don't want to be a nuisance," she purred in what she considered was her deepest, sexiest voice.

"We'll only be a tiny minute, just to ask a question, you understand?"

The clerk remained steely jawed, clearly unmoved by either of the appeals for time with Mr Darius.

"Can I make an appointment for now?" Charles Andrews persisted, expert at getting his own way in the cut-throat world of American business. This fine example of pure Englishness was certainly a tough nut to crack.

The clerk merely stared ahead, saying nothing. His pen threatened to drip onto the appointments book as an ink globule grew fatter at the nib.

"You don't *look* very busy!" Madeleine exclaimed, losing her cool. She twisted exaggeratedly from the waist, flailing her arms to emphasise that the reception area was completely empty of needy clients. "There's not even a coat or hat on the rack, so don't tell me he's got a client with him!"

At that moment, Mr Darius himself appeared to see who was causing the disruption. He caught sight of Charles, an acknowledging nod showing tightly restrained pleasure.

"Ah. Mr Andrews – just the person . . . I hope Anthony here has been looking after you." It was a comment rather than a question. Madeleine felt it best not to point out exactly what a cold fish Anthony had turned out to be in helping achieve a meeting with the solicitor.

Charles Andrews was surprised to have walked in on such a coincidence, keen to know exactly what Mr Darius wanted with him. He and Madeleine trotted obediently after the elderly solicitor, who had the slow creep of a tortoise. As a parting shot, Madeleine tossed her head dramatically to show Anthony just how unimportant he was in the whole scheme of things.

Once everyone was seated in the flock wallpapered inner sanctum, Mr Darius clasped his hands together on the green leather-topped desk, peering at Charles directly. "It's very fortuitous you're here, Mr Andrews. I've been contacted by your wife's lawyers in America. She asked for a copy of her will to be sent to me. I can only assume she wanted to get everything in place before moving back here."

"Moving back?" Charles blurted, stunned by the news.

Interrupted by the information whilst appraising the sheer amount of green in the room, Madeleine's mouth gaped open in a perfect 'O'. Mr Darius took this as a cue to continue.

"Your wife's solicitor contacted me to say that her intention was to contest her father's will. You understand that Professor Ambrose left both Fig Tree Hall and the income from his invention patents to his son, Peter Beresford?"

"Peter, the policeman," Charles nodded.

"She felt that perhaps her father had made a mistake, as they had apparently lost touch for some time before his disappearance. Your wife wrongly assumed her father ignored her letters, having no contact with him for over twenty years."

Charles Andrews nodded as the situation became clearer.

"Of course," Darius continued, "your wife had no idea that due to a degenerative condition, the professor had actually taken his own life in a tiny office behind the book shelves in the library. Thaddeus Ambrose certainly did like his secrets."

Andrews nodded again. His wife had always pretended she regularly wrote and received letters from her father in England. Barbara even regaled Charles with intricate details of the contents of the correspondence – village life in Milford, new inventions her father was working on, and requests that she visit soon because she was so badly missed. *Clearly all completely fictional accounts, conjured in Barbara's mind because she couldn't accept that her father might have alienated her.*

With his business brain now firing rapidly, Charles asked, "Did she stand any chance of getting Fig Tree Hall – is that why she was planning to come back to England? Since I've been here, I've discovered the policeman was the illegitimate child of a cook who still works at the Hall."

Madeleine nodded fervently.

"Surely Peter Beresford can't have a true claim . . . What about if he keeps the income and I – as my wife's next of kin – continue with her claim on the property?" His eyes glinted in an altogether greedy way that Mr Darius found most distasteful.

"I'm afraid it doesn't work like that. Professor Ambrose left a legal will making his feelings perfectly clear. He wanted his son, Peter, to inherit the Hall *and* income from the inventions."

Charles Andrews stared ahead, processing the information, finding Darius had more to say.

"He was a very clever man who clearly wanted to protect his investment. It would make no difference to that decision, legally speaking, if your wife had been resident in England or not. Ultimately, her father's wish was to leave things as they were in his final will, otherwise he would have arranged to see me to make changes."

"But Barbara, born Dorcas, was his daughter – from his marriage to Evelyn. They were very happy as a family. My wife told me her father had guaranteed that one day, she would be a very rich woman. Her brother died young and she was the only one left to inherit anything." A hint of anger had crept into Charles Andrews' voice. This, suggested to Mr Darius that the other man was losing his argument.

"That may well be the case, but perhaps it was said before your wife became aware she had a half-brother?" Mr Darius smiled in a sympathetic and understanding way. He knew this because he'd practised it many times; sometimes in front of a mirror in the privacy of his own home, just to make sure he was conveying exactly what he wanted to convey.

"I see," said Andrews, although this was not strictly accurate. "Barbara only became aware of her sibling *after* the discovery of her father's body. A telegram from the British police, informed her that her father's corpse had been found, ending years of speculation. The telegram mentioned Peter Beresford as the new owner of the Hall, an illegitimate child she had no knowledge of." Charles Andrews assumed the news had been so curtly delivered because there was only so much space on a telegram, but doubted the information could have been sugar-coated in any way. He recalled his wife's anger, her wish for some sort of retribution. But now she was dead, unable to express her dissatisfaction.

"Your wife's lawyer informed me that Mrs Andrews was going to write to Mr Beresford about this. I strongly advised a matter this sensitive should really be dealt with through proper legal channels. I suggested that I write a letter informing Mr Beresford of your wife's intentions, but I heard no more on the matter."

Charles Andrews assumed a pained expression, completely forgetting that Madeleine was there. Darius continued doggedly.

"I assumed your wife wanted to tie up loose ends in America, putting her plan into action once here. Which brings me back to why I wanted to speak with you, Mr Andrews. A few days ago, I received a telegram from your wife's lawyer, a Mr Richard Griffin Junior. He told me to expect a copy of your wife's will forthwith, at her request. I now have the document and it makes interesting reading."

"Oh?" said Andrews, his eyes lighting up once more.

"Before I continue, might I suggest that the young lady leaves the room?"

Squaring up to the inference, Charles replied gruffly, "There's nothing you can say that can't be said in front of her. She's been my secretary for five years and she knows all my affairs."

Madeleine gave a loud sniff. She was sticking by her boss's side without fail. Her tight black skirt felt constricting – she would have preferred to get up and walk about, but needs must.

"As you wish," replied Mr Darius evenly. He opened a drawer in his desk, instantly reminding Charles of why they had come. The solicitor's grey head dipped as he peered to locate the document he was after.

It had become his practice more recently to place items pertaining to current dealings in the drawer for convenience, avoiding the need to ask Anthony to search the filing cabinets. Mr Darius, being old school, found it easier and quicker to do a job himself. "Ah, here we are. The will is very . . . Well, see for yourself."

Charles Andrews leaned forward with the expectation of being handed the sky-blue envelope containing his wife's will. To his surprise he found that the legal gentleman hung on to the document firmly. Mr Darius opened the envelope, carefully unfolding the page inside as if at a grand awards ceremony in anticipation of announcing the winner.

"'I, Dorcas Elizabeth Ambrose, etc., etc. . . . leave nothing to my cheating, lying husband, Charles David Ambrose, who only married me because he thought he could get his hands on my father's money. It is my belief that Fig Tree Hall, my childhood home, truly belongs to me and I shall fight this injustice for the rest of my days. In the event that I die before this matter is finalised but technically in my possession, I wish to leave Fig Tree Hall to the Milford Historic Society. They should make the Hall into a museum in honor of my father, Professor Thaddeus Cornelius Ambrose, and his marvellous inventions that have changed the world.'"

Charles looked thunderstruck. "She knew? How could she possibly know I was having an affair with Madeleine? We kept it a secret, and in any case, it will be ending pretty soon."

Whether intentional or not, the words slipped from his lips in a way that suggested to Mr Darius that he was glad to get it out in the open.

"Well," Andrews continued, refusing to look at Madeleine's shocked face as tears threatened to spoil her perfect make-up, "Barbara always was clever like her Pa. We met when she applied for an internship at one of my companies – she was head and shoulders above the other candidates."

Madeleine sniffed again, only louder.

Charles thought quickly on his feet. *I need to get the old coot out of here and find that safety-deposit key.* "Would it be possible for me to have a copy of my wife's will?" he asked hopefully.

"You'll need to apply for one at the local registrar of births, marriages and deaths. There is a small charge. They'll ask in what capacity you make the request, so you may need to show a marriage certificate."

Charles Andrews looked irritated, bureaucracy thwarting his plan. "What about the address of my wife's lawyer in the States – are you allowed to give me that information so I can contact him on my return?" It was almost a throw away comment, an observation of how unhelpful everyone in England seemed to be unless you had the paperwork signed in triplicate.

Mr Darius gave an enigmatic smile. "I'm a solicitor and I deal in facts, so I *can* help you with that request. If you would accompany me, we shall go and have words with Anthony. It will take but a moment." The old solicitor hauled himself from his comfortable chair, walking slowly on stiff legs from his office as Charles Andrews followed.

Finding herself alone, Madeleine crossed to the desk and wrenched open the right-hand drawer. The interior held nothing but papers, and Barbara Andrews' precious will sat on top of them. Opening the left drawer revealed a moulded metal tray with various compartments. A small silver key glinted in the afternoon light; Madeleine snatched it up, slipping it into her handbag as she heard Mr Darius having muted words with Anthony. Closing the drawer, she retook her seat, hoping to make it appear as though she had not moved in the last couple of minutes.

As they entered the room, Andrews smiled widely, handing her a small sheet of paper upon which was written the address he had requested. Scowling viciously, Madeleine shot to her feet – impeded again by her skirt – and ran from the room.

Mr Darius mused that she had not fled into the comforting arms of Anthony. "Do you wish to go after her?" he enquired, knowing that in such matters of the heart, it was always best to suggest it.

Charles Andrews shook his head. "No – as I said, she was going to be history when we got back to the States anyway. Perhaps it's for the best. I guess now I'll have to advertise for a new secretary." Andrews than had a thought that amused him. "I don't suppose Anthony would be interested in relocating to America and working for me out there?"

Mr Darius gave him a candid look, wondering whether Charles Andrews would ever again see the address of the American lawyer he had just provided. "I think we both know that's not going to happen. Now, is there anything else I can help you with?"

When Charles Andrews nonchalantly strolled into the foyer of The Crown Hotel, nothing appeared to have changed. He had no idea what he'd been expecting. Perhaps rocks to be flung at his head, or Madeleine ready and waiting, foaming at the mouth, her claws unsheathed for vengeance. But all seemed serene as he was greeted by the buoyant hotel receptionist.

"Hello Mr Andrews! How are you today?"

Charles was not in the mood for light-hearted banter with a non-acquaintance. He replied dismissively, "Fine, just fine." As the receptionist's sparkly little eyes continued to probe, searching his very soul, Charles enquired, "Has Miss Turner been back at all? She wanted some fresh air and went for a walk around the village."

The receptionist continued to hold his unwavering gaze. *And if you think I believe that load of old codswallop, you must be two fishes short of a pond.* "Miss Turner breezed through here about ten minutes ago, sir," the receptionist informed with delight, hoping it would lead to some friction. "The young lady got into the lift, or as you prefer to call it, *the elevator.* She arrived back here in reception very shortly afterwards with her suitcase packed."

Andrews bristled but said nothing.

"Then she slammed the room key down on the desk. Miss Turner scowled in a most unbecoming way, saying, and I quote, 'That horrible pig can pay my *beep, beep* bill, 'cos I'm not going to *beep, beep* pay it'. You can fill in the blanks, sir, as I certainly can't repeat such language in an upper-class establishment like this."

With a deep sigh, Andrews nodded, knowing it was no better than he deserved. *At least I didn't have to actually witness one of Madeleine's hellcat screaming fits*, he thought with relief. They were always monumental, often utilising and launching available objects as missiles, with the ultimate aim of hitting him squarely in the face.

The receptionist grinned widely, adding a sympathetic tilt of the head.

I'm well rid of her, and that's a fact, Charles Andrews congratulated himself, only falling short of actually patting himself on the back. *I just have to get my hands on that key Madelaine's stolen. It's due to come into the possession of a law-abiding policeman of this parish . . . soon to be the unlucky half-brother who gets what's coming to him . . .*

Lies Trip Easily from the Tongue

"I'm sorry to call so early, Peter, but something strange has occurred." The worry-laced voice of Mr Darius registered sharply down the telephone line. Peter was instantly awake, the interrupting boom of the grandfather clock in the hallway announcing it was eight in the morning.

Peter clutched the telephone receiver, anticipating news of another death from arsenic poisoning that he was about to be sued for. He spotted a shadow moving at the end of the corridor. Seb was waiting there unnecessarily, trying to catch some juicy information in his widely cast net of nosiness.

To avoid arousing suspicion Peter merely replied, "Tell me."

Mr Darius took a deep breath, speaking closely into the telephone. "Well, as I say, most odd. The key to the safety-deposit box that we spoke of . . . It's gone."

"How?"

"I have no idea. It was there at the opening of business yesterday, I'm sure of it. As a matter of fact, Dorcas Ambrose's husband came to see me . . . I know the key was in the drawer when I came into my office – I saw it in my desk as I looked for a certain document."

Pondering on the news about Charles Andrews' visit, Peter wondered what the solicitor expected him to do about the missing key.

"I see," Peter said, still aware of Seb's presence, "but it's a tricky one . . ."

"Oh, no, no. You misunderstand me! I know there's nothing you can do personally, that's why I've already telephoned the police. No, I wanted to inform you because you were to be the recipient of the key, once everything is dealt with."

"What did they say?" Peter asked, hoping the intelligent old solicitor would realise that Peter meant the police response to the disappearance. He already knew it would be difficult to determine where the key had gone.

"You understand, I'm not at liberty to say?"

"Well, it's good of you to let me know," said Peter, unsurprised. "I hope it turns up soon–"

A shrill ring from the brass front door bell, accompanied by some thunderous banging made Peter spin around as he replaced the telephone receiver. Seb dutifully beetled down the hallway to answer it. His heart pounding in anticipation, Peter stood ramrod straight by the banister rail, his feet not moving from the spot. Seb eagerly opened the door, allowing trouble to enter. A blast of chill air pervaded the hallway with ominous intent.

"My name is Sergeant Whittaker of the Milford police," announced the strangely cuboid officer who stood in the doorway, his bovine features thrusting forward in an attempt to make his authority understood.

Seb regarded him with little respect, failing to invite the officer inside.

"I'd like to speak to Constable Peter Beresford, please." Whitaker barked as a command rather than a polite request.

Seb stood aside, making a sweeping gesture with his hand to indicate that the man was free to enter.

"Ah, Peter," said Sergeant Whittaker curtly, catching sight of his colleague standing in the hallway. Whittaker peered around in awe, taking in the grand surroundings that had become home to the junior officer. He made no comment on the sheer luck of some people.

"I've just received a call from Mr Darius from Darius, Cummings and Bennett in the High Street. It appears that a certain key has gone missing. I understand it was due to become your property, when the investigation into Dorcas Ambrose's death is complete."

Peter stared benignly, realising the connection between Barbara Andrews and Dorcas Ambrose had been made.

"Because you're involved in the case and you failed to inform us that Mrs Barbara Andrews was, in fact, your half-sister, I formerly have to ask your permission to make a search of these premises. If you fail to comply, I'll take action, obtaining a search warrant to complete the task."

Seb's eyes shone like hot coals. He shut the front door on the outside world, concentrating on the unfolding drama within. Seb refused to meet Peter's gaze, knowing his employer would prefer it if he retreated to the kitchen instead.

Nodding to his colleague, marvelling at his over-zealous and officious tone, Peter said, "Treadmill, could we have some privacy please?"

Treadmill, is it? Seb acknowledged delightedly, knowing Peter must be under pressure if it was surnames only . . . *Or perhaps he's just trying to show off that he's got servants, now he lives up at the big house . . .* Without a word, Seb darted back into the kitchen, leaving the two policemen to battle it out alone.

"Gawd!" screamed Kitty, a hand flying to her chest in shock. "You nearly gave me apoplexy!"

Nella Barnes nodded, scowling in Seb's direction from her seat at the kitchen table. "What's occurring then?" Nella asked, having picked up the phrase from a recent television programme, deciding she would use it at the first available opportunity. She remained seated, but broke from her task of planning the dinner menu as Kitty continued washing the remainder of the breakfast things.

"Peter's in trouble!" Seb dramatically informed the two women, caring not a jot for the worry this would cause Nella. "Police have just come for him because he tried to conceal that Barbara Andrews was really Dorcas Ambrose, his sister! What do you think about that then?"

With his eyes still shining with excitement and glee, Seb pulled out a chair. He plonked himself down at the table as though he'd already done a day's work and was entitled.

"What on earth?" Nella blurted uncomfortably. "Do I stay in here, or should I go and help him?" Immediately recognising that she didn't need Seb's permission or advice, Nella began to fret over the best course of action.

"Something about searching the premises, apparently," Seb supplied further, drip-feeding nuggets of information to cause the most anguish, as he saw fit.

"They *haven't* arrested him, then?" Nella challenged, deciding that the rangy little scroat of a man sitting next to her could infuriate for England.

"N-no," said Seb with caution, "just a search to find a key, apparently. . ." he trailed off miserably, seeing that Nella was furious with him for unnecessarily causing worry.

"How are they ever going to find a key in this place?" Kitty asked, as the infinite possibilities of various nooks and crannies jostled in her brain.

"Don't be so silly!" Nella snapped, "There is no key, or else I'd know about it. Peter wouldn't take a key, he's honest as the day is long!"

The comment rolled off Seb's back. He consoled himself that the bovine policeman must be asking questions and poking around the Hall for a reason.

"Why's that Sergeant here then?" Seb ventured bravely. "The police must think they have something to go on."

"That's ridiculous! You seem to forget that Peter *is* the police!" Nella thundered, pushing her wooden kitchen chair back with her ample bottom. She took herself off to the far end of the kitchen to cool down, her striped blue and white apron flapping with the momentum.

♥

"What on earth are you doing here?" Lily asked, open-mouthed as Peter walked into the library in plain clothes. "I thought you were working. We didn't have a lunch date, did we?"

"No, but I need to talk to you urgently," Peter muttered, causing Ida Pritchard to rapidly lose interest in the back cover of the romance novel she'd just selected from the shelves. She continued to gaze blindly at the book, ears pricked at full attention.

"I'm closing in five minutes," Lily replied, loud enough for Ida to hear. "Unfortunately, Ida," she informed the stout woman directly, knowing she was still all ears, "because Mr Lucas is still in hospital, I'll have to shut the library while I take my lunch."

"Oh!" cried Ida, taking it as a personal slight not to be included in the discussion, "Can't you just eat it here? I won't tell anyone, and you can have your little chat at the same time . . ."

There was an element of hope in Ida Pritchard's eyes and Lily saw this as a sign – a sign that the woman would be hard to shift. "Well now, Ida," Lily said with as much Acting Head Librarian authority as she could muster, "if I broke the rules, that would be very unprofessional of me, even if I made an exception–"

"For your policeman, you mean?" Ida chirped with amusement. "Looks a bit harassed, if you ask me. Probably more trouble with arsenic, I'll be bound." She remained firmly in place by the romance titles. Lily decided the woman had only come into the library because rain threatened.

"Talking of being bound," Lily quizzed, "I hear you've been helping your neighbour out with pastry for his pigeon pie. That was very nice of you." If a direct request failed to work with a stubborn library patron, buttering up was always the next arrow in Lily's quiver.

"It was," confirmed Ida, chest swelling with pride. "And how was I repaid? Up and down to that outside lavy all night, he was. Flushing like there was no tomorrow, and all because the silly old beggar probably didn't cook those birds properly. I ask you!"

Not wishing to discuss Bert Buttermere's bowels just before her lunch, or at any other time for that matter, Lily decided she had to be firm. "Can I ask that you pop back later, if you can't see anything you like at the moment? Might be some returns this afternoon, something you haven't already read."

Ida shot Lily a look of purest umbrage. She stomped out of the library, pulling her capacious rust-coloured winter coat – worn all year round – across her frontage like battle armour.

"Well, that's got rid of her," Peter sighed with relief. "I hope she doesn't cause you any trouble later."

"Oh," said Lily, watching the slowing momentum of the swing door in Ida's wake, "I know how to manage the likes of Ida Pritchard. I've got a steamy romance under the counter to fob her off with. That'll keep her quiet. Now, what was it that you wanted to tell me?"

"I had a visit from Sergeant Whittaker first thing this morning. He wanted to search the Hall because that safety-deposit box key has mysteriously disappeared from Darius's desk drawer."

"What?!" cried Lily, "You mean that someone actually broke into the solicitor's office and took it?"

"I have no idea," replied Peter, tired by the drawn-out nature of the investigation into Dorcas Ambrose's death and all the twists, turns and implications that went with it.

"I got a call from Darius at eight this morning before I left for work, then Whittaker was knocking down the door soon after because Darius had reported the disappearance. I won't say theft, because there's no evidence that anyone stole it. He may have even misplaced it himself – he is getting on a bit."

"But how could anyone actually get at the key?" Lily asked, her intrigue growing rapidly. "Surely, they would have been seen, if someone either entered or left the building?"

"Or they were in plain sight all the time, entering as a client and leaving the same way. How else could anyone get into Darius's office? Perhaps they distracted him, grabbing the key from his desk when he was out of the room."

"Do you think that's what really happened?" asked Lily, eyes wide.

"Well I can't see anyone climbing up the drainpipe outside of the building in full view of passers-by in the High Street. That would be too risky. It has to be someone who got in via normal methods, posing as a person needing legal advice, maybe."

"Surely they don't suspect you?"

Peter shrugged. "I suppose they're pursuing every line of enquiry. I just happen to be suspect number one – cast as the grasping half-brother who got the Hall, the patents income, and who now wants the safety-deposit key to complete the set."

Lily nodded sympathetically.

"They know that Barbara Andrews was really Dorcas Ambrose . . . Whittaker came in like a lion but went out like a lamb, losing interest when he realised there was little point in asking me questions, or searching the Hall. I mean, if I'd taken the key, I could have buried it in the grounds. They just don't have the manpower to do the spadework in a search like that."

Lily pursed her lips, desperate to be supportive as he continued.

"I got the impression Whittaker was only showing willing because Inspector Reed had sent him. He didn't expect to find anything much," Peter concluded.

"Just a minute," Lily said, waving her outstretched hand. "Who would want that key, unless they knew what it was for and what they could potentially gain? There's only you and Mr Darius who know the key fits a safety-deposit box left to Dorcas. . ."

"Which is why they potentially suspect me of taking it. Although as I was never alone in Darius's office, it's hardly likely that I managed to get in and out with that key unseen." There was undeniable sarcasm in Peter's voice.

Knowing the idea was preposterous, Lily asked, "Is that what Mr Darius is saying then, that you took it?"

"Not in so many words. But as Darius didn't take it himself, that only leaves me."

"What if old Darius *has* lost it, mistaken it for a locker key or mislaid it somewhere? Or he might be in on it, as he isn't getting any younger – take what was in the deposit box for himself and retire in comfort?" Her breathing was rapid as the idea took hold, seeming to make more and more sense to her.

Peter shook his head. "Hardly likely, the man's scrupulously honest. No, it has to be someone else. Maybe that solicitor's clerk – definitely a cold fish."

"Wait a minute!" Lily screeched in a way that was becoming far too frequent for Peter's liking. "Yesterday – when you telephoned here . . . we spoke about it, the key! I remember, I said it would be exciting to finally find out what's in that safety-deposit box."

"And?" asked Peter, puzzled.

"*And* I'd just been speaking to Bert about his troubles. He left and I went to get the poisons book. I thought that someone else must be in the library because the door was still swinging slightly, but I didn't see anyone. What if someone overheard me talking about the key, the fact that it was all that Dorcas was left by her father?"

"Well, it's certainly an explanation, but it's no good worrying about it now. That information wouldn't be very interesting to most people, so who do you think it might have been?"

"That's just it!" Lily exclaimed with frustration. "I didn't *see* anyone, although there was a faint whiff of perfume, so I suppose it must have been a woman."

"It certainly wasn't Bert!" Peter quipped, glad to break the tension.

"How about we go and ask if he saw anyone? I'll close up here and we'll go along to his cottage."

"What, *now*?" Peter asked, not really in the mood for the overwhelming odour that was Bert Buttermere.

"Why not?" Lily chirped as she enthusiastically went to fetch her jacket.

Lily knocked firmly on Bert's peeling yellow door, keen to get some answers. She was prepared for the smell this time, and had squirted a small amount of flowery perfume, kept in her handbag for special occasions, onto a clean white hanky. The plan was to touch it to her nose occasionally, feigning imminent hay fever.

The door finally opened and Bert appeared, dressed in a pair of khaki army shorts and a bright red fez hat, the black tassel dangling playfully in front of his rheumy blue eyes.

"Hello again. Do you want to come in?" Bert muttered, failing to move aside to allow entry.

"Please," nodded Lily.

"I've got no biscuits . . . I've got a tin of sardines."

"Right," said Peter as he and Lily shuffled forward in an attempt to get Bert to move.

Once inside the grubby lounge, Lily asked, "Do you remember yesterday, when you came into the library and we were talking?" Her eyes were hopeful, but Bert shook his head.

"No charge for it, is there?"

"It's not about a book. No. It's just that, I think someone came into the library when we were chatting, but I didn't see who it was."

"How'd you mean?"

"Well," Lily tried to explain patiently, "when the library door swings, I know that someone's just come in or gone out. Only I didn't see either, because we were talking."

"Probably got a ghost then," Bert suggested, giving his considered opinion.

Lily repressed the urge to tut and continued. "Did you see anyone come in or go out, while we talked yesterday?"

"Why?"

"Because it's important," she said tightly.

"I only saw a bit of black hair behind one of the shelves. Thought you knew someone was there, otherwise I would've taken more notice. Didn't know there'd be twenty questions."

"Anything else?" Peter asked, sensing that Lily might raise her voice in irritation if she didn't get a straight answer.

"She wore those clacky, tall shoes that made a noise as she moved . . . Bit o' perfume in the air too." Bert sucked his teeth loudly. "Lily of the Valley, I think it's called."

"How do you know that?" Lily asked, stunned the man even knew the name of something that smelled so lovely.

"My mother used to wear it," he informed them, moving closer.

"Thank you, Bert," Peter said, holding his breath while Lily lifted her handkerchief to her nose.

Back inside the library, Lily shared her spam and pickle sandwiches with Peter. They sat at one of the scratched little tables provided for quiet research work, although they tended to get piled with books when browsing patrons failed to place them back on the shelves.

"So, we've got someone with black hair, wearing perfume and high heels," Lily summarised, failing to see where this had got them.

"And if you put that together with Charles Andrews visiting Darius yesterday afternoon, we have our culprit."

Lily took a bite of her sandwich then said, "We do?" spraying myriad crumbs over the table. She chewed determinedly before asking, "What, Charles Andrews in a black wig?"

"No! I mean his secretary, Madeleine Turner! She must have come into the library yesterday and overheard you talking to me on the telephone. She obviously passed that very interesting piece of news to Andrews. He then went to see Darius, making up some excuse to get him out of the office and pocketed the key."

"Oh, very good," Lily nodded in admiration, the remains of her sandwich held mid-air. "But I can't imagine the likes of Charles Andrews' secretary frequenting a library, she's not the type. Her sort's more likely to paint her toenails a vivid shade of scarlet than to read a good book, I should imagine."

"Not a very charitable attitude, if I might say – I think she's fairly harmless. It all fits though, whether she uses the library back home in the States or not, I think it's the most likely explanation to who's got that key."

"Right then, so what do we do now?"

"I have absolutely no idea," Peter replied, his eyes shining with excitement as a plan began to form.

The foyer of The Crown Hotel was busy that lunchtime with people arriving to check in, check out, or trying to push their way through the throng of bodies and suitcases to enter the restaurant. Peter slipped quietly towards the stairs, unnoticed by the preoccupied receptionist. *Some things are better tackled alone,* Peter told himself, guiltily thankful that Lily needed to re-open the library that afternoon. He easily climbed the two flights of stairs to the second floor, heading to room 24. Peter gave a sharp knock, despite the DO NOT DISTURB sign.

"Come!" the occupant said sharply. Peter did as requested. The pink chintzy room was identical to when he'd discovered Dorcas's letter.

"Mr Andrews, do you mind if I have a word?" Peter came further into the room, watching Andrews throw a pile of folded shirts into his gaping leather suitcase on the empty bed next to his own. "Going somewhere?" Peter observed with interest.

"What's it to you?" Andrews muttered with annoyance at having gained an audience, his back to Peter.

"I was just wondering if you intended to leave Milford, as you appear to be packing. It would be inadvisable, until the investigation into your wife's death is complete."

Andrews whipped around to face the interfering busy body of a policeman, who had no business being in his room.

"I was told you'd been thrown off the case because you might have something to do with it! Who are you to ask me questions?"

Patiently, Peter stood his ground. "I've been advised not to have any involvement in the investigation in my police capacity, but this is a private matter."

"Oh?"

"I want to know if you took anything yesterday from Mr Darius's office, when you visited him?"

"Again, what's it to you?" Charles Andrews asked rudely, continuing to snatch socks and underwear from the chest of drawers, throwing them into his suitcase.

"Well, because of reliable knowledge acquired by your secretary, I wondered if you'd taken possession of a certain key?"

Andrews stared at Peter as though he'd lost his mind. "I have no idea *what* you're talking about – what key!?"

"Oh, come now, you know exactly what I'm talking about," Peter continued, slightly unsure of where this was heading. *If he's going to deny all knowledge, I'm not going to get far.*

"Perhaps we should ask your secretary about it? I happen to know she overheard a private conversation in the library yesterday, meaning she definitely knows all about the key."

"She may well do," muttered Andrews. *Did Madeleine take the key from Darius's desk, like we planned? There wasn't chance to ask before she hurried away and booked herself out of the hotel. But what does it matter? The key is no longer important . . .*

He caught Peter's enquiring look and provided, "She's gone back home. We decided her secretarial position was terminated, meaning there was no need for her to stay."

Peter nodded, knowing there was more to it. "So, you don't have the key, is that what you're saying?"

Staring into Peter's solemn blue eyes, Charles Andrews nodded by way of confirmation. Peter knew that he was telling the truth.

You're a Long Time Dead

"It's all over the village!" Lily informed Peter as he walked into the kitchen after a stroll in the grounds that evening. Having just arrived, she was flushed after hot-footing it up the Fig Tree Hall driveway to share the news.

As Peter wondered what he'd walked in on, Nella put him in the picture. "Poor Ida, she's only my age and now look what's happened . . ." She shot a look across the scrubbed wooden table. Seb remained sensibly mute, but considered nipping out to the Gassy Herring pub for a quick half. Nella's gaze then travelled across to Kitty who, shook her head in disbelief.

"Would somebody mind telling me what's happened?" Peter asked calmly, already having an inkling the news wasn't good.

"She's in hospital, half-dead with arsenic poisoning!" his mother informed him matter-of-factly. "She was taken badly this afternoon and Bert Buttermere called the ambulance! Lily was just saying that Ida didn't come back to the library, like she said she would." Nella looked to Lily for corroboration.

"That's right," Lily supplied, taking up the baton. "You remember, she said she was coming back?" she implored as Peter took a seat at the table.

I wonder where all this is leading, he thought, pouring himself a cup of tea from the big brown pot in the centre of the table. "Not that it's important, but as I recall, she stomped out because you wanted to close for lunch. What happened after she left the library to land her in Milford cottage hospital?"

"Apparently, by the time she reached her cottage, she had terrible stomach pains and sickness. Bert found her struggling to get her key in the lock. He was just going out, luckily, so he called an ambulance as she could barely stand by that point."

"How do you know it's another case of arsenic poisoning?" Peter asked Lily.

"Because I rang the hospital to ask if she was all right. I thought I could take her that romance novel to cheer her up. The nurse said I could visit tomorrow, because it takes a few days for arsenic to leave the system."

"She actually said arsenic? Unlike them to give away a piece of information like that," Peter said with surprise. "They usually say something noncommittal, like, *the patient's as well as can be expected*, or, *the patient is resting*."

Lily hung her head, a deep rose hue climbing up her neck and onto her cheeks. "I might have told the nurse I'm Ida's daughter," Lily muttered, "only out of concern, you understand?"

Peter shook his head but said nothing while Seb grinned inappropriately.

"It's like someone's going around the village trying to bump people off," Kitty supplied.

"Now that's just silly!" Peter chided. "There's no serial arsenic-ist. All the cases can be accounted for sensibly. I'm sure the reason Ida has succumbed will be explained the same way."

"But how can you be sure?" Seb asked, daring to speak, although he knew Peter was unhappy with his snooping. "An innocent woman, sitting in her cottage and visiting the library a couple of times a week. Where's the motive to poison her like that?"

Peter gave Lily a look but said nothing.

"I don't suppose you've been told anything, after the early morning raid today?" Seb went on, judging that he'd come this far. "I assume they told you not to come into work, as you changed out of your uniform once the sergeant had left?"

Peter resented Seb overstepping the mark, refusing to fuel the fire. Aiming his reply at Lily, he said, "We'll go and see Ida tomorrow, take her some fruit and that novel after we've finished work."

The inappropriately-named Belcher ward, so called after hospital founder, Sir Jeremy Belcher, was quiet. Patients were tucked neatly in their beds for the evening, having sat up and taken nourishment, of a sort. Hushed visitors spoke with their relatives and friends under the eagle-eyed gaze of Matron Carmichael. The austere woman paced in no-nonsense black brogues supporting a hefty walrus figure, her ridiculously feminine blonde curls framing a battle-axe face.

"And you are?" she challenged as Lily and Peter dared to make their way towards a stricken Ida in the farthest bed by the window.

"Here to see Mrs Pritchard," supplied Peter, sensing that only close relatives were allowed near, and this relationship might have to be proved first with blood and stool samples.

Matron Carmichael scrutinized Lily with uncomfortable closeness. "Are you the daughter? I must say, you don't look a bit like her. She won't be allowed those," she pointed to the brown paper bag of crisp little apples that Lily was carrying, making to snatch them away.

Flinching instinctively, Lily quickly thrust the apples, that were too good to lose, into her capacious handbag. She nodded nervously, intimidated by the huge woman's over-bearing air of authority.

"She's over in the corner," informed Matron Carmichael, her mouth forming a flat line as she confirmed what they already knew.

Lily nodded, preparing to escape quickly.

"Don't be too long mind. Your mother's tired and she's had her stomach pumped." Her authoritarian presence bustled away to attend to something far more important. Lily and Peter were left to cross the wide expanse of scuffed, corned-beef coloured linoleum towards Ida. Numerous visitor's curious eyes tracked their progress.

Trying to convey her sympathy, Lily bent over Mrs Pritchard's vulnerable, sheet-clad form. Her feet had been immobilised by a folded pale blue blanket, tucked tightly across the bottom of the bed to prevent escape.

"Ida, I'm so sorry that you're in hospital! Bert told Flossie Draper from the fish shop, who told Mr Jenkins at the Post Office, who let his customers know. So, Hamish Bodkin told Mr Blewitt, who told me." Lily took a deep breath, Ida's grey face reflecting her annoyance at being the current topic of juicy gossip throughout the village.

"I'll get us some chairs," Peter said, crossing to the opposite corner to take possession of two worse-for-wear orange efforts, the foamy padding showing prolific seepage. Visitors' eyes followed his every move, their own conversation – or that of the prone patients they had come to see – clearly not enough for them.

He tucked the better of the two seats under Lily's bottom and she sat without breaking eye contact with Ida. Peter positioned himself quietly on the other chair, behind Lily in Ida's line of sight as the bed-bound woman twisted towards her two visitors.

"So," Lily chirped, believing Ida would appreciate it, "what do you remember?"

"I wasn't unconscious!" Ida cried, tutting loudly. "I was fully *compass mantis*."

"Don't you mean– oh, never mind . . ." said Lily generously, deciding there was no point in correcting the other woman's mispronounced Latin. "Tell us what happened," Lily encouraged.

"Nothing *happened*," muttered Ida, deciding it was all too much effort. "I felt ill and Bert saw, so the interfering old beggar got an ambulance to me."

"You must have been very bad, for him to be that concerned," said Peter, wondering if they would achieve their purpose of getting any useful information.

Ida merely nodded.

"I've brought you a romance – *And He Took Me in His Arms* by Philippa Philpot. I know you like her books." Lily placed the novel on Ida's over-bed table, seeing the woman had no interest, lacking the energy for thanks.

"I did bring you a bag of lovely apples too," Lily continued, "but Matron wouldn't let me give them to you." She stared as Ida's face became a bilious green and the woman struggled to sit upright. Panicking, Lily wondered if she should call someone.

"They think it might have been them what did it," Ida managed, gagging dryly then flopping back onto the pillows, exhausted. "They pumped out lots of apple pulp, apparently – from the pie I made."

"Ohhh!" Lily exclaimed with a mixture of interest and disgust.

"And that's what they told you – that the apples had upset you?" Peter interrogated as Lily looked queasy.

Ida nodded again, gesturing for some water. Leaping up obligingly, Lily poured some from a worn plastic jug with an orange flip-top lid that sat on Ida's bedside locker. She handed the equally tired plastic beaker to Ida who canted her head, drinking deeply from it.

"So, you made an apple pie," Lily summed up in what she judged was a helpful way. "That doesn't sound too harmful to me."

Peter glanced at Lily with wide eyes before continuing the information extraction. "I assume they tested the contents of your, err, stomach, coming to the conclusion that arsenic made you sick?"

Again, Ida nodded, seemingly keen to continue. "I had the symptoms of poisoning. The apples were given to me, cookers they were, and I decided to make a big pie. I ate it over two days, although the sickness and stomach trouble started the first evening. I just thought I'd got the same bug as Bert." Ida handed the beaker to Lily so she could place it back on the locker.

"I can see now why you wouldn't fancy those apples I brought you," Lily said, not sure she wanted to eat one either now Ida had put her off the idea. "Although, I can't imagine anyone eating a huge fruit pie, all to themselves."

"You're a long-time dead," Ida replied curtly.

"We'd better let you get some rest," said Peter kindly, shooting a look of utter disbelief at Lily, sensing that poor Ida had probably had enough. "Can you just tell us one last thing – who gave you the apples?"

Ida shook her dark head, her hair matted and flattened against the pillow. "I've no idea. They were left in a basket on my doorstep."

Madeleine Turner sat in the guest lounge of The Orchard Hotel in Wenham. *It's certainly not in the same league as The Crown,* she considered, taking in the tatty beige wallpaper and chipped cream paint. She sat next to a three-bar electric fire, only two emitting a modicum of heat to mar the inner chill of the room. *But it will do.*

She hadn't even bothered to unpack her suitcase after being shown to an equally disappointing room, dimly lit and decorated in muted shades of mushroom and beige. *I'm only planning to stop the one night. Just long enough for me to do the deed . . .*

The Crown Hotel receptionist clutched the telephone receiver tightly, waiting impatiently for room 24 to answer. He had counted five rings, his inquisitive eyes riveted to the desk in front of him. He dared not look up to meet the gaze of the very stern police sergeant. Instead, he decided that the unfortunate-looking man resembled a sturdy bullock and willed Mr Charles Andrews to quickly answer his call.

At last, Andrews – who had pushed the persistent ringing into the background – snatched up the telephone by his bed. "What is it?" he barked.

Relief and shock flooded the receptionist. *But then*, he mused, *I'm used to this kind of abuse from people who are devoid of manners.* "Mr Andrews? This is reception. I have a police officer here who would like to speak with you." *There! Message delivered, job done.*

Andrews sighed deeply. *He's here again – when will I get some peace?* "OK, show him up."

"I think it's more the case that the sergeant is expecting you to come to him, *sir*," the receptionist provided with a hint of sarcasm.

"Really?" Andrews replied politely. "Well thank you . . . what was your name again?"

The receptionist felt a blush coming on under the eagle eye of the sergeant. The officer didn't have time to be messed about while he and Mr Andrews got to know one another on first name terms. "It's Tristram, sir. Shall I inform the sergeant that you'll see him in the hotel lounge shortly?"

"If you could do that, Tris, I'd be grateful," replied Charles Andrews in his most charming voice.

Replacing the receiver, Andrews viciously hurled a glass ashtray snatched from the bedside table, watching as it rebounded against the door with a loud crack. "Better not keep the flatfoot waiting," he announced to the room, slipping out into the corridor and giving the door a hefty slam to show just how tiresome he found the whole pantomime.

To his surprise, Charles Andrews discovered that it was Sergeant Whittaker rather than Peter Beresford waiting for him. He occupied a particularly comfortable, burnished chestnut leather armchair in the hotel lounge.

Andrews took the chair opposite, ensuring his face gave nothing away. A young housemaid, dressed in black with a frilly white apron and cap, headed over to the real fire. She dutifully built it up with logs from a gleaming brass bucket on the huge stone grate. Tristram, who had detected a distinct nip in the late May afternoon air, had instructed her to light it.

Once the maid completed her task and left the room, Sergeant Whittaker folded his hands in his lap. He sat forward, reminding Andrews of a farm animal eagerly searching for fodder.

"What can you tell me about your movements yesterday afternoon?" began Whittaker, fixing the other man with small, searching brown eyes.

"When exactly do you mean?" Andrews met his gaze with innocence, determined to be as obstructive as possible.

"Well now, let's just focus on your visit to see Mr Darius the solicitor, shall we?"

"As you wish." Andrews shrugged, folding his hands in his lap to mirror the sergeant. *A way of implying, without words, that I'm on the same wavelength as you,* he thought tactically, *even though I most definitely am not.*

He gave a look of forced concentration and continued, "I went to see him about my wife. Darius explained he had wanted to meet anyway. Apparently, unbeknown to me, my wife was planning to come back to England. She'd started fixing things up with her lawyer, then died before the plan was put into action – the lawyer had already sent Darius a copy of her will."

"Yes. I got all that from Mr Darius himself. What I don't understand," Whittaker paused, staring unblinkingly at Andrews for longer than was comfortable, "is why you went to the solicitor's office in the first place."

"Excuse me?"

"Why did you go and see Mr Darius – without an appointment?" The stare continued.

"That's my business," Charles Andrews said, throwing a savage glare back at Whittaker. *Mustn't lose my cool with this chump, otherwise I'll never get to leave this god-damned country!* he reminded himself.

"I think you'll find that it's actually *police* business, Mr Andrews. Can you provide me with a valid reason why you went to the offices of Darius, Cummings and Bennett – without having made an appointment – then demanded to see Mr Darius?"

"I did not *demand* to see him," Andrews said in his defence.

Whittaker patiently unfolded his shovel-like hands, then folded them again. "Did you have a valid reason for being there, Mr Andrews? Were you, for example, intending to make an appointment to discuss your wife's estate, but decided to enquire whether Mr Darius could see you anyway?"

"Something like that. I knew he'd been the solicitor to my wife's father. I hoped he could tell me when this whole thing might be over with." Charles Andrews assumed a hurt expression, aiming to convey that he was the victim of circumstance. Furthermore, he'd lost money from missed business deals after being advised to stay in England.

"So, you merely dropped in on the off chance?" Whittaker probed. "Because Mr Darius was formerly Professor Ambrose's solicitor, and once you got to see him, he informed you of your wife's intention to return here?"

"Yes."

"Was that the extent of your conversation?"

"What? Oh . . . a few other things were said, about my wife's will, how she had it in her mind to get Fig Tree Hall back one day."

"And had your wife ever conveyed this desire to you?"

Andrews shook his head adamantly. "No. I thought we were happy. She didn't have to work and could please herself, seeing her friends for lunch and so on."

"She never mentioned taking possession of her childhood home?"

"She never said anything, not a word. I guess this all came about after she discovered Fig Tree Hall wasn't hers. It came as a shock, after all these years, to hear her pa was discovered dead in his secret room. She always did play her cards close to her chest."

"But you both turned up in Milford, you and Mrs Andrews, and you brought your secretary along too. Surely, your wife must have given some inkling of why she wanted to come back here?"

Charles Andrews shook his head. "It was just a light-hearted suggestion, that my wife visit Milford where she grew up. I'd been planning a business trip to London for a while, but at the last minute, the guy blew me out. Barbara said we should come here instead, and Madeleine too – so I could do some work while Barbara looked around her old haunts."

"She didn't want you to see the sights together?" Whittaker asked.

"Evidently not. She told me a few places she intended to go, but I got the impression I wasn't actually invited. We went to the village fayre as she said it was an annual tradition, but I came back to the hotel after I'd seen it and Barbara stayed on – it meant more to her than it did me. I've already explained all this to another officer after they found her body in the grounds of the Hall." Andrews affected a sniff of distress that did not fool Whittaker.

"And your secretary – what of her?"

"You mean while I was at the fayre, or yesterday, with Darius? She's already told you her whereabouts before my wife was found. As for yesterday, we had a difference of opinion over a work matter. We mutually agreed that she should leave my employ – nothing would be gained by forcing her to stay, making her travel back to the States with me . . . Whenever that might be."

"I see."

The void of silence stretched infinitely, urging Charles Andrews to fill it.

"Look," confided Andrews, changing both his tactics and his tone, "we're both men of the world. My relationship with Madeleine was a little more than just . . . well, you know.

Darius informed me that my wife knew about our affair and Madeleine was there with me at the time. Things got a bit heated. I said she was getting too demanding – I'd already decided the relationship was over . . . And then Madeleine stormed off. You know what women are like."

Whittaker choose not to comment on a subject he knew very little about.

"And that was the last I saw of her."

Whittaker nodded, having already had a full account of the situation from Mr Darius himself. "So, as far as you're aware, Miss Turner is now heading back to the United States?"

"I assume so, yes."

"Then we'll leave it there for the time being, Mr Andrews. But I may need to question you again at a later date." Whittaker made to leave, failing to catch the expression of sheer annoyance clouding Charles Andrews' face.

Madeleine Turner emerged from *Wenham Hardware* with a precise copy of the safety-deposit box key secured in her purse. It was now time to execute the next stage of her plan, a slight diversion from the original, but satisfyingly tantalising, given recent events.

That cheap pig will get exactly what he deserves, she thought charitably, crossing the road to a wooden bench and sitting herself down. She opened her purse – *known in this country as a handbag* – she told herself, the thought tickling her. Madeleine's other purchase, just prior to having the key cut, was a medium crepe bandage from the local chemist a.k.a. pharmacy. This translated to *drug store*, a far better description for the purpose of the business.

Undoing the clean white paper wrapping, Madeleine quickly applied the bandage to her right wrist, taking the stretchy cream fabric around the four fingers of her right hand. She finished the job by neatly tucking the end under the tight folds on her palm. Crumpling the empty white paper wrap, she pushed it between the bench slats then stood, making her way to The Orchard Hotel reception.

The lank, yellow hair that hung around the receptionist's face reminded Madeleine of a greasy Afghan hound. The young girl failed to smile, and Madeleine wondered if the gormless article would actually have the wherewithal to carry out the task she was about to request. She approached the untidy reception area, enquiring politely, "Would you be able to write something for me – I've sprained my wrist?" Madeleine waved the heavily bandaged joint stiffly, conveying frustration. "It would be the hand I write with, wouldn't it?" She smiled generously, her poppy red lipstick parting to reveal perfectly straight white teeth.

"What do you need?" asked the girl without enthusiasm.

"Well," Madeleine continued, rummaging in her purse with her un-bandaged hand, "I have to return a key to the Countyshires Bank in Milford High Street. I wonder if you could write a note and the envelope, so it can be posted back to them?"

The girl looked unsure. "I suppose I could just hand the key in to them when I go home tonight. I live just outside Milford, but it would mean taking two buses," she suggested, rather than agreeing to the original request.

"Oh, I really wouldn't want to put you out. If it's posted tonight, it will arrive by morning," Madeline gushed, having no intention of letting the girl take charge of the precious object.

"As you wish, madam."

Madeleine placed a plastic bank bag on the counter with exaggerated difficulty, having extracted it from an internal pocket of her *purse*. "The key's in there. If you could write a little note for me?"

"Saying?"

"*Please find enclosed the key Charles Andrews took without permission.*"

The girl's badly plucked eyebrows rose but she did as she was asked.

"And an envelope please," Madeleine directed.

A small envelope was selected and the girl scribbled the bank's name and address on the front. "Do you want it to go into the mailing tray marked first class?"

Madeleine nodded, congratulating herself that she had wiped the original key clean of her own fingerprints.

Immaculate Deception

Peter wondered when it was all going to end. He made his way once more to Chief Inspector Reed's office, summoned, apparently for a 'little chat'. *Could word have reached Reed about my visit to see Charles Andrews? Perhaps I'm about to get a verbal warning not to stick my nose in.* Once Peter was in front of the terrifying man, all became clear.

"I wanted to see you because we're not making progress with the Dorcas Ambrose case."

Peter stood immobile as realisation dawned, waiting to be told where exactly he fitted into the investigation he'd been warned to keep clear of. It now seemed common knowledge that Barbara Andrews was actually Dorcas Ambrose.

Very little fresh air circulated inside the Chief Inspector's office, impaired further by a firmly closed window and a full-pelt fan heater, belching oppressive and unnecessary warmth. Peter felt dizzy as Reed continued; the words jumbled and Peter only caught one in ten as his mind reeled, fogged by oxygen depletion.

"It's come to my attention that you're carrying out a mini-investigation of your own, asking questions around the village and so forth. I've come to the conclusion this may actually be of use to us, although technically, you're still off the case, Beresford."

Peter nodded. "Thank you, sir."

"I suppose it's to be expected," Reed continued, "that you would want to see this nasty business over with, doing all you can to move it along. There's not enough evidence to charge anyone with your half-sister's death. The coroner wants to hold an inquest to determine if it was accidental death or murder – if she was deliberately poisoned."

Swaying slightly, Peter corrected his balance, forcing himself to stand straight. "Yes, sir," he managed in as convincing a way as possible.

"Now, as you're aware, there have been a number of arsenic-related incidents around the village. So far, we've not been able to tie them down to one source, accidental or otherwise."

Peter cleared his throat and nodded.

Reed fixed Peter with a beady stare and said matter-of-factly, "My money's on the husband – it's usually the spouse in ninety percent of cases. Whittaker questioned him yesterday. Evidently, the man was having an affair with his secretary. Pound to a penny he wanted his wife out of the way, it's as old as the hills."

Peter nodded again. He was unsure of whether Reed expected him to give his opinion of Charles Andrews, and whether it was likely that he killed Dorcas.

"And then there's this business with the missing key. I suspect the husband of that too, but we can't pin it on him. No one's sure of what happened before the key disappeared, so unless it turns up or there's further information, we can't charge him with theft. What are your thoughts?" Reed's intense stare becoming more penetrating.

Peter blinked, trying to force sensible thoughts now a burning headache was forming across his temples. "It seems there was very little communication between Mr and Mrs Andrews, from what I gather."

"Meaning?"

"Meaning that she didn't want to share her plans about contesting her father's will and trying to win back the Hall. Perhaps she was planning on leaving her cheating husband and settling back in England."

"Yes, it certainly looks to be that way," Reed agreed. "But I don't know how we can get a confession out of him – if he went as far as killing his wife, for whatever motive."

"What about questioning the mistress? Has anyone asked her what she knows?" Peter suggested tentatively. *It's not my*

*place to direct the course of the investigation
– Madeleine Turner's probably already been
asked for her version of events.*

"Good suggestion, Beresford. The affair
only came to light when Whittaker
questioned Andrews. We have no reason to
suspect the secretary of any wrong doing,
but they may have planned the death
together."

Peter pursed his lips, sure he was going
to faint any minute if he didn't get out of
Reed's office.

"Well, that's all for now, Beresford. I
wanted to keep you appraised of the
situation, get your views in case you could
bring anything new to the table. I'm sure
you're itching to do more than deal with lost
dogs and shoplifters, but that's bread and
butter policing. You can go now, but could I
ask that you keep me informed of any
developments you may get to hear of
pertaining to the Dorcas Ambrose case?"

"Of course, sir," Peter managed, surging
from the stifling room into the wonderfully
oxygenated corridor beyond, his head
pounding. Taking himself off to the gents'
toilet and flinging the window wide, he drank
in the late-May air until he felt normal again.
*Reed is asking what I think because he's
desperate,* Peter told himself. *If they've got
nothing, it's unlikely this will be anything*

*more than an accidental death, but even that
needs to be proved . . .*

Madeleine Turner purposefully entered the
Countyshires Bank in Milford High Street.
She'd chosen to dress completely in black,
although she wasn't planning a hold up at
gunpoint. Teamed with her patent black
stiletto boots, she wore black leather gloves,
her right wrist and hand now unencumbered
by the discarded bandage.

Madeleine swept confidently past the
counter clerks, industriously dealing with
withdrawal and deposit requests. She was
only challenged on entering the corridor
beyond, leading to the manager's office and
vault room.

"Excuse me, madam, may I help you?"
asked a grey-haired, sallow man with the
face of a hawk, appearing out of nowhere.

Madeleine had not expected to gain entry
to the safety-deposit box without being
stopped and questioned. She turned a wide,
friendly smile on the man. "I was told to
come this way by a member of your counter
staff," Madeleine lied, maintaining eye
contact with the suspicious, hooded stare.

"I very much doubt that, madam," replied
the man with authority. "Entry to the safety-
deposit area is on an appointments-only
basis with either myself or Mr Carruthers,

the manager." He maintained the pursuing stare of a hunter.

"Then I must have misunderstood – my apologies," gushed Madeleine, trying to reduce any drama regarding her true motive to a minimum.

"Let me accompany you," the man suggested, striding forwards at a pace on long spindly legs. Madeleine hurried to keep up, not wanting to let the man out of her sight.

They passed through a meeting room into another corridor where a door bore the name, MR ARCHIBALD CARRUTHERS, MANGER, in gold letters. The pair then reached a box room with no windows. The man flicked on an electric light and a sulphurous yellow glow flooded the room from several fat bulbs above.

Madeleine registered the wall of steel drawers of varying sizes on one side of the room. On the other there stood an enormous metal safe, sporting a large carbuncle combination dial to its front.

Hovering nervously, Madeleine said, "I understood I'd be allowed to access my safety-deposit box alone . . . I would prefer it to be private."

She tightened the belt on her charcoal raincoat to show she meant business. Madeleine slipped her black leather purse strap from her shoulder, unzipping an inside pocket to access the newly-acquired key.

"Just a moment, madam," the man continued in a belittling voice.

Madeleine shook her head with a degree of irritation, the safety-deposit box key held mid-air as she urged the omnipresent, overly diligent bank employee to leave.

"I have to enter some details into a special register as a permanent record. If you wouldn't mind providing your name and then waiting for a couple of ticks, I'll be back shortly." He stared the stare of a dead turbot on a slab, waiting for her name.

"It's Barbara Andrews," Madelaine said curtly. Once alone, she toyed with opening the deposit box, snatching up the contents then leaving again, feigning having changed her mind. *If I stay, they'll discover I gave the wrong name for the register. That key's in the name of Dorcas Ambrose,* Madeleine recalled, growing flustered. *I really should have thought this through. No doubt, the key number is recoded somewhere in her maiden name, or her father's . . .*

The door to the small room burst open and a portly little man waddled in, his sparse hair Brylcream slick, failing to conceal a wide area of pink scalp. Small round glasses only served to make his eyes appear nondescript. He also sported a rather startling moustache, resembling the back end of a ferret. "I'm the manager of this branch and I demand you tell me what you think you're doing?" the little man insisted, with an air of genuine authority.

Madeleine looked about her, noting the absence of windows offering no means of escape. *I'm going to have to tough this one out,* she told herself as panic began to rise. Taking several deep breaths, she found this did little to calm her hammering heart.

The Deputy Manager appeared ready to pounce.

"I'm here to access my safety-deposit box. No crime in that, is there?" Madeleine challenged sarcastically, waving the copied deposit-box key under Carruther's nose to show she wasn't bluffing.

"I have reason to believe that key does not belong to you. The police have been called." Mr Carruthers stood his ground, secure in the knowledge that he was completely correct.

"I *beg* your pardon?" Madeleine exclaimed, affecting surprise and clasping her free hand to her chest to demonstrate the injustice. "I came here today in all good faith, and here I am, being treated like a criminal."

"That box is not yours to access, and you know it," Carruthers replied coldly. "We have to guard against keys being mislaid or stolen and we have certain procedures in place. I happen to know that the key you're holding belongs to a lady by the name of Dorcas Ambrose. You are not she."

Knowing the game was up, Madeleine replied brazenly, "And how can you be so sure?"

"Each of our keys," informed Carruthers with ill-disguised contempt, "is assigned a number that appears on the key itself. That number is entered into our register every time a client wishes to access the box they've hired from us. Our deputy manager saw there was no number on your key. He checked it against our records and a list of absent keys that we have."

"He didn't have time to do that and relay the information to you!" cried Madeleine in astonishment. *He was only gone for a few moments . . .*

"It's an extremely short list and we're a very efficient bank. We're not in the habit of allowing our keys to be lost or stolen but occasionally, one goes astray. The key in question was signed over to Mr Darius, to pass it to Professor Ambrose's daughter at the appropriate juncture."

"But I *am* Dorcas Ambrose, and my married name is Andrews!" Madeleine almost screamed. "The contents of that box are mine – they were left to me!"

"They most certainly were not," Carruthers replied. "You're no more Dorcas

Ambrose than I am. It's well known around the village that Dorcas – whose name was changed to Barbara – died last Saturday at the village fayre."

"You knew her then?" Madeleine said, astounded that she had not considered this possibility.

"I most certainly did, from when she was a small child living at Fig Tree Hall and her father first opened a savings account in her name. I've been at this bank for over thirty-five years, so I'm very familiar with the fact that Professor Ambrose left Dorcas the key to that very safety-deposit box in his will."

Madeleine looked crestfallen.

"Ahh!" Carruthers broke off at the sound of footsteps in the corridor, "it sounds as though the police are here to question you."

The determined little bank manager stepped to one side from the guard dog position he'd assumed. Sergeant Whittaker and Detective Constable Cribbens nodded to Carruthers as they entered the room.

"*Miss Turner*," said Whittaker with some amusement at catching her red-handed. "We understood you'd left the country – another ruse cooked up between you and Charles Andrews to throw us off the scent?"

Madeleine stared at the flagstone floor, saying nothing.

"But here you are," Whittaker continued, "trying to pass yourself off as Dorcas

Ambrose, from what I hear. How did you come by that key you're holding, and what exactly did you hope to achieve here?"

The sergeant assumed a look of wide-eyed expectation. Solving the case of the missing key would bring them one step closer to finding out what really happened to Dorcas Ambrose.

"I got the key from Darius's desk, and you know I did," Madeleine blurted unattractively, her crimson mouth forming a sulky pout.

"So, you weren't obtaining the key at the request of Mr Andrews then? Cribbens, write that down!" Whittaker instructed, watching as Detective Constable Cribbens extracted a police-issue notebook from his jacket. Flipping to a clean page, he scribbled fervently with the stub of an old pencil he kept rammed in the spine.

"We talked about it, yes," Madeleine admitted, refusing to make eye contact. "I was the one who told him about the key in the first place! He decided it would be a good idea if we got the key to see what was in the safety-deposit box – to find out what all the fuss is about!"

Whittaker read her face like a book. "You already know what's in there, don't you Miss Turner? But you also needed to know the whereabouts of the key."

Tutting with irritation, Madeleine repeated the overheard conversation between Peter and Lily in the library. She then turned her gaze directly on Whittaker, taking in the look he gave her, realising that ramping up her feminine charm was not going to work this time.

"You still haven't answered me. You already know what's in that box without even looking, don't you?"

"Shouldn't this interview be taking place at the police station? I thought you Brits liked things done *just so*," Madeleine spat viciously.

"The Countyshires Bank is as good as the station, Miss Turner. We have Mr Carruthers present, and you're here holding a copied key, which is technically the property of the bank. It will be handed back to Mr Darius for safekeeping now we know its location. What's the reason for wanting to access this particular box?"

Madeleine sighed deeply. Without warning, she suddenly threw the key to the floor where it landed awkwardly against the ink-black, highly polished left boot of DC Cribbens. He swooped to retrieve it, holding it tightly between his left thumb and forefinger in the event that Miss Turner might attempt to snatch it back.

"I'll ask you one last time, Miss Turner. What were you hoping to find? It seems likely that your former boss wanted access to Dorcas's property to prevent Peter Beresford being left Professor Ambrose's estate. Why the interest is that little key?"

"Charles knew nothing, he just thought he was being clever!" Madelaine blurted. "He wanted that key purely to cause maximum disruption – to the investigation, to Constable Beresford, to his wife's memory for all I know."

Whittaker nodded for her to continue.

"That's what he's like! When I told him what I knew about the key, an obsession came over him and he just had to have it. He frog-marched me down to that solicitor's office with the instruction that I was to grab the key while he kept Darius talking. Although he already knew it, he asked Darius for the address of his wife's s lawyer in the States. The old boy had to go out of his room for it, so I took the key while he was gone."

There was a knock on the door and the Deputy Manager went to answer it, returning swiftly. "I'm sorry to disturb you, Mr Carruthers, but the morning post has just arrived. I thought you might like to know that a key's been sent to us. It appears to be the twin of the one without its serial number." He handed the small silver key to the manager who placed it in his palm, turning it over and over again.

"Can you explain this?" Carruthers asked Madeleine Turner directly.

"Oh, come on! You can't possibly connect that key to me without any kind of evidence. Anyone could have put it in the post!"

"But anyone didn't, did they?" Whittaker said solemnly. "I believe you copied the key and that copy is what DC Cribbens is holding." Madeleine's eyes grew wild but she said nothing.

"You posted the original key back here," Whittaker observed. "Doing it that way, you needed to memorise the box number. But it had its advantages – the Deputy Manager wasn't able to recognise it quite so easily." Whittaker shook his head at the schoolboy error in putting the original key in the post, rather than the copy, or posting either key at all for that matter.

Close to tears, Madeleine realised her mistake. "I guess old eagle eyes here spotted it for a fake when I took it out of my purse. Charles really didn't have anything to do with it – he just came along for the ride. *Yes*, I know what Dorcas has been left in the deposit box, but that's only because I have insider knowledge . . . ."

"Do go on, Miss Turner," Whittaker implored. "We'd all love to know what would drive you to such great lengths."

"Maybe I just want to hang on to the secret for a little while longer?" she said obstinately.

"Easily sorted," Whittaker decided. "Mr Carruthers, if you'd like to do the honours?" He gestured to the copied key that Cribbens still held in stiff white fingers, his grip so firm, he'd cut off the blood supply. Carruthers crossed the room, taking possession of both the fake key and the genuine version as he passed. He then joined Madeleine in front of the corresponding safety-deposit box.

"I'm almost too excited to actually open it," Carruthers provided, a brief moment of frivolity before the secret was revealed. He slid the copied key into his waistcoat pocket for safekeeping.

The genuine key slipped easily into the lock and with one turn, the mechanism clicked to release the drawer. Carruthers slid the metal box from its casing with the precision of a surgeon, placing it with unnecessary delicacy onto a wooden table in the far corner of the room. With his back obscuring the view, he opened the box and gasped.

In a millisecond, Whittaker was by his side, getting his first glimpse at what resided within.

"What is it?" he asked in puzzlement, staring at the fat white tube of sturdy card bearing a printed number. He peered closer still, making no sense of the reveal.

"It's an invention patent, Sergeant Whittaker," Carruthers explained.

Whittaker looked again at the casing and then at the bank manager. "I don't understand," he said, all professionalism knocked from him.

"You British policemen certainly do have a reputation for being knife-sharp," Madeleine blurted with derision, "but you seem to be letting the side down. Instead of having your full wits, you've only come half-prepared – shall I fill you in?" Madeleine took centre stage, a leading lady, standing equidistant to all parties in the small space. She raised her voice without need so no one missed what she was about to say.

"It all began during the war. My mother was a top-of-her-class secretary, so good she was asked to work for the United States Government. She was seconded to work with Professor Ambrose, who was asked to produce a military enhancement drug to overcome combat fatigue. My mother did all his typing. She had to sign an official document and was sworn to secrecy because that drug formula is worth one heck of a lot to the US Government!" She pointed a shapely scarlet nail at the innocent-looking document tube for emphasis.

"But surely," Whittaker said, stunned, "the US Government kept copies at their end, as they were paying Professor Ambrose?"

Madeleine shook her dark head. "You would think that, but no. It wasn't allowed under the Professor's strict instruction. He agreed to do the work because it engaged his interest, but he demanded sole ownership of all relevant paperwork."

A look passed between Carruthers and his deputy.

"But, of course, that information needed to be seen by the secretary typing up the document. Although my mother was breaking the Official Secrets Act, before she died last year she told me that this document existed. She knew Ambrose had paperwork at his home in England. When I overheard the ginger girl in the library talking about a safety-deposit box key to her policeman boyfriend, I put two and two together."

"How very astute of you, Miss Turner," Whittaker observed. "Now, if you'll accompany me down to the station, you'll be formerly charged."

"With what!?" cried Madeleine. Thoughts swam, predominantly featuring the cold stone walls of a British jail.

"Theft and fraud, Miss Turner, unless Mr Darius decides not to press charges. But I shall strongly advise against that course of action." Whittaker threw Madeleine Turner a cold look, gesturing it was necessary to leave the small room, sandwiched on either side by himself and Cribbens. *I've spared her the indignity of being handcuffed and escorted out of the bank. But if she tries to make a run for it,* Whittaker decided, *Cribbens can go after her because my corns are playing up.*

Lily replaced the telephone receiver and stared around the empty library. *I know that Mr Lucas would never do such a thing,* she thought, *but under the circumstances, surely, he wouldn't begrudge me leaving five minutes early?*

She nodded, her decision made. There wasn't a great amount in the way of fines on the premises, just a matter of a few pennies, so no need to make a detour to the bank. Resolute, Lily grabbed her olive-green jacket, turned off the lights and firmly locked the door.

Lost & Found

Technically, Lily thought, *I'm actually on library-related business, so I really have nothing to worry about.* She made her way from her place of work with the guilt of leaving slightly early still stinging. It felt as though Mr Lucas had hauled himself from his hospital bed, traction and all, to observe her through binoculars as he squatted awkwardly behind the post box.

Entering Willow Lane, Lily found all was quiet as she knocked on the door of the first cottage she came to. Noises from inside told of definite signs of life. The door finally opened a crack and a pair of washed out brown eyes stared from a deathly pale face.

"Ida!" Lily greeted the other woman cheerily to lift the invalid's spirits. "It's so good to see you back home again." She grinned inanely, waiting to be invited in.

"What do you want?" Ida replied rudely, preventing her door from opening any wider with a firm hand. "I'm only just out of hospital this afternoon."

"That's why I'm here, sort of," Lily faltered, wondering if she was going to get any further than the doorstep. "Can I come in for a mo?"

A heavy sigh escaped from between Ida's pale lips. The door suddenly opened to reveal the woman standing in a baggy pink skirt and a shapeless bobbly grey jumper. The look was topped off by a pair of muddy green wellington boots. As Lily entered and closed the door, Ida rounded on her, eyes narrowed.

"So, you heard then?"

"Heard what?" Lily asked in all innocence.

"That I discharged myself," Ida announced indignantly, her snub nose raised in defiance.

"Oh! I err . . . No, I hadn't heard that. One of the villagers told me you were back home, that's all." Lily felt embarrassment overcome her as she stood in the untidy front room, telling of Ida's hurried departure the day before yesterday.

"And I bet I know which one as well!" Ida continued brusquely, her hands on stout hips.

"Sorry?"

"Which villager. There are always tongues wagging in this village, no matter what."

"Err, well," Lily replied, regretting her decision to call. "I just wondered if you had everything you needed, and to check that–"

"I know exactly what you came to check!" Ida interrupted. "You wanted to make sure I brought that library book back home with me and not left it on the ward. It was my stomach that was affected, not my brain!"

"No, of course not," Lily said, taking a step nearer the door.

"And do you know why I decided to leave? Well, I'll tell you," Ida ranted on, seeing Lily shake her head in submission. "I left because of the food – I've never seen such muck!"

"But surely, you weren't in a position to–"

"Nothing solid, they said. No potatoes or a good meat pie. I was given some watery gnat's widdle, passed off as vegetable soup. I can tell you, it had never seen a vegetable! Not even from a great height."

Lily looked suitably sympathetic.

"And then I was offered some grey grouting mixture, posing as porridge. I can't even begin to describe the taste of that foul concoction, but I wouldn't feed it to my worst enemy. I was only in hospital for a day and a half, but look how emancipated I am!" Ida grabbed her stretched elasticated waist band and tugged viciously to emphasise that her billowing skirt was now roomier than ever.

Lily bit her tongue, resisting the urge to say, "I think you mean *emaciated*." She gave a concerned nod and began, "It must have been terrible to be–"

"Anyway, if you want that book back," Ida exclaimed, whirling around to locate it, "you can take it with you now. I had a flick through but it didn't grip me."

Lily spied the corner of *And He Took Me in His Arms* under a pair of discarded fuchsia pink bloomers, cascading over a brown crocheted cushion on the settee. About to protest, she didn't get the chance.

Ida snatched at the loose dust jacket of the book, retrieving it with a hand that appeared slightly blue in colour. She thrust it in Lily's direction. "Here, have it back, as it's what you came for. I would have looked after it you know!" The harried woman had the look of a slapped kipper.

"Really, I didn't come specifically for that," Lily protested, holding her hands up in surrender. "I was only asking if you needed anything. If you're sure there's nothing I can get you, I'll be off. If there's anything, let me know." Lily made her escape as Ida stood stock-still, glaring mercilessly without a word of thanks.

A look of puzzlement clouded Sergeant Whittaker's face as he read the report on the samples taken from *All Buns Glazing*, tested for arsenic. "I don't understand it," he muttered, shaking his head and pursing his lips into a thin line. His comment, directed at

Detective Constable Cribbens, yielded a questioning glance by way of response.

"Would you credit it?" Whittaker continued. "Every single one of those samples from the tea shop has come back negative – the hair, the kitchen utensils, the refrigerator, and even the counter tops. It's nil all the way down the page!" He smacked the sheet of paper with his hand.

"So where does that leave us?" Cribbens enquired warily. He knew there had been no luck with this investigation, and it looked as though the trend was set to continue.

"I'll have to let the Chief Inspector know, then we'll need to put our thinking caps on." Lost in thought, Whittaker failed to see Peter emerging from the filing room after a futile effort to match new information with an old crime. A door key was reported missing from beneath a flower-pot some two-months previously. Now the owner of said flower-pot claimed her cat may have knocked it over and buried the key in the vegetable patch. Mrs Catchpole was advised to get the locks changed in case a would-be burglar took their chance. News of the potentially buried old key therefore appeared somewhat irrelevant.

"I'd say, *What I wouldn't give for a nice, genuine crime*, but we've already got one of those in the village," Peter joked, waving the thin brown folder he held. Noting Whittaker's blank expression, he continued. "Last year, Mr Travis also reported having a house key stolen from under a flowerpot, suggesting there might be a spate of these thefts, but none of the details match Mrs Catchpole's account about her key. Then of course there's Tiddles, the cat burglar . . ."

His colleagues nodded simultaneously. "No good news here either, I'm afraid," Whitaker muttered. "The Chief said we should share any new information about the Ambrose/Andrews death with you, but it's another blind alley. The test samples came back showing no arsenic present at the tea shop." Whittaker looked demoralised by this turn of events, although a spark of inspiration suddenly occurred to Peter.

"The fruit in the turnovers sold at the fayre! Where did Mrs Pargitter get it from?" His eyes shone as a thought took hold.

Detective Constable Cribbens shrugged. "Local greengrocer's, I suppose."

"But the greengrocer hasn't been questioned, has he?" Peter continued, hopeful of a new lead.

"No," said Whittaker with interest. "I don't think any connection's been made with who supplied the actual fruit as a potential source of the arsenic. There's no greengrocer in Wenham, so the Pargitter woman must have come into Milford to do her shopping." He looked mildly harassed, adding, "I've got a report to write and we can't send you, Beresford – it'll have to be you, Cribbens."

Cribbens assumed a purposeful look and nodded fervently, keen to do some real policing.

"Mr Cox?" Cribbens addressed the greengrocer, trying to inject as much authority as possible into the two words.

"That's what is says over the door," the man replied.

Expertly twisting the corners of a brown paper bag filled with pears, he handed it to a customer. She extracted her purse to pay, hoping to hear more. Mr Cox gave her a direct look, telling her the conversation was strictly private and the customer shuffled out of the shop with a look of disappointment.

"I'm here to ask if you sold some apples to a woman who runs the tea shop in Wenham? It would have been just over a week ago." Cribbens fixed his gaze on a tray of russet pippins rather than the fierce-looking Mr Cox, the enquiry sounding like an accusation.

"I've been asleep since then. You'll have to remind me what she looks like," Mr Cox replied gruffly, stroking his gingery beard in thought.

Cribbens faltered, having only come face-to-face with the indomitable Diane

Pargitter on one occasion. He decided to describe the things he remembered most clearly about her. "She's forty-something, big woman with dark curly hair and small piggy eyes. Unfortunate manner as well – calls a spade a spade, if you know what I mean?"

Mr Cox pondered for a long moment, then shook his head. "I know *of* her. She's been in here before, complaining about some King Edwards she said were all eyes. I don't remember her coming in recently though."

"So, she didn't get any cooking apples or peaches from you? She might have been boasting about running the cake stall at the village fayre – she's the type who likes to inflate her own importance."

"No, definitely no fruit. If she bought some, she didn't get it from me. Sorry, I can't help you." Mr Cox signalled this was the end of the matter and turned to assist a new customer; a stocky young woman with an empty basket he hoped would soon be full of purchases from his shop. Mystified, Cribbens made his way back to the police station to report yet another dead end.

Whittaker seemed angry, although it was difficult to tell. Peter returned from lunch to find yet another unsettling development had occurred, with the finger of blame wavering in his direction again. "It's more trouble for you, lad" Whittaker announced, coming to stand directly in front of the enquiries desk where Peter had been posted that afternoon.

"Why, what now?" Peter replied, almost afraid to ask.

"It's that Mr Hawke, the RSPB man you had some truck with a while back. The one that rallied half of Milford into action when those birds died of arsenic poisoning . . ."

"He's not complaining again, is he? I thought the whole business with the birds was firmly in the past. You're not telling me it's happened again – more birds dead?" Peter waited as his brain helpfully provided: *it's probably a swan on the village pond this time, and all swans belong to the Queen, so now you're really in trouble . . .*

"Apparently, Hawke's dead. And to make matters worse, they're testing for arsenic. I've just had the pathologist on the blower, telling me all about it," Whittaker said grimly.

"You're having me on? There's been another death in the village, but no obvious link to how it happened?"

Whittaker nodded. "Reed wants me to question the owner of the local timber yard, because they use arsenic preservative up there. I'm not holding out much hope – they follow so many rules to make sure everything's safe. It's unlikely to be arsenic from that source." He let out a deep sigh.

Peter waited, knowing there was more.

"And Cribbens says the greengrocer couldn't tell us anything about the fruit. We'll know by the end of the day whether arsenic definitely killed Hawke, but as for how it got into his body . . . let's just say, the plot thickens."

"Why has arsenic been suggested as the cause of Hawke's death?"

"I personally think the pathologist just jumped to that conclusion. As far as I could determine, Hawke didn't have any of the symptoms. But then if he had a gyppy tummy, maybe he didn't shout about it, and then it was too late."

Peter shrugged, knowing fingers would be pointed if the man *had* died from arsenic poisoning. *Members of the Milford Resident's Association might think I'm to blame because he accused me of doing away with those damn birds . . .*

"I suppose we'll just have to wait to find out the truth," said Peter, praying for any cause of death other than arsenic poisoning.

As Peter was about to finish for the evening, the call came. The pathologist seemed to have no reticence, sharing the findings in the case of Mr Oswald Hawke. Peter realised this may be because a written report would follow the verbal, thwarting any effort Peter might have been planning to hide something.

"It's arsenic poisoning all right – throughout the tissues. By the looks of him, he'd been exposed to the source over a long period, because arsenic breaks down the body cell by cell. The effect it's had on him is clear to see."

"So," Peter asked with interest, "does that mean the way the arsenic killed Hawke could be different to how it killed Dorcas Ambrose?"

"Well," said the pathologist, taking time to choose the right words, "the way it got into the body doesn't appear to be via ingested food. But the tricky thing with arsenic is, it can act quickly or slowly after exposure to the source. Less than one-hundredth of an ounce can kill. Hawke could equally have come into contact with the source a while ago or quite recently . . . No, I'd say that the sources are different, although the same substance has resulted in both deaths."

"That's very helpful, thank you." Peter hesitated for a long moment before adding, "Do you feel able to say whether Dorcas died accidentally, or whether it was murder?"

The question hung in the air and Peter heard the pathologist take a deep breath at the other end of the line. "I'm afraid that's something only the coroner can tell you," was all he said.

Peter began the short walk home to Fig Tree Hall in a contemplative mood. Had the pathologist meant, *I can't tell you, because you're a suspect*, if it was murder, or *I can't tell you,* because the pathologist simply didn't know if the arsenic in Dorcas's body was accidental or on purpose?

Making his way up the driveway, Peter quietly placed his key in the lock and crept inside. He wasn't in the mood for questions, or Seb's increasingly furtive behaviour. Instead of entering the kitchen, he headed straight along the hallway to the library, where the atmosphere was incredibly still.

Poisons and Their Uses still sat where Lily had left it on the solid oak table. Peter snatched it up and headed for the most comfortable armchair in the room, setting himself and flicking to the chapter on arsenic. An hour later, Peter closed the book, having discovered all there was to know on the subject. He began to put the information to use, matching the most relevant facts to the two deaths.

The following day, Milford police received a telephone call from the neighbour of Mr

Oswald Hawke. Peter hoped to determine some useful detail but after the neighbour had finished speaking, Peter's heart sank. *Just a report that Mr Hawke's cat hasn't been seen for two days.* Peter assured the caller he would pop along later to have a look around. The neighbour appeared very keen that this take place.

"You go to Hawke's place," Whittaker agreed, "the neighbour might know something about the man that we don't."

Peter left the station, walking the short distance to Hawke's rambling cottage. There was no sign of the neighbour who'd called, supplying the elusive animal's name as Ming, an over-fed Siamese who never missed a meal if he could help it.

The cat had failed to peer with squinting blue eyes into the neighbour's window when it got no response from its owner, which was most unusual behaviour. The neighbour had expected to see the hungry cat, following Mr Hawke's death.

The path to the side of the cottage was uneven, overgrown with buddleia attracting several butterflies. The garden beyond was not huge, but held plenty of nooks and crannies for a curious or sleepy cat to lose itself for a period of time. Tentatively, Peter called for the animal, swinging around in a circle with the expectation of a cream and brown feline emerging from the undergrowth.

Ming did not appear and Peter began to realise the exercise may take longer than anticipated. He made his way across the lawn to the back of the property, peering through a rather dirty window. On every shelf and piece of dark wooden furniture inside sat a stuffed bird of some description. As Peter stared, he was sure one was still moving, but decided he must be imagining things.

He moved to a small sash window where he could see a short hallway inside. Peter tried the window and found it gave easily, opening by a modest crack. A flower-pot containing a vivid red geranium plummeted from the end of the sill to the stone slabs below, the contents of the pot showering his black boots with soil and petals.

Peter shook both of his feet in turn, gazing at the sad mess before pushing gently on the window frame to encourage it to open some more. It obliged, allowing him to get his upper body through the gap. It was at this point that getting stuck first entered Peter's mind. *Lucky Whittaker knows I'm here, or I could be wedged tight until the neighbour finds me*, he mused. Wiggling his backside, Peter found that something gave way, so he was able to ease his legs through the window.

Once inside, the cottage had the smell of stale, unwrapped biscuits. Peter saw that the walls of Hawke's cottage were sombrely decorated and the place hadn't been cleaned for some time. Heading through a doorway, Peter found himself in the room he'd seen from the outside. The dark wood floor was strewn with newspapers, books, several apple cores and unwashed cups, still half-full with cold tea. *The multiple birds really are quite intimidating at close range*, Peter decided, *with their beady little black eyes following me around the room . . .*

He left quickly, hoping to find this was the full extent of the horrid little beasts. Standing in the hallway once more, Peter realised the layout of the cottage involved the kitchen and living room behind him. He assumed a bedroom and bathroom lay beyond the remaining two doors.

The hall carpet underfoot was dark brown and sticky to the soles of his boots. Stepping forward, he opened the door on the left. A small bathroom had been inexpertly divided to also serve as a kind of workshop. A work in progress sat in the far corner; a bird with a fan of iridescent tail feathers. Peter had never encountered a similar bird, although the shimmering blue and green reminded him of a picture of a kingfisher he'd once seen in a book. The specimen emitted a foul odour of decay, the preservation techniques having been curtailed by the amateur taxidermist's death.

Peter pulled a long cord that hung from the ceiling, finding it had a greasy quality. The overhead light sprang to life and the full scene of taxidermy tools and jars of chemicals met his eyes. Peter picked up a bottle labelled FORMALDEHYDE, rapidly replacing it on the chemically stained wooden shelf erected for the purpose. A small box next to the bottle read TAXIDERMY SOAP on its faded cover.

A wail of epic proportions then met his ears. Peter stood stock-still as terror flooded his body. He did not believe in ghosts, but the noise was unlike anything he'd ever heard before; unearthly and piercing, penetrating his very bones. He forced himself to move away from the discoloured porcelain sink, his fingers turning white as he gripped it tightly. The wail came again and Peter found his hands were shaking.

A stuffed, jet-black crow sat on the side of the bath, mocking him. Its head, positioned at a jaunty angle, followed his every move. *Most people have an arrangement of dried flowers or a bottle of bath salts as a decoration,* Peter joked to himself, trying take his mind off the source of the wailing noise.

Back in the sticky hallway where a small pile of post had already formed on the doormat, Peter placed a hand on the final door knob, tentatively turning it. Inside the room he could just make out an unmade bed and an imposingly large wardrobe. Thick curtains were drawn tight, letting little light into the room. Heaps of clothes lay on the floor and he almost tripped and went flying. *The smell's worse in here, despite that half-stuffed bird in the bathroom*, Peter decided, the aroma of recent animal waste pervading his nostrils.

As he was about to make his escape, his vision acclimatised to the gloom and something caught his eye on top of a stout chest of drawers to his left. The colours were muted, but the shape was definitely familiar.

Between two dark figures with pointed beaks and outstretched wings was a stuffed cat, curled there as though it was sleeping. *Perhaps it's Ming's predecessor*, Peter thought with sympathy, knowing pet owners were extremely sentimental about their animals, mourning them deeply when they died. He edged closer in the gloom, a hand outstretched.

The Proof of the Pudding

The cat opened its narrow sapphire eyes at being disturbed, but did not move. Peter staggered back, horrified at the evident reanimation of the stuffed creature that suddenly seemed incredibly life-like. The cat emitted another loud yowl that Peter recognised as the ethereal noise he'd heard from the bathroom.

Regaining his balance, he managed to enquire, "Ming?" of the cat. This didn't encourage the animal to confirm its name. Nor did the animal provide a full account of how he'd been shut in a bedroom, unfed, for two days with only two inedible stuffed birds for company.

Peter hurried from the oppressive room with a sigh of relief, heading for the kitchen. Ming followed closely to ensure the human intended to prepare some food for him. After a brief search of the cupboards, a tin of cat food was located. Peter set about opening it as Ming emitted encouraging wails, twisting himself around Peter's ankles in a helpful way. A bowl of water was also provided and Peter watched as the cat ate and drank contentedly.

"What are we going to do with you?" Peter asked the cat, not expecting a sensible answer. Ming looked up from his licked-clean food bowl, staring with mesmerising blue eyes.

Peter crossed the brown kitchen linoleum to stroke the cat's ears and Ming pushed his head up to meet his hand. "I'll take you to see Lily, she'll know what to do," he told Ming. The cat seemed to agree and trotted to heel as Peter unlocked the back door with the key in the lock, stepping outside again. "Just a minute," he shouted, darting back inside to close the sash window where he'd gained entry. Ming waited patiently while the human locked the door. *What do I do with the key?* Peter wondered, tucking it into the pocket of his jacket for safe keeping and heading to the library with an obedient Ming by his side.

"Who's your friend?" Lily asked, spotting Peter and the cat purposefully approaching the enquiry desk. "He's gorgeous, aren't you, Pudding?"

"Pudding?" Peter said with a smile as the cat seemed to appreciate the remark. "I thought he was one of those upper-class pedigree cats, hardly a pudding."

"It's a term of endearment," said Lily, coming out from behind the counter to give

Ming a long stroke from ears to tail. The cat purred loudly as Lily duly provided more attention. "So, where did he come from?"

Peter told Lily the story of Mr Hawke and his apparent fascination for the taxidermy of his feathered friends. He explained how Ming wouldn't really fit in at the station, where stray dogs were sometimes brought in without a lead, barking and growling in protest. "So," he summed up, "I was wondering if you had any ideas?"

"Well," said Lily, pondering the problem as she continued the cossetting process, "I suppose he could live here at the library. It's always warm and there are plenty of places for him to curl up or explore. Plus, dogs have to remain outside, and he would deter any mice."

"Like a good read, do they?"

"They love the book, *Of Mice and Men*," Lily grinned.

"What about during the night, if he wants to go out on the prowl?"

Lily straightened up and nodded, seeing the problem. Mr Lucas might have something to say about it as well. "I'll look after him today and take him back home with me tonight. Mum loves cats – he'll be company for her when I'm at work or with you."

"He seems quite vocal," Peter informed her, "not that I want to put you off. But, I suppose, with your mother being so deaf, it's a good match . . ."

"That's settled then, isn't it, Pudding?" Lily addressed Ming directly. She tickled the velvety brown fur between the cat's ears, observing that he seemed in full agreement with the idea.

"His name's Ming," Peter supplied.

"Yes, but I shall call him Pudding."

"Why *Pudding*?"

"Because his colouring reminds me of a big Christmas pudding with lots of cream," Lily said simply.

The new arrival at the library made himself thoroughly at home. After a long sleep on the windowsill in the afternoon sun, he was ready for some intellectual stimulation.

"Now," Lily told the cat, who now sat on top of the enquiry desk, listening intently. "Peter said your former owner was interested in taxidermy – that's stuffing and preserving dead animals – although I expect you don't need to know that."

She glanced at Pudding in case she'd offended his sensibilities but saw, to her relief, that he seemed happy to continue.

"I've just found an interesting book on the subject and I'm now going to see if there's a link between taxidermy and arsenic. Perhaps it's used as a preservative, like when Mr Buttermere told me timber is treated with an arsenic substance to stop it rotting. I know you've never met Mr Buttermere, and you probably wouldn't want to, with that sensitive nose of yours . . ."

The cat dipped its head slightly and Lily took it as a nod. The library door swung open and a man in a black trench coat strode in. He caught sight of Lily and smiled warmly.

"Hello there. I wonder if you could tell me where I might find a Mr Peter Beresford – I gather he lives here in Milford?" His green eyes twinkled below straight dark brows, the colour of ebony.

Two sets of blue eyes – one pair belonging to Lily, the other to Pudding – stared at the newcomer. The cat trusted Lily to handle the situation. "Who wants to know?" she said, a wary tone entering her voice. *He seems pleasant enough*, she assessed, *but what could a complete stranger possibly want with Peter?*

"I wanted to ask him a few questions about his father," the visitor replied in what Lily recognised was a hybrid British-American accent. He smiled again, showing perfect white teeth.

"I see," she nodded, stroking Pudding in an effort to calm herself down. "You'll find him at the police station just along the street. He works there – he's not being detained due to some sort of public order offence or anything. . ."

As soon as the words left her lips, she wanted to kick herself. *Why on earth did I say that? He's going to think I'm an absolute idiot,* she chided herself. To make matters worse, Pudding shot her a questioning look.

"Thank you kindly," the man said with a grin, adding as he left her to wallow in her own embarrassment, "great cat, by the way. I've heard about you eccentric Brits." Lily cringed, hoping she'd never encounter the green-eyed stranger again.

"Is there somewhere more private we can go?" the mysterious man asked Peter, catching interested glances from Whittaker and Cribbens. Giving a nod to his colleagues, Peter led the man to a nearby interview room, equipped with windows in the event that things turned nasty. *That's assuming Cribbens or Whittaker are still paying this much attention*, Peter thought.

Eager to be told why the man wanted to speak specifically to him, they both took a seat on hard chairs. Without a word, the man placed a black briefcase on the table between them. For a moment, Peter imagined a gun was about to be drawn from inside. Instead to his relief, the man withdrew a business card.

"Sorry it's all a bit cloak and dagger. My name's Jeffries – I'm a representative of the US Government." He placed his card in front of Peter with a smile.

"I see."

"This probably seems very odd, but I'd like to ask you some questions about your father. He was working on a formula during the war on our behalf – a military enhancement drug."

"For what purpose?" Peter managed, an iron fist gripping his insides.

"To overcome combat fatigue. We thought the documentation was lost without a valid patent number to trace it. It's recently come to our attention that the patent for that particular formula has been located."

"Oh?"

The man nodded. "In a safety-deposit box in the Countyshires bank here in Milford."

Peter tried to control his bewildered expression as the man continued.

"We also know there's more paperwork than just the patent document itself. It figures that must be in your possession, as you were left your father's residence and all his research work." The man drew breath as the information hung heavy in the air.

"How did you discover that this patent had been found?" Peter asked with curiosity, his brain piecing details together.

"Your half-sister's lawyer in the States – a Mr Griffin – has been in contact with a Mr Darius. Darius is involved with your relative's affairs here in England. Recently, a young woman pretended to be your half-sister, to access the safety-deposit box containing the missing patent left to her by Professor Ambrose."

Peter raised his eyebrows.

"The bank recognised her for an imposter. Mr Darius has assured us that the document is secure, but that it now belongs to you, as next of kin following the death of your half-sister."

"That makes it a lot clearer," said Peter, although this was far from the truth, given the complexity of the situation. "So, what do you want from me, exactly?"

"As I said," Jeffries continued, leaning keenly forward to close the gap between them, "your father had paperwork pertaining to this formula in his possession. Because this concerns a military enhancement drug, it's very valuable to us."

Peter nodded, still not fully understanding how he was implicated.

Jeffries sensed this and put it in the simplest terms. "Basically, you keep the patent and the profits. We take the paperwork giving us the research behind the formula so we can reproduce it under licence."

"I've no idea if there *is* any such paperwork and if it does exist, where it might be! When I discovered my father's body last year – and I didn't even know he was my father at that time – he was in a mummified state in a tiny little study he'd created behind his library. I never even met the man, let alone spoke to him about his work!"

As the memory of the unpleasant discovery returned, Peter had a flashback of Professor Ambrose's terrifying death stare, his wizened body stretched grotesquely over his suicide letter. He'd taken a deadly toxin because he was suffering from a degenerative nerve disorder, affecting his work. Peter gave an involuntary shudder, meeting the other man's interested gaze.

"I appreciate what you're saying," Jeffries nodded, "but we really need that supporting paperwork. You mentioned your father's study – has that been cleared out at all since his death?" His penetrating green eyes were filled with hope.

"Err, no, not really. Not at all if truth be told. It's all been such a whirlwind – finding out I was the Professor's son, that he'd left me the Hall and everything. What with one thing and another, I've left my father's secret study untouched as it hasn't been a priority."

"Sentimental reasons?" asked Jeffries rather strangely, his dark eyebrows arched. "It's only to be expected, putting off sorting through a loved one's possessions."

"Look, are you asking me to go through all the papers in there to see if I can locate this formula information?" Peter asked directly, wanting this rather unorthodox interview to be over.

A smile of satisfaction spread across Jeffries' lips, knowing he'd achieved success. "That's exactly what I'm asking."

"Right, well I'll do what I can," Peter provided, with some irritation.

"When exactly can I expect to hear from you?" Jeffries persisted, pushing the business card with his contact telephone number even closer.

"I'll get on to it tonight," Peter confirmed with a sharp nod, hoping Lily would be in the mood to help him.

Lily arrived in a buoyant mood, keen to attempt the task that Peter had outlined over the telephone. Shortly after she'd received his call at five o' clock, Lily informed Pudding that he would be going to a new home to be loved and cared for.

Pleased that she'd brought her bicycle to work so she didn't have to take the cat on the bus, Lily carefully locked the library door.

She scooped Pudding up from where he sat on the stone steps, placing him in the wicker basket on the front of her transport. As she started to pedal, Lily was pleased to see Pudding enjoying the breeze in his fur, settling himself into an acceptable position so he could watch the world go by.

The introduction to Mrs Forbes had been brief, but satisfactory to both parties. Lily's mother cosseted the newcomer – her deafness and his loud meows a perfect partnership. She put the gas fire in the living room on specially, an act of kindness that Pudding fully appreciated.

Lily bid a hurried farewell to them both, slipping out of the front door to jump back onto her bicycle. She caught her mother telling the cat that Lily was always rushing off, now that she was 'engaged to that policeman'.

Pedalling quickly, Lily soon arrived at Fig Tree Hall, free-wheeling up the driveway in anticipation of getting stuck into Professor Ambrose's copious collection of research papers.

"At least that smell's gone," Lily observed, remembering only too well the acrid stench of death that had pushed its way down her throat when she and Peter discovered the body of Professor Thaddeus Ambrose the year before. The space behind the library fireplace still seemed too small to house a study area. Lily recalled that she'd been too scared to enter the tiny cubby, especially as Peter had advised her not to because the mummified remains weren't a pretty sight.

Squeezing her way through the gap created by opening the false door next to the fireplace, Lily found herself in a tiny Victorian laboratory. She admired an ornately carved desk along one wall and a small glass-fronted cabinet across another. It housed bottles and jars containing brightly-coloured liquids Lily imagined were probably lethal. The distillation equipment Peter had described was still in position, a teetering pile of research papers occupying a large area of the remaining floor space.

"Do we work in here or take the whole lot into the library where there's more space?" Lily asked. She wondered how Diane Pargitter ever managed to squeeze her bulk into the compromising vestibule, to gawk at the dead Professor and have a good nose about.

"I think it's swings and roundabouts," Peter replied, shaking his head. "There's no room to spread things out and make piles to keep or discard. It'll mean lots of trips back and forth though."

"I think the second option might be best, as it keeps it all tidy," Lily decided, knowing she'd rather be in the main library. She grabbed a sheaf of papers to make a start. "We have to be systematic about this, so the next lot of papers will go under this one, and so on. It keeps things in order, if there is one." She shot a dubious glance around her. "Great opportunity to clear some of the rubbish out though."

"How do we know what's rubbish and what we should keep?" Peter asked. "I wasn't given a name for this formula or drug, so unless there's a document entitled 'US Government', I'm not holding out much hope." He gave a loud sigh, casting a resentful glance at the enormity of research work Professor Ambrose had produced.

"I know what you mean, but if we put aside anything that obviously *isn't* the formula, that will narrow it down to the stuff that might be."

Peter nodded half-heartedly, scooping up the next section of the pile. He followed Lily through to the library and they both tried not to drop anything vital in the squeeze back through. As they neatly brought through and stacked papers on the library table, the pile in the library grew larger and the one in the cubby diminished steadily. The process took time but eventually, everything was transferred.

"So, now the work finally begins at a quarter to seven!" Lily said far too cheerily as Peter flopped, exhausted into an armchair.

"Can't we do it in shifts?" he groaned. His stomach rumbled loudly and he developed a mental block against the task.

"If you like, I'll get on and you can just sit there for consultation purposes. I don't mind this kind of thing. . . in fact, I love it," Lily said with enthusiasm, grabbing the first sheet of papers and reading the title.

"Well, there's a bit of luck," Peter quipped guiltily, hoping he would manage not to fall asleep with boredom.

Two hours later, Lily's shout interrupted the gentle snores coming from Peter's chair. "I think I've got it!" She cried excitedly, waving a sheaf of papers and jumping up to splay them like an open fan.

"Wha–"

"You managed to doze off! There's a lot of technical stuff here, but I suppose that was to be expected. I managed to find a pattern in the way the papers were placed in the pile – it looks haphazard, but it's actually a really good filing system. And here it is!" she waved the yellowing document with curled edges again.

"Are you sure?"

"I can't find anything else that relates to what you've been told by Jeffries, and it does say here, COTHADDIUM – US GOVT." She pointed helpfully with her left index finger, grinning widely as she did a little dance of joy on the spot.

"Wow, thank you so much," Peter said, feeling there wasn't enough gratitude in the world to express his relief. Lily not only gone through the mountain of papers, she'd actually found the very one that was needed. "What did you say it was called?"

"Cothaddium – C-O-T-H-A-D-D-I-U-M," Lily replied, spelling it out, "obviously derived from his name – Thaddeus, and the fact he was working with the American Government." She crossed the gap between them, wiping a hand theatrically across her brow. "What a relief! Let's go and have some supper now, I'm famished!"

Peter extended his arms to hug her, catching sight of his watch to see it was almost nine. "I'll just give Jeffries a call and say I've found the document he wants – get him off my back. He's staying at The Crown."

Raising her eyebrows, Lily said, "*You've found*?" teasingly, following it up with a giggle.

"Well technically you, but I don't want him to know anyone else has seen this precious paperwork. Remind me to take it with me tomorrow – I'll just go and make that call."

Lily nodded as he released her from his arms and she headed to the kitchen in search of food. Peter went in the opposite direction, along the hallway to the telephone. He searched his trouser pocket for the little card Jeffries had provided, transferred carefully from his uniform jacket pocket.

As he turned his back to make the call, Seb glided effortlessly from the shadows. He quietly entered the library, heading for the table where he spied a document that had been separated from the others. *This is something important*, he mused furtively, *as it's taken them hours to find it . . .*

Entering the kitchen after speaking with Jefferies, Peter peered around the room. "Where's Mum and Kitty?" he asked with astonishment.

"Gone to see Jailhouse Rock at the cinema – they left a note," Lily informed him, pointing to a scrap of paper on the table. He sat down and she placed a loaf of bread and a breadknife before him to do the honours.

"You know what big Elvis Presley fans they are – couldn't wait to get on the bus for the nine-thirty showing!"

"She never said . . ."

"Were you expecting a cooked meal? You'll have to make do with sandwiches. There's some cold pork, Nella says, and homemade apple sauce."

"Sounds good," Peter enthused, being a big fan of cold roast meat between two slices of bread. "I'm glad we're alone actually, so I can tell you what Jeffries said. I notice they didn't invite Seb along, so he could still wander in to act the gooseberry."

"And I've got some news for you about arsenic after the research Pudding and I did this afternoon, but you go first." Lily tried to contain herself as she fetched the butter dish, cold pork and sauce from the refrigerator while Peter carved the springy white loaf into slices.

"Jeffries didn't say much really, just that he was pleased the papers had been located. We arranged to meet tomorrow lunchtime so I can pass them over to him. I hope I'm doing the right thing, I mean . . . is it what my father would have wanted? Maybe he didn't hand over his own notes on the research process for a good reason. . ."

"You can only do what you think is best," Lily soothed, pulling out a chair and plonking herself down eagerly. "And as you've been specifically requested by the United States Government to hand over the paperwork, I don't see that you really had any choice."

Peter nodded, bread knife held in mid-air.

"*And*," Lily added, fixing him with a serious look, "I'm very pleased to announce, I've found a link between the art of taxidermy and the use of arsenic in the process. I know it's not my place to say so, but I'll bet that's what killed Hawke – years of using taxidermy soap."

"Soap – what, to wash the chemicals off his hands?"

"No, it's a soap containing arsenic that's used on the skin of the birds, or whichever poor creature is being stuffed. It keeps it soft when the taxidermist is mounting the specimen." Lily blushed, dropping her gaze in embarrassment. "Sorry – that sounded a bit rude!"

Peter grinned. "I think I get the picture – the arsenic is also a preservative, like we've heard from Bert Buttermere when they used it in the timber yard. Years of exposure to taxidermy soap could be the reason Hawke's now dead. It could be how a high level of arsenic got into his body. I'll let the pathologist know in the morning."

"Still doesn't explain Dorcas's death though, or the other cases of non-fatal poisoning around the village," Lily sighed, disappointed that her information had only solved part of the riddle.

"But it's a start!" said Peter before taking a huge bite out of his sandwich.

Arsenic is Forever

"So, the arsenic came from taxidermy soap?" Whittaker said, eyebrows raised with intrigue. "And the pathologist agrees that's what killed him over time?"

Peter nodded. "Apparently. There are stuffed birds everywhere in the cottage, suggesting he'd obviously been using the soap frequently. Who would have thought an innocent pastime could be so deadly?"

Whittaker shook his head by way of reply. "Good work, lad. Now all we have to do is find the source of arsenic that killed Barbara Andrews." He peered at Peter. "The coroner's arranged an inquest at two this afternoon."

"Has he? I just can't see a connection. If Charles Andrews didn't deliberately add arsenic to his wife's little snack at the fayre, how did it happen? And, according to the arsenic testing at *All Buns Glazing*, there was neither the opportunity or the knowhow from there." *Thankfully, nothing much has been made of Barbara being Dorcas . . .*

"Perhaps we should have questioned your favourite tea shop tenants again, before the coroner got involved," Whittaker said. He missed the furtive look that followed, failing to realise that Peter had already done just that.

"I'll go along to the inquest, if you like. See what's said," Peter offered, trying not to sound too keen.

In his lunch hour, Peter headed for The Crown Hotel, finding Jeffries waiting for him in the bar.

"Do you want a drink, or is that not really allowed on duty, ha, ha," Jeffries asked with the expectant grin of a man who knew he was about to get what he'd come for.

"I won't, thanks," Peter replied, shaking his head. "I haven't got long – have to be somewhere else."

"I see," the other man replied, lifting a shot of whisky to his lips. "You do have the papers we spoke of – you said you'd located them?"

Reaching into his inside pocket, Peter withdrew the folded document and passed it to Jeffries with a touch of misgiving. "So, what happens now then?"

Jeffries eagerly took possession of his prize, turning a questioning glance on Peter. "Nothing, I'd assume. Once I hand this over, you won't hear any more. What were you expecting?"

"Oh, I don't know. Perhaps some sort of receipt to acknowledge that my father's background research work on this drug is now in the hands of the US Government?" Peter replied with more than a hint of sarcasm.

The grip of doubt in Peter's stomach grew steadily more substantial until he had the compulsion to reach out and snatch the papers back. His hand hesitated forward but he consciously withdrew it again, knowing that it was already too late.

"I can write a receipt if it bothers you, but it won't be on official headed paper."

Peter knew that Jeffries would never have been sent to do the job unless he was equipped with a thoroughly unstinting streak of ruthlessness. Jeffries glared obstinately, his fake smile now deemed unnecessary.

Still stinging with irritation, Peter walked at a pace to Milford library in search of a listening ear. The weather was bright and cheerful with a glorious warm breeze, but this did not match his mood; his gut told him that he'd undoubtedly just been conned.

"Oh, how lovely to see you," Lily said, her face lighting up at the sight of him.

"You might not think that when I tell you how I feel," Peter said morosely. "Jeffries took the papers like a fox grabbing a chicken, then he ridiculed me for wanting a receipt of some kind."

Lily's mouth formed a perfect 'O' as she imagined the scenario. "That's awful! I can't believe he just took it, and didn't even give you a dated chitty."

He chuckled, in spite of himself. "Well, that's cheered me up at least. Listen, are you going to the inquest this afternoon? Should be interesting."

"Oh, I can't abandon my post!" Lily replied, dreadfully disappointed to be missing out. Peter was about to suggested an extended lunch break when she continued. "*And* I've got Mrs Pritchard over there, between modern romance and local history, showing no sign of budging," she gave an exaggerated nod in Ida's direction. "Shame about the time, I'd like to have heard–"

Peter put his index finger to his lips as he spied Ida making her way over to them. "I'll see you afterwards then," he said briskly, exiting through the swing door. The thought of getting caught up in another of Ida's conversations, where she held everyone else responsible for her recent situation, was just too much.

Ida stared after his departing, uniformed figure and shook her head. "No sense of community, these policemen. He could have asked how I am, updated me on any development about the poisonings, as I've experienced it first hand, but no . . . ." Her fleshy mouth pursed into a tight pucker as she handed another Philippa Philpot classic, *Promise You'll Love Only Me* over to Lily, which she duly stamped without a word.

Milford Village Hall had become a makeshift coroner's court for the inquest. Peter entered to take a seat next to Diane Pargitter and immediately, the overbearing woman turned and scowled.

"Were we expecting you?" she asked with heavy resentment. "You should have let them know you were coming here today." The statement was distinctly unwelcoming and Peter sighed, masking it as a cough. Diane, however, was not done.

"*And* we don't want you in here if you're going to cough all over the place, spreading your germs!" she added. Diane's hands flew to protect her nose and mouth, her piggy eyes glaring little chunks of jet.

"I know this is a nuisance. They're trying to get this whole thing over and done with, so the coroner needs to ask a few questions."

"Harrumph!" Diane responded loudly. "I thought you were warned off this poisoning case because they think you might have done it?"

"That's not something that should concern you," Peter said, already too tired to argue. "Can we just wait quietly and let the coroner go through things – it won't take long."

"I hope they don't need Felicity as well, if it's about the business. There's bound to be more bad news, probably that we'll need to close down for good. Felicity's going over the books again to see if there's any way we can manage for a bit longer – before going cap in hand to the Salvation Army. *Yes,* that's how bad it is!" Her round face grew savage with the effort of becoming annoyed, reminding Peter again of a sweating beetroot.

The short, unassuming figure of the coroner – a little man with sparse hair – entered the room, seating himself behind a desk facing the crowd. In a commanding voice in contrast with his stature, he suggested, "Can we begin, please?" There followed an examination of the evidence given by Peter, Charles Andrews and Madeleine Turner before the coroner turned his attention to the formidable Diane Pargitter.

"*Mrs Pargitter*," the coroner said, waiting for the woman to identify herself by raising a hand. "Can you confirm that it was you who made the fruit turnovers for the fayre?"

"Oh, not this again!" Diane erupted. "Look – I've already told them everything I know. Why don't the police concentrate on that girl

I read about in the *Milford Advertiser* – the one who stole that key from the solicitor's office and tried to break into the safety-deposit box at the bank? She's the sort of criminal you ought to be going after, not the likes of me!" Diane Pargitter's florid complexion turned magenta and critical, worrying Peter that some kind of collapse might be imminent.

"Could we please stick to the investigation into the death of Barbara Andrews?" the coroner said sternly.

"*And then*," Diane continued with no sign of letting it go, "there's that poor Mr Hawke from the RSPB. The paper said he was found dead in his garden by the postman – is that true?"

"Mrs Pargitter! I'm not here to provide *you* with information about ongoing police cases. Can I please continue with my intended line of questioning? I'm trying to establish whether Barbara Andrews was murdered, or whether her death was accidental," the coroner barked.

Diane's thin eyebrows rose. "But how can you be so sure there isn't a murderer stalking the village?" she countered. "Two unexplained deaths and the police are no nearer to solving them, so I've heard . . . The writing's on the wall–"

"If we could move on. Perhaps your answers will be of some help in solving the case in hand," the coroner suggested. His purposeful glare dared her to interrupt. "Now, if you don't mind, can I ask where you got the fruit for the turnovers you made?"

"Where did I get the fruit?" Diane repeated in a bewildered voice, as though she was having difficulty understanding the question.

The coroner nodded. "Did you buy it from a greengrocer?"

Shaking her head slowly, Diane replied in a small voice, "No . . ."

"Then where?"

"Well . . . I had a couple of old tins of peaches at home in the cupboard. Frank used to like them in a cobbler, but since he died, I couldn't face eating them as it would only remind me–"

"So, you decided to use the fruit in your baking?" the coroner interjected gently, in contrast with his earlier tone now that he was finally getting somewhere.

"That's right. I had to sell the house because there was no money. I needed to clear everything out. Frank's life insurance wouldn't pay out – some technicality over a clause he wasn't covered for. You'd think being in the business, having arranged his own life insurance he'd have covered every eventuality, wouldn't you?" Diane gave a meek smile and the coroner recognised a woman who dearly wanted to talk about the misfortune that was her husband's death.

"My condolences, Mrs Pargitter, but could we continue?"

"Well, life goes on, as they say. There was also very little money released by selling the house because it all went on bills. But who'd have thought I'd end up running a tea shop with Felicity Manners-Gore, of all people!"

The coroner nodded, not wanting to get side-tracked. "What about the apples?" he asked casually.

"What about them?" Diane asked, seeming surprised.

"Where did they come from?"

"I picked them from the garden – masses of them on the ground, there were. They would have rotted away if I hadn't decided to use them in the turnovers."

"Cooking apples?" the coroner asked as Peter was reminded of something he'd recently heard.

"The apples were cookers, yes, and they came from the little orchard behind the tea shop. Shame to let them go to waste. Money is so tight, you see. I wanted to do something for the fayre, but I didn't want any expense, so I used what I could find." Diane looked quite pleased with herself as the coroner decided how to phrase his next comment.

"Did you know that the fields around Wenham are tainted with arsenic, because the farmers formerly used it in a pesticide?"

Diane nodded and replied, "Of course, Constable Beresford told me. I expect he remembers," she shot a look at Peter. "I accused him of buying us the lease on a business that's sitting downwind of fields sprayed with poison."

The coroner nodded again. "Arsenic is a cumulative poison – the soil in the whole country is tainted with arsenic at varying levels. It's only when there's enough for it to become dangerous that there's the possibility of fatality."

In contrast to her earlier complexion, Diane's face now blanched white. "So, what are you saying? That the apples I put into those pastries were poisonous, because they'd been grown in arsenic-rich soil?"

"I would have exercised some caution in using those apples . . ."

"But nobody told me *not* to use them! It should have been on a public warning notice, or outlined clearly in the property deeds when we moved in." Diane cast the accusation, screwing up her eyes in a vicious squint that almost lost them completely from view. She turned to Peter with contempt. "Did you know there was a large amount of arsenic in the orchard behind the tea shop!?"

Peter looked horrified. "I only know about the local area. No one grows anything on that ground, as it's common knowledge."

"Not to me, it's not!" Diane cried. "So, because I put apples from the orchard into my cooking, I killed that woman, is that what you're saying!?" Her hands then flew to her face as she began to hyperventilate dramatically.

"You *are* responsible for her death, yes," the coroner confirmed.

"Ohhh!!!" wailed Diane. "I shall go to prison and the other inmates will be nasty and difficult, and the food will be atrocious! *Ohhh!*" She continued so loudly, Peter wondered whether sedation was called for.

"Being responsible for a death is not the same as murdering someone," the coroner continued in an effort to appease. "I believe you when you say you didn't know about the high arsenic levels, and I don't think you intentionally baked poisoned pastries that anyone at the fayre could have bought and eaten."

Diane nodded, mouth gaping.

"I intend to rule the outcome of this inquest as accidental death. You will not be held responsible for Barbara Andrews' demise or be charged with murder."

"But I still killed her, however you dress it up! She ate something I cooked and died because of it. Oh heavens – Ida Pritchard!"

Diane looked as though a fit of apoplexy was imminent, fists clenched and piggy eyes bulging.

The coroner nodded that his investigation was now complete and people began to disperse. Peter whispered to Diane, "Ida mentioned that someone had left a basket of cooking apples on her doorstep, but she wasn't sure who. Did you know she was hospitalised after making a pie and eating rather a lot of it?"

"Another arsenic poisoning?" Diane asked rather too loudly for Peter's liking, her expression stricken.

"Yes," Peter informed, "she had to have her stomach pumped. Ida told Lily that she hated being in hospital so much, she discharged herself. Ida's doing fine now though, I saw her in the library before I came here."

"Thank goodness for that," Diane blurted, causing a few straggling villagers to look around with interest. "She's such a good friend and we think alike on almost everything."

I bet you do, Peter thought, keeping it to himself. "I'll have to go back to the station and let them know the coroner's verdict, and what's emerged – about the arsenic originating from the apples you put into those turnovers."

He rose from his seat and made for the door, knowing there was nothing else to say. *Thank goodness Barbara Andrews being Dorcas Ambrose doesn't seem to be an issue,* Peter thought. *That would have really complicated things . . .*

"Must you tell them?" Diane called after him in a barely audible voice.

"I must," Peter assured her.

"Good work Beresford, identifying how the arsenic got into the pastry that killed Barbara Andrews. Whittaker's just told me you put two and two together at the inquest," Chief Inspector Reed said warmly.

"Thank you, sir. It's good to know the coroner's findings have drawn a line under what's happened."

"You understand why I had to take you off the case? You're now completely in the clear of any lingering suspicion about how you half-sister was poisoned. It was a bad business and it must have been very difficult at times, but I always knew you were completely innocent."

Peter nodded with embarrassment.

"I hear you also showed great ingenuity, discovering the source of the arsenic in the Hawke case. You must be commended for that," Reed announced. He fixed Peter with the probing eyes of an entomologist, peering through a magnifying glass at a particularly interesting beetle.

So, they knew all the time that Barbara Andrews was once called Dorcas Ambrose? Peter realised with amazement. *There was no need to torture myself, worrying . . .*

"Thank you, sir," Peter said again.

"–Therefore, in light of your recent work, bearing in mind the way you also solved the mystery of your father's inexplicable disappearance last year, I'm recommending you sit your Sergeant's exam." Reed sat back in his comfortable chair and beamed widely, showing several discoloured teeth.

"Sir! Oh–"

"I know," Reed interrupted, raising a hand, "no need to thank me, you've earned it. Now, get back and continue the good work."

Peter gave an involuntary salute and left in a daze. He walked on cloud nine as the dream he had been chasing since he joined the police force came rapidly into focus.

"What's up with you?" Whittaker asked as Peter joined him behind the front desk.

"Nothing, it's just a good feeling to have another case tied up – very good in fact."

"And good to know you're in the clear," his colleague nodded, unaware of Peter's other victory.

♥

Nella, Kitty and Seb were already gathered around the kitchen table when Lily entered, closely followed by Peter.

"I've just been telling Lily the good news," he announced with a grin, causing the occupants of the table to simultaneously turn their heads towards him.

Lily nodded to back him up.

"Chief Inspector Reed told me this afternoon that as I'd discovered the different sources of arsenic involved in the poisonings, and because I solved the Professor Ambrose mystery last year, he's going to recommend me for my Sergeant's exam!"

"Oh, that's wonderful news!" cried Nella, jumping up to give Peter a hug.

"Well done, Peter!" chimed Kitty, standing to give an unnecessary little curtsey.

Seb sat stony-faced, giving a nod as all eyes fell on him to follow suit.

Lily grinned, pleased at the outcome, but a small irritation niggled her. *It was me who made the link between taxidermy and arsenic, plus I found the Cothaddium paperwork . . . And I suggested pushing the heart-shaped mouldings on the fireplace in the library last year, revealing the secret room where Ambrose's body was hidden. . .*

"So anyway," Peter said, ignoring the joyless little butler-cum-valet who wore a completely disgruntled expression, "I thought we could all go to The Crown for dinner to celebrate! What do you think?" He gazed around the sea of happy faces bar one, only to find Nella smiling but shaking her head.

"I shall cook something special!" she declared. "Now you're almost a Sergeant you can have a double celebration – make an honest woman out of this lovely librarian here!"

Lily didn't know where to look.

Nella beamed, crossing the kitchen to open the refrigerator and peer in. Lily and Peter exchanged looks but said nothing. Nella had taken to dropping heavy hints at every available opportunity about beginning work on the wedding cake, so that it had time to mature.

"What do you fancy – steak and kidney pudding?" Nella said, turning from the very modern kitchen appliance. Peter nodded enthusiastically, suspecting his mother wanted to do this for him because she was so proud.

"If you're sure, Mum," he said. "Thought you'd all jump at the chance of a night off and a slap-up meal at a posh hotel!"

"So," Lily interrupted, "you were saying that Mrs Pargitter just hadn't realised the soil behind the tea shop contained a high level of arsenic? I can't believe she put the apples that had fallen to the ground into those pastries. I'm really glad I didn't have one now!" she said with a shiver. "But why did it kill Dorcas when Ida had similar, but just became very unwell?"

"Well, not to be rude, but Ida is built like a brick you know what house and Dorcas, by comparison, was only a very slight woman. It's the same principle as the donkey and the birds – the bigger animal became ill after ingesting the arsenic in several pastries but didn't die, whilst the birds succumbed because they were much smaller, even though they ate less."

"But what about Bert Buttermere?" Lily questioned. "He's skinny as a string bean and he didn't die, just had a very bad stomach." *That he needed to share every detail about*, Lily recalled, feeling queasy.

"Ah!" Peter said, raising his right index finger in a knowledgeable and – Seb decided – ultimately big-headed manner. "Bert became ill after eating the pigeons in a pie, but their bodies had already absorbed some of the arsenic. It had taken much less to kill them, so it was a smaller dose by the time Bert decided to consume the local wildlife. Plus, he probably built up some level of tolerance during his exposure to arsenic at the timber yard where he worked for years."

"Isn't he clever?" Nella beamed. "My son, the policeman!"

Everyone clucked in agreement with one exception. Seb slowly pushed his chair back from the kitchen table. He made his way cautiously to the door, head down, posture stooped.

"What's wrong with you, misery guts?" Nella chided sharply, annoyed he hadn't congratulated Peter on his achievement. She watched him creep away.

"Just going for a lie down. I'm not feeling like celebrating," Seb grumbled, leaving them to it.

The police pathologist telephoned Peter that evening. It was unexpected, and Peter appreciated the fact that Seb wasn't hanging around to eavesdrop.

"I wanted to let you know for definite," Mr Graves told him. "With the information from the inquest, I've just completed the paperwork confirming Barbara Andrews' death as accidental. We've known for years that some areas are very heavily polluted with arsenic – it's just an unfortunate turn of events that the apples found in that little orchard in Wenham were actually eaten. I'll send a written report and let you inform your solicitor. Thought you'd be glad this loose end could be tied up."

"Oh, I am, believe me!" Peter said with relief, wondering why the kind old gentleman was still working so late into the evening. "Thanks for taking the time to let me know, Mr Graves – I hope you don't mind me saying, but I've always thought your name was very apt, considering the job you do. . ."

"Oh, trust me, you're not the first to say that. I believe it's called nominative determinism – when someone works in a profession that suits their name, like Mr Cox the greengrocer, I suppose."

"I'd never thought of that one!" Peter chuckled. "You should go home, it's late!" he added, full of gratitude that the difficulties of the last few weeks were finally over.

"I never leave here early – that's how I keep my wife happy!" He replaced the telephone receiver and Peter listened for a few moments to the somewhat comforting buzz on the line.

Epilogue

Peter called into the offices of Darius, Cummings and Bennett, equipped with a copy of the coroner's report that had very speedily arrived at the station that morning. As the first port of call at the reception desk, Anthony threw an unwelcoming glance at the new arrival, knowing full-well that he did not have an appointment.

"I need to inform Mr Darius of a development in a police case," Peter said amiably. He noted that Anthony's expression did not change, deciding he may as well have saved his breath.

"But you don't have an *appointment*," Anthony exclaimed with extreme sarcasm.

"No, but I thought–"

"Then you may not see him until you *do*. Shall I make you one now?" Anthony asked brusquely, opening the appointments diary. He took up his ink pen, head lowered, mouth pursed as tight as a cat's bottom.

"There's no need, Anthony!" cried Mr Darius, hurrying forward to greet Peter. He ushered him into his overly green office before the solicitor's clerk could blink. Darius shut the door firmly, gesturing that Peter should sit. "It's just a matter of formality, given the turn of events I've very recently been informed of by Chief Inspector Reed," the little man said, sliding deftly behind his desk.

"I was actually calling in for the same purpose, I think," Peter informed the solicitor. He was unsure which angle of the investigation Reed had conveyed, but knew this would truly be the end of the drama created by Dorcas Ambrose. He handed Darius the report, assuming Reed had already told him of the coroner's findings.

"The safety-deposit key came back into my possession following the . . . incident, I suppose you'd call it, and I assure you that the copy has been destroyed. I can see why Miss Turner wanted to take possession of the document, given the strong association with her mother. . ."

Peter nodded, sensing that the only reason Madeleine Turner had tried to break into the deposit box was to ingratiate herself with the American Government. "I was told that both she and Charles Andrews will be flying home after the funeral with no further charges."

"Ah, yes . . . a most unfortunate business. I understand that the funeral has been arranged for Friday at eleven a.m. It's dreadful to think that the event will be so poorly attended, although I'll be there."

Peter nodded again. "Yes, just her husband, you and me. I think my mother would want to pay her respects too, but that's only four people – not much to show for a person's life . . . ."

"But let us proceed with the matter in hand!" Darius cried, springing to life suddenly as though jump leads had been attached to his ears.

"Please," Peter agreed.

Darius opened his desk drawer and whisked the safety-deposit key out of his tray, handing it to Peter in one smooth action.

"It's yours now that Dorcas's death has been confirmed as accidental. I'd advise that you place all of your father's patent documents in a large deposit box at the bank . . . for safekeeping, you understand? God forbid, a fire at the Hall damaging the patents you have stored in your safe . . . ."

"I will, thanks." Peter smiled briefly at Darius, prickling at the unpleasant suggestion of a fire. "And thank you for everything you've done. It can't have been easy, having to deal with a lawyer from another country." He stood in readiness to leave, proffering his hand for Darius to shake. The man took it modestly and gave a surprisingly firm shake in return.

"It's my job Peter," was all he said.

♥

Peter called into the library after he'd seen Mr Darius to tell Lily the good news. He rested his hands casually on the enquiry desk as Lily moved closer from behind it. She indicated with a surreptitiously pointed finger that Ida Pritchard lurked with intent in the romance section.

"How does she get through them so quickly?" Peter whispered, nodding towards Ida and marvelling at her capacity for reading.

"She only reads the last chapter so she can find out what happens!" Lily said under her breath, following it up with a giggle that caused Ida to scowl in their direction.

Stifling a guffaw, Peter said, "I've just seen Darius and that's all sorted now." He leaned in further so he could close the gap. "I can't quite believe it's all over – the suspicion and accusations, wondering what people were saying when my back was turned. . ."

"Well, I never heard anything nasty about you," Lily soothed.

"I don't think people would say anything to your face, knowing we're together, but I'll bet that behind the scenes–"

"Try and forget it. It's all come right in the end, although I think it'll take Diane a long time to get over the fact that someone actually died as a result of eating her cooking." Lily gave a conspiratorial look after checking that Ida wasn't in earshot.

"How do you know that?" Peter asked with interest.

Lily leaned in even further, her lips almost toughing his left ear. She succeeded in knocking a date stamp to the floor with a loud thud. An audible tut came from the romance section and Peter pointed to a wooden painted sign on the desk that read, QUIET PLEASE, making Lily cackle sharply. After she'd recovered, Lily replied in a hushed whisper, "Apparently, Diane told Ida that she never wanted to bake anything ever again. Ida also said that the turn of events had knocked Diane for six – she's said that she doesn't want to go on with the business."

"I suppose that's understandable," said Peter generously, "but it might do her good to just carry on, get back on the horse, so to speak. If they re-open the business now, it'll get lots of customers coming in because of all the grisly publicity."

Lily cackled again earning her an, 'Oh, really, some people!' from several bookcases away.

"Sorry," Lily said, lifting a finger to her right eye and wiping away a tear that was rapidly forming, "but can you imagine Diane, trying to get on a horse?!" She stifled a hearty laugh, nearly choking on it.

"Don't you mean *mounting*?" whispered Peter wickedly, causing them to both dissolve into helpless and uncontrollable fits of laughter. This only grew worse when Ida Pritchard marched past and out of the library, throwing them both a very hard stare.

That evening, Peter let himself into Fig Tree Hall, telling himself that some days, everything just seems to go right. He spied Seb looking shifty by the staircase and corrected, *perhaps not everything . . .* The skinny man approached and Peter saw he still appeared to be stooped, a physical affectation that Seb had recently adopted. Peter hoped it wouldn't be a permanent fixture. Coming further into the hallway, Peter drew closer, noting that Seb Treadmill was now wringing his hands with anxiety.

"Are you all right?" Peter asked as an opening gambit. "You seem to have been a bit off-colour lately." He stood directly in front of the miserable wretch, who refused to make eye contact with him.

"I need to tell you something, something that might be relevant to the case . . ."

Masking his surprise at the news, Peter said, "Go on–"

"I've been fretting since it happened, wondering what would transpire if I confess. It's eating me up and I've got to say something, but I hope you won't think . . . Ohhh!"

The man's distress reminded Peter of Diane Pargitter's reaction, on being told she was responsible for Barbara Andrews' death. He assumed his most serious policemanly expression and then said, "Just tell me . . ."

Seb cringed away from Peter as though he'd been physically struck. He remained quiet for a long moment before finding the courage to speak. "On the day that I found your relation dead in the grounds . . . there's something I didn't tell you. I didn't tell anyone, and I can't help thinking I should have said something at the time. . ."

"What on earth is it?" Peter asked gently, feeling Seb's torment.

"I saw her . . . I saw her throw down the bag!"

"What bag? You mean the bag she had over her shoulder?"

"No!" Seb shrieked, "The brown paper bag that had the pastry in it!"

"Oh! *That* bag . . ."

"Yes," Seb said, although he appeared not to care, so intent was he on continuing now that he'd begun. "I saw her open the bag as she was walking along the path behind the Hall. She ate the turnover then made her way over to the big oak tree – the one with the initials carved on it. Then she wiped her hands on the bag, screwed it up and threw it into the grass."

Peter nodded but didn't dare to interrupt. "She obviously didn't see I was there, but I wasn't having that – dropping litter! So, I marched over as she made herself comfortable under the tree and challenged her about it. She sort-of screamed, said I'd scared her by creeping up like that. I snatched up the bag and held it in her face. Anyway, she didn't care – she just laughed and said this was her house and her tree, then she pointed at the initials!"

"D.A. – Dorcas Ambrose. Of course! When Cecelia Morris saw those initials carved on the tree last year, she thought it was to do with one of the clues from the murder mystery weekend. I suppose, that's just what it's turned out to be!" Peter lost himself in a maze of thoughts, another piece of the puzzle finally slotting into place.

Seb shook his head, wondering why he'd bothered.

"But I deliberately kept quiet about it – took the bag away with me and put it in my pocket. Then I went back to patrolling the grounds," *I'm not going to tell him I actually went for a little sleep under a tree*, Seb thought sensibly. "When I next went past where she'd been sitting, I found her laid out under the oak, dead."

Peter gazed at Seb, knowing that he'd taken the opportunity to have a snooze, rather than seeing to his security and parking duties on the day of the fayre. "It's of no consequence now, so don't worry about it," was all he said. He reflected on the fact that, as an adult, Dorcas had died under the very tree where she'd carved her initials as a child.

"But you don't see what I'm saying!" Seb persisted. "The bag contained fruit pulp that had oozed through the brown paper, plus it had Dorcas's prints on it – vital evidence! I kept it because I thought the police might blame me for her murder – I was the only other person around when she died!"

"What did you do with the bag?"

"It's at the back of my sock drawer."

"Well for goodness sake, take it out and throw it away! It was an accident that Barbara Andrews died, nothing more than that. The pathologist got all the information he needed from her stomach contents – if he'd wanted her fingerprints, he could have had those too! There was nothing that could be gained from having that bag as evidence."

Peter paused for a moment, wondering if he'd gone too far, but the look of relief in response said it all. He smiled and added, "You're completely in the clear and you've done nothing wrong. No one ever suspected you of murdering the woman."

Seb grunted his approval.

"But just because you didn't do it this time, doesn't mean I won't suspect you if anything happens in the future." Peter arched his eyebrows to show he was only half-joking.

"So, I'm not going to prison than?" Seb asked. He stood straight and tall, throwing Peter a cheeky grin.

"Not this week, no."

Now a changed man, Seb strode confidently towards the kitchen. Peter smiled to himself, hoping this was a lesson that would make his unruly member of staff better behaved for a while. He shook his head and went to join Seb, Nella and Kitty, knowing it would only be a matter of time before the man was back to his old tricks.